WOKE UP
in a
STRANGE
PLACE

Eric Arvin

Dreamspinner Press

Published by
Dreamspinner Press
4760 Preston Road
Suite 244-149
Frisco, TX 75034
http://www.dreamspinnerpress.com/

Woke Up in a Strange Place

Cover Art by Paul Richmond   http://www.paulrichmondstudio.com

ISBN: 978-1-61581-795-5

Printed in the United States of America
First Edition
February, 2011

eBook edition available
eBook ISBN: 978-1-61581-796-2

To Dad, by the riverbank

As with any novel, this one could not have been written, and certainly never published, without the help and inspiration of many. Miranda Maxwell (a wonderful friend and editor), Andrew Barriger, Craig Gidney, Ruth Sims, Carey Parrish, and Carol Strickland are just a few, as well as the entire Dreamspinner family. And then there's the music. Always music. Nick Drake, Jeff Buckley, Elliot Smith, and Townes Van Zandt for the purpose of this tale especially.

PROLOGUE

"I CAN see heaven," Lou said. He was holding Joe, cradling him in his arms as they lay on the nighttime beach. They combated the crisp breeze with warm sweaters and a tight embrace. The sound of the water beating the rocks and the shore soothed them.

"You can see past the clouds?" Joe asked, playing along.

They had spent the month traveling the coast of New England—the Gay Grand Tour. They had rested at B&Bs that had been recommended along the way. Their golden retriever, Spooner, had been left with Joe's mother. They missed him terribly but needed the time alone.

Things had been strained lately. They needed to focus on each other again. Joe's position as a book editor—mostly tomes on mythology and folklore—had taken up a lot of time. And Lou's mother was a bit of a menace.

"Absolutely, I can see it," Lou replied. "Just up there. It's not so far." He pointed to a vacant patch in the sky. "It's just past that star you can see shining through that cloud clearing."

Joe laughed comfortably. "You're a silly man, Lou," he said, snuggling into Lou's chest, smelling his cologne.

"What would you do if I died?" Lou asked. His voice took on a slightly more serious tone.

The question took Joe aback. He raised his head from Lou's chest and looked him in the eye. "What kind of question…? We're too young to be talking like that."

"We're not too young. I just turned thirty. People die every day."

"Well, not us," Joe replied bluntly. Granted, they hadn't been taking terribly good care of themselves lately—lots of take-out and an expired gym membership—but talking about dying just seemed odd. Like an insurance commercial. "We're together forever. I'd go crazy without you. Absolute bonkers."

"You've got more courage than that. You would survive."

Joe didn't say anything, but he knew Lou was wrong. He couldn't think of a world without him. Not anymore. Not after all he'd been through, all the disappointments and searching.

"Would you wait for me?" Joe asked quietly, his head resting again on Lou's strong chest.

"Where?"

"In heaven. Beyond the clouds and the stars. Would you wait for me?"

"It wouldn't be heaven without you. Of course I'd wait. I'll always wait for you, Joseph. Waiting for you, the anticipation, it's what drives me. You're my life-force."

Joe sighed, tears in his eyes. "Smooth talker. You always know just what clichés to use."

"Go to sleep, baby," Lou whispered. "I'll be here in the morning."

A BEAUTIFUL PLACE TO GET LOST

VARIOUS echoes. That was all he heard until he opened his eyes.

With a last snap of his synapses like lightning charging back to heaven, Joe found himself in another place altogether. The stale argument of biology versus spirituality became moot. In the end, none of it mattered. One wonders why there needed to be a right or wrong answer at all. Joe realized then that love had only ever been about content, not form.

It was a repositioning, a new form of situating himself. He was lying on his back in a summer field of barley now. How he had gotten there, he had no idea. Maybe the sky had dropped him. However it happened, he was lucid. Everything still felt real. Still felt... *tangible.* Stalks surrounded him. In the afterlife, most people wake up in fields of gold. This has been so since death began because it's what most humans know of peace, beauty, and ease. He knew the feel of the barley as it scratched his skin; he smelled the fragrance of summer as it blew past him, over him; he tasted the sweet humidity; and he hummed with the lulling sound of honey bees making love to nearby wildflowers. There was a perceptible heaviness to the smell of the breeze, though. Like a frost was soon to set in. A few of the stalks were dead and fallen.

There was no discomfort in the barley's touch. It was a pleasant itch, like a tickle. In fact, there was a tickling sensation to everything, an almost untamable giddiness. He heard a giggle issue forth from his own being as he lay on the golden blanket, stretching his arms and legs out to their full extent.

He could remember nothing of before, our hero. The last vestiges of imagery had become sepia, like a dream, clouded around the edges. His memory was receding like the tide. This accounted for his lack of frantic anxiety, for his complete acceptance of an otherwise absurd situation. Only he existed in the barley, free of caustic worries. The few dead barley stalks were interesting but not worrisome.

Memory? What was memory? Me-mo-ree. A strange word. A distant concept. Laughable. Lacking in description. For all he understood, the whole ball of existence was set above and around him and had always been barley and gorgeous sky.

There was only one thing he was certain of, and that was simply because the thought had attached itself to him so fiercely, like a stubborn root digging deep into the soil. His name was Joe.

Joe. Was that it? Three letters? J-O-E. Three tiny symbols of some ancient script signifying an existence. There was more, right? There had to be more. There must be strength and vitality and vigor wrapped up in those letters somehow, for he was *of* the barley now, of the very same fortitude and determination. He felt it inside.

Joe (as he remembered his own name with some glee) lay staring at the sky. It was different than what he thought a sky should look like. Not a single solitary shade, but multi-layered, like a cake. Like sweet eats streaked and decorated with purples and pinks and oranges.

He lounged and gazed upward, feeling no need to move. There was no urgent call to stand and appropriate a functional demeanor. He felt only the impulse to melt or sink into earth or sky.

He was not alone where he lay but could sense curious rodents and lisping reptiles passing around him. Yet he felt no fear or repugnance at the thought of them. They were of the barley as well. Everything was one.

A wisp of some sweet redolence wafted over him as he relaxed hidden in the tall, thin stalks of golden grass. It was familiar, like an echo.

The sound of something wading through the barley raised Joe's curiosity. He rose to his knees, peering over the tips of the stalks as they swayed lazily.

He saw a figure. Another someone moving steadily through the grain waves. The barley flowed around the form as it slowly approached.

Soon, it became clear to Joe that this new form was that of a young man. He possessed a slender face, a strong nose and brow, a cleft chin, and dark black hair that blew with the wind at his bare shoulders. He looked tired. His face was pale, and dark circles marred his worried eyes. Farther behind the Stranger (and even more curious), almost like an afterthought demanding to be seen, was a golden retriever that leaped high enough into the air to see above the gorgeous field, ears flopping and tongue hanging loosely.

Joe got to his feet and waited for the young man with a rush of excitement, though it was a mystery as to why. He ran his hand over the top of the barley that flourished hip-high around him, the tips tickling his tender flesh.

"You're here," the young Stranger said, looking quite breathless. A hint of expectation lay in his expression. It was as if he wanted to tell Joe something urgent. The muscles in his jaw flexed and striated. It was a lovely jaw, one that might have been carved from stone.

"I'm here," Joe repeated. "But where's here?" Joe's eyes were wide, keenly observant. His peculiar feeling of intimacy with this mysterious man grew as the Stranger spoke. Joe felt a closeness, a need for this individual. Potent desire had now supplanted his previous complacency. His very breath quickened in this new presence and matched that of the Stranger's own.

"Here's where you're supposed to be." The man smiled with a shrug. His tired eyes were misty and full of emotion.

"That's a stupid thing to say." Joe grinned. "But it's nice. It's really nice here." He looked around at the flowing field of gold and the ecstatic canine in the distance, if only to keep from staring so obviously at every tiny detail of the Stranger's face. *What lovely eyes!*

"Well, it's been waiting a while for you." The Stranger couldn't seem to take his sad eyes from Joe.

"I know you," Joe said, drawing closer through the barley. He recognized that the Stranger was naked, but then, he realized, he was too. He hadn't noticed this fact before but felt no disgrace in it now. "Who are you?" he queried softly.

"You're right," the man smiled with slight mischief. "You know me. You know me very well, Joseph." He stared at Joe, swallowing a lump in his throat. Again, that look of urgency, of some tale to be told.

Without thinking, Joe put his hand to the Stranger's chest. He felt as if it were an altogether natural thing to do. He felt the warmth of skin, but there was no rhythm beneath it. There was no beat or cadence in the toned chest. Joe gasped as a sudden maverick echo shocked him like a jolt of electricity. The chill of grief and loss rippled through him, and the image of a towering structure appeared in his mind, a lighthouse from a distant memory. It lasted only for a moment, passing quickly, but it made him draw his hand away. The Stranger grabbed it gently. A soft breeze sprinkled over them, birds in the cake-like sky, butterflies in the field just above the flaxen waves.

The Stranger smiled again. *Nostalgia.* His eyes brilliant blue hints of past joys. *Memory.*

"I know you... who are you?" Joe choked out, all at once very moved.

"I have to go now, Joe," the Stranger said as he let go of Joe's hand. "I just had to see for myself if it was true. And it is: you're really here." With teary-eyed reluctance, he turned and began walking away. He appeared not to see the dog that bounded ahead of him.

"Please!" Joe shouted. In that moment, he felt the odd sensation of something being torn from him, something deeply cherished. "Where am I? Can I come with you?" He began trampling through the barley toward the Stranger. More of the stalks looked haggard and frostbitten.

The Stranger turned with a smile, a tear traveling slowly down his face. "You will. But it takes time. You've got to *remember* it all first."

Joe felt that want, that painful need to be with this young man.

"I will be there when it all comes back, Joe. But it has to come back slowly, like these waves of gold."

"And you'll be waiting?" Joe knew he sounded desperate. But his desperation did not feel baseless.

"As long as it takes. You know I will," the Stranger said as he lifted his hand to wave. "Have courage. Great courage."

The horizon very quickly changed to a deep violet and seemed to draw itself around the young man like wrapping paper. His lovely form became a silhouette and then vanished altogether into the darkening air as if he had not been there at all. The golden retriever disappeared as well, with a reverberating call for play. The Stranger's leaving brought the dusk.

Joe stood bewildered and shaken. A dim light shone on the stalks about him from the sky's devastating moonlight. He felt he would cry, like a child ripped from the comfort of loving arms. He questioned what to do, looking about at the darkened field that now began to glitter with tiny bugs. It seemed colder now. That frost was settling in.

He perceived a penetrating restlessness in his core, a surge of ambition to get underway so that he might be with the Stranger once again. After all, he had said he would be waiting. This was no time to wallow in the tragedy of things lost. This was a time to begin a search for answers. Joe could not remain in the field. He had to walk on. And though there was no trail or path that he might follow, he placed one foot in front of the other and began.

His journey was now underway.

As he made his way through the violet night, his grief faded and was assuaged by the serenity he had first known lying in the tall grass. The tips of barley again brushed and tickled his hands, groin, and thighs as he walked. Every step he took gave him hope, though he was more aware than ever of the dead stalks.

Off on the horizon and high above him, indeed all around him, he saw thousands of glittering lights of all colors blinking and winking their way across the sky. Some left exuberant streaks to show their passage in the night; others were almost imperceptible. It was a hypnotizing show, and it delighted him.

Once he had decided to start walking, tokens of past experiences came more easily to him. Remembrances in little droplets, like dew forming on a leaf. He remembered now his dislike for ketchup but his love of hamburgers; his favorite color, green; and his favorite time of day, dusk. All of these tiny personal accents collecting now like little dewdrops finding their ways to the center of the leaf. And as he peered into the night, his earliest memories came back to him.

HIS very first memory was that of standing in front of his mother's full-length bedroom mirror in his diaper. The mirror had a crack in the lower right corner that probably needed to be fixed, but she liked it there. It added character and strength, she had said once. A Dusty Springfield song played on the clock radio on the nightstand beside his mother Veronica's bed. The smell of lasagna wafted in from the small kitchen; it was almost dinnertime.

The image in the mirror returned his awakening gaze. He was coming to a new understanding about himself. Something—some indefinable thing—was different about him. It was something his fresh, new mind could not yet comprehend.

From there, memories were whispered to him pleasantly and with ticklish fervor by the grains. Not always linear, a stream of consciousness swam through him, brushing past the banks of his mind. Even the mundane occurrences of toddlerhood were nothing less than amazing experiences at the time: his first trip to the zoo; playing on a Slip 'n' Slide on the lawn (how the grass irritated his legs, but he didn't really seem to care); a boy named Peter who would become Joe's first great friend; and the amazement at a fuzzy bee and the sting of its betrayal. All of these memories glided around him like spirits in the night air, as if memory was an entity in and of itself.

There was one thought, though, one floating vision on the current that Joe remembered with particular enchantment. He was walking hand in hand with his mother down the busy street of their small hometown.

Traffic was never much of a problem there except for the one weekend in the year when a chautauqua of the arts came to town. Handmade loveliness and foods that were not available for much of the year could be purchased for far more than they were worth. As Joe walked, smiling up at the beautiful Veronica who peered down at him with love, he made a game of trying not to step on the myriad of cracks on the concrete walkway.

Soon they stopped walking long enough for Veronica to look at a few odd trinkets and arts and crafts at an outdoor boutique. Joe looked around him in search of anything that would render itself up to his excitable mind. Right next to him stood another little boy whose mother, a very thin-looking thing (Joe thought she looked a bit mean, like a witch), also regarded the trinkets and doodads. Joe watched the boy intently and felt an immediate draw to the blue of his friendly, playful eyes. He held a vanilla-and-chocolate- swirl ice cream cone (which happened to be Joe's favorite as well) that dripped in messy streams down his hand and forearm and onto the summertime sidewalk. Ants were already marching to the sticky substance.

It seemed to Joe that this messy little blue-eyed boy wanted to say something—either grunt or make some other attempt at communication. Nothing came, though. Neither of them said anything. They just stared at one another until the mean-looking woman looked down at the blue-eyed boy to let him know it was time to go. Joe raised his hand to wave goodbye. (At that age, the world is a small place, and it's completely believable that everyone can see everyone else again just around the next corner.)

The little stranger took in the greeting, and then, having no real idea what to do with it, stuck out his tongue—not necessarily a spiteful gesture; it was just the only thing that occurred to him to do. At least, that was how Joe chose to interpret it.

"Louis!" the mean old woman said as she jerked the little one away.

Joe only stared after the two as they walked off. He'd see him again. Joe knew it even then. It was a small world, after all.

FRUIT TREE

JOE was not aware of how long he had been walking. The exact measurements of time and distance had escaped his care as memory was rested upon memory. He was still in fields of halcyon grass and fireflies. Above him twinkled an infinite number of perfect, tiny lights. For anything other than this simple knowledge, he cared not. Even when, on a whim, he looked behind him to survey the distance he had traveled, there was no trail to be seen. No tracks of his passage were there to give any hint of the yards or footsteps taken. The stalks of barley had sewn up the trail between then and now as quickly as he had passed through, coming together again as if they were thin soldiers filing into ranks. He delighted in this observation and walked backward a little, watching the tall grass merge anew in the wake of his passing.

As Joe journeyed on and reveled in the beauty around him, he heard the unmistakable sound of musical notes. They were very faint at first, a whispered melody. His initial reaction was to look to the grain, as if it were enchanted with tune. Why not? But then, as he continued walking, the music grew clearer. Closer. A single-stringed instrument. Joe did not search for the source, though his curiosity was piqued. He did not feel rushed. He would eventually get to the origin of the music, he was certain. So he simply let it guide him as he danced in dreamy circles with the fireflies. The somber, lilting, plaintive chords washed around his naked self and through the air. He merely followed its ebb and flow.

In a very short time, it seemed, though he could not know for certain how long his carefree promenade had been, Joe arrived at the melody's source. He stood in front of it, though he could not see any physical manifestation thereof. The sky was still too dim for Joe to make out anything more than silhouetted forms.

Then, in a flash, it was as if the night sky was peeled away to reveal a new dayspring with a sky of azure blue. Just like that, with no warning at all, it was peeled right off like an orange skin. And there in front of him (surely it had been there the whole time, only hidden by some trick) was a massive tree that took up so much space and shot so high in sculptural elegance that even the aureate grass around it seemed to recline in awe at the sheer height. The roots stretched out in gnarls and great gray hills. Its limbs were thick and strong, and they reached out, grabbing at the sky with their foliage, large leaves the size of human heads. Various fruits sprouted from it. Perfect fruits. Apples, mangos, pineapples, oranges, strawberries, kiwi, and not a rot in one of them. They all shone as if recently polished, full of juicy life and richness and ready to burst.

Joe walked under the shade of the tree, where it was considerably cooler. The branches hung quite low, so he pushed them gently aside. Only an occasional glint of sunlight filtered through the canopy. Joe marveled at what he saw as he gazed upward into the underside of the brachia. It was a home, a place of life and for living. A tree house of such marvelous design that he grinned in boyish excitement. One with level upon level, not crudely constructed with scrap wood and nails, but solid, strong, and meticulously carved and conceived.

The music floated from one of the lower tiers, cascading down the circular steps around the tree's curvaceous form like a warm waterfall. Joe could see the notes if he squinted hard enough. He approached the sturdy staircase and began to climb, wading through the falling music and holding onto the simple wooden rail as he went. Each step felt cool and smooth on his bare feet. Fireflies that had escaped with him from the nightlift into the shade of the tree trailed after him as he ascended into the branches.

The music grew louder but no less melancholy as Joe slowly climbed the winding stairs past floors of constructed comfort. Finally, he came to the tier from which the music emanated. At the opposite end of the tier, situated in a wickerwork rocking chair, was a man. He had his back turned to Joe as he played a guitar and looked out into the foliage. One shoeless foot was positioned on a rope that was tied between two posts on opposite sides of the deck, and the other was tapping the floor to the chords issuing forth from the instrument. His jeans were ragged and worn, frayed at the bottom. And he wore a white T-shirt over which hung longish, black, scraggly hair.

The guitar player was at once still. No music. No foot tapping. Yet it wasn't as if Joe had startled the musician. The guitarist had simply sensed Joe's arrival. He took his other foot off the rope and put the guitar on the floor to his side.

"So here you are," he said in a gruff but youthful voice. He still looked out into the leafy arms of the tree. "And in all yer nekkid glory too."

Finally, he rose from the chair and, over his shoulder, gave Joe a sideways glance with a teasing half-smile.

The guitarist turned to face Joe completely. An unlit cigarette hung loosely from his bottom lip. Joe once again felt a strange surge of acquaintance, but this wasn't the same way he had felt in the barley with the naked Stranger. This was more of a fleeting familiarity than an intense recognition. Still, he felt an undeniable connection to this new figure.

Joe took him in. He was a scruffy-looking man, but handsome, with a bristling shadow of dark facial hair across his jaw. His eyes were small and dark and hid kindness behind their seemingly indifferent, unexcitable glance.

"Are you a singer?" Joe asked, feeling a bit anxious. It was all he could think to say.

"And a songwriter. Yeah, I wanted to be," the guitarist said. "I tried to be, but it never really worked in my favor." He looked Joe up and down with some sort of suspicion coupled with an odd expression of pride.

"You're very good. What I heard was beautiful. You should give it another go," Joe said. He was still just getting acclimated to his own voice, its pitches and intonations. He couldn't tell if it masked his kindled anxiety.

The guitarist smiled and played with the cigarette in his mouth. "Maybe I will," he said in his swarthy drawl. "You're Joe." He extended his hand. It was a big hand. Hardy, but with long, dexterous fingers. It secured a tight grip around Joe's own. "It's nice to meet you, Joe. I'm called Baker. It is I, my nekkid friend, who will be yer guide."

Joe looked at him awkwardly. "Guide?" he asked. He scratched an itch on his thigh.

"Shee-it." Baker grinned. "You expectin' to get around this place alone? But then, I guess you ain't really seen too much of it. Trust me, though, ain't no way, son! It's too big here. I've got a lot to show you, and you got lots to see, which means we got a lot to do." He leaned down and picked up the guitar, pulling the strap over his head so that the instrument rested diagonally across his back. "We should get goin'," he said. "Do you want somethin' to wear? Otherwise, son, you're gonna be floppin' all over the place."

"Uh… maybe something light," Joe said, feeling just the tiniest bit self-conscious. "But where are we going?"

"Let's get you some threads," Baker said as he walked to the stairs.

Joe followed, perplexed. They climbed higher into the tree, past levels of varying size and delectable scents. They were joined by the odd squirrel or chirping bird as they made their mount. The wood creaked and moaned around them in a strange song. Breezes played with the leaves and branches.

"Are we going all the way up?" Joe asked, looking as far as he could upward.

"No, but close," Baker answered. "I live at the top. I can see out over everything. Well, everything that's known to me, anyway. But we're goin' to the place just below mine. To my favorite guest flat." The shade from the tree was comforting, relaxing.

"You have guests here?" Joe asked as he looked around at the thick, gnarled limbs and brachia. He knew the field of barley was just below them and that it stretched out for acres, but Joe could see none of it due to the prominent foliage that encircled them.

"All the time," Baker said. "You just missed one. He wasn't wearin' any clothes either. There's a lot of that around here. Mostly by new souls, like you. But some older ones too like to skip around singin' and a-dancin' the day out. Kinda funny."

Finally, they stopped at a large, open level. "Here we are," Baker said.

Joe looked backward and downward at the myriad of stairs they had just traveled. The steps wound like smooth, brown, polished piano keys around the body of the tree.

"You should be able to find somethin' to wear here. There's the wardrobe," Baker said, pointing to a very large, simple wardrobe carved from the tree. No designs of twirling vines or whatnot over-stressed its elegance, and yet it was crafted with great care and built to last.

Joe walked to the wardrobe and opened the large doors. Baker sat down on an old rocking chair in the corner. The guitar was once again on his lap, and he began to strum it idly.

As Joe looked through the items of tried-and-true clothing— mostly jeans, jackets, and T-shirts—he asked the question that had been itching for an answer since he had awoken in the barley. It came out very matter-of-factly now. Easy as water from a faucet. "I'm dead, right? I've died? That's why I can't remember everything. That's why everything here is so... crisp. So new... like unused words being spoken for the first time."

"Dead?" Baker rolled the question over his tongue as he slid a finger along a guitar string. "That's a weird concept, death. Truth is, Joe, and it's a cliché, but we never die. We just exist differently, that's all. We're always around. We live in a last moment of life before we move on to another. It's the Eternal Second."

Joe picked out a pair of baggy jeans with holes in the knees and along the thighs, much like the ones Baker was wearing, and slid them on over his bare flesh. He was trying to understand what he had just been told. "So, this is heaven? I got in?" He pushed his hair back from his eyes.

Baker laughed. "Heaven's another interesting concept." He looked at Joe's pleading face with a thoughtful expression, then shook his head. "But, yes. If there were a heaven, this is it. You got in, kiddo. There are no gates here, though. No barriers at all... of any kind. Everybody gets in, Joe. No matter what your beliefs once were. No matter what you've been told before. And there ain't no angels here. That's why you need a guide in the beginning. It's just so damn big. Bigger'n any place you've ever been. This place ends only where you want it to."

"This is heaven," Joe whispered to himself. He closed the wardrobe doors, lost in a moment of disbelief and excitement.

"Yep." Baker smiled and stood. "This is your big heaven, my friend. Everything you want is here." He pointed to the jeans. "Is that all you need? Just the jeans?"

"I think this will do," Joe nodded.

Baker pulled the guitar over his shoulder and gestured Joe to follow him back down the circular stairs of the tree.

"Baker, why can't I remember everything from before? Everything that happened in my life? I mean, I get a sense of familiarity from things, but it seems I should be learning from mistakes or something."

"That's why I'm your guide, Joe," Baker said. "That's why I'm here. To help you recall your past, or reclaim it, until you don't need me. Until you can do it on your own. You gotta know it before you move on. You gotta recognize yourself. Understand the lessons. If you cain't make no sense of it, well then, what use was it?"

"So, it'll come back to me in time?"

"Time?" Baker smirked. "Yeah, it'll come back if you want it to."

"Why wouldn't I want it to?" Joe asked in surprise as they rounded the trunk.

"Well, kid, things happen. Bad things. Memories hurt just as bad here as they do where you came from." He turned on the steps and faced Joe. "Be prepared, my friend. Some things you're gonna see... well, they're gonna hurt. Hurt like hell."

AT THE base of the tree, the leaves hung low with their ample produce. They brushed the ground with playfulness when any light wind stirred them. Baker grabbed a perfect apple from a perfectly strong branch. Joe did the same. For Joe, the first bite into the apple was a new experience, exciting and with a sweet taste that was overwhelming. Better than candy or vanilla-and-chocolate-swirled ice cream.

They pushed their way through the massive foliage until they both finally stood on the other side of the tree, which was located on sloping ground. The roots jutted from the grassy dirt like tentacles, as if the tree could move. As if it were simply resting for a bit and would soon get up and stroll about the land with thunderous strides.

The barley fields were behind them now, and Joe and his new guide stood on the top of the sloping mound and faced out onto a flat area of high grass through which ran a small creek. It seemed to reach on and on. There was a dense forest of much smaller trees in the distance into which the creek wound its way as it grew in width and depth. And yet, those were only the very first and simplest characteristics of what waited ahead of them, of the map that they were to follow. The entire landscape beside and surrounding the plains and the waterway drew an astonished gasp from Joe as his eyes widened. It was an orchestra of ridiculous impossibilities.

High above, suspended in the sky like great festival ornaments, were planets. Spheres set so near the ground it would seem their rounded edges could almost be reached but for the distance of the wild fields. The largest of these celestial satellites was a huge orange globe with three wide rings circling it. Great winged beasts flew in silhouetted flocks over the surfaces of these marvelous worlds.

And then, too, on the ground, in the opposite direction from the creek, strolled about ten massive animals. Giant dinosaurs that walked slowly and without concern. They followed an incongruously small figure, possibly a child, in a sort of uniformed march.

Across the creek, on the side opposite Baker's tree, there was a small camp of families. Their tents were solid and round, and Joe could discern nothing but sounds of joy coming from them. The people wore simple clothes and did simple things, and yet it seemed they did not want any more than what they had. It was enough.

Beyond this, beyond the plains, there were hills and mountains that held things Joe could now only guess. This was a plain of peace and wonders. Who knew what else the mountains hid?

"We follow the water," Baker explained. He took a bite from his apple, first remembering to remove the cigarette that still hung from his lip and placing it behind his ear. "You ready for this, chief?" he asked with his mouth full. There was a gleam of excitement in his otherwise apathetic eyes.

"Yeah," Joe breathed out anxiously. Ready for what, he was not sure. So far this Baker fellow was not too forthcoming with details. He had not sufficiently prepared him for dinosaurs and planets.

They walked down the pitch and onto the level ground, passing through the grass, over which fluttered the occasional wide-winged butterfly or the shadow of a beautiful eagle. Soon they were traveling alongside the creek. The water made the sound of wind chimes as it hit the curves and rocks of the small brook. Joe glanced into the waters, watching the silver ripples and striations. Clear, clean water. It literally glimmered and sang. He could even see faces in the current made of light and water, all in mid-song, their mouths in the shapes of choral Os.

But then Joe noticed something else: *himself.* He caught his own reflection in the stream and froze on the spot, dropping the half-eaten apple to the ground. He ran his hands over the body he saw in the water, over the chest and abdomen.

"This is *me?*" he whispered in shock.

It was not the body he had expected to see but rather the body he had always wanted. That is to say, the memory of his former body came rushing over him. A few droplets of self-knowledge were allowed. He remembered the struggles with his old body. The hours of discipline and starvation that had never paid off. He remembered with some hostility the pursuit of the Ideal. But *this* body was much better, much more in line with what he had longed and fought for. The baggy jeans hung low, showing off a sculpted physique. Well-toned, but not too muscular. A perfect V was formed by his hip muscles leading down to his groin. His abs were painfully well-defined. His chest was strong and shoulders broad.

"This is me?" he said more loudly, as the creek held his image like a mirror even as it flowed onward. He pushed back a strand of brown hair from his brow.

"Yep." Baker came to his side. "That's you, chief. You musta hit the weights a lot, huh? Stayed away from the pizza?"

"I guess." Joe grinned at himself, still stunned.

"Would you like to be alone with yourself?" Baker jabbed playfully. "Come on. There's more creek. You can walk along it. Besides, this is that guy's *heaven*, as you put it." Baker gestured across the water at a beautiful young man lying at the creek's edge, enveloped in his own reflection. He was nude, with golden locks of hair that played at his pale shoulders. His eyes were lost in admiration toward the waters. The youth sighed with intoxication and vanity, completely unaware of Joe or Baker. He would try and touch the water to grasp the reflection, but just as his fingers skimmed the placid stream he would jerk his hand away, not wanting the ripples to detract from his view of his mirrored self.

"Who is that?" Joe asked, entirely charmed by the youth.

"He's been there forever. Even before I got here. The kid's not interested in finishin' any kinda journey. His guide finally gave up on him." Baker chuckled. "She left in a huff."

Joe was still unsure of the identity of the young man.

"Search your memory for mythology. Who do you think it is?" Baker said. "You've got an education."

Joe looked at Baker with his first semblance of doubt since he had arrived. A dubious grin broke across his face. "No way," he whispered.

"Hey, every myth comes from some sort of truth. Here that fella can stare at himself as long as he wants without worrying about starving to death. Poor Echo's love remains unrequited."

Joe smiled in skepticism and looked quickly down at his own reflection to ascertain that it was still there. That he hadn't changed suddenly. The pull of the pool *was* addicting.

"Come on," Baker urged again. "Let's not steal this dude's thunder."

"*Really?* That's really him?" Joe asked as he pulled himself from the fixed position and continued to walk.

Baker simply nodded, finishing off his apple and throwing the core into the creek. It splashed like a windchime struck. "Wait 'til you see Medusa," Baker joked.

Joe continued to glance at his own reflection as they journeyed along the stream. When, as it happened, he lingered too long in awe and fell behind Baker, he felt the touch of gentle eyes upon him. It was Baker waiting up ahead, cigarette back in mouth. Joe ran to meet up with him once again.

"Sorry," he said with an embarrassed half-grin.

As the sojourn progressed, however, Joe became more respectful of Baker's position and did his best to stay at his guide's side.

The creek chimed louder as it grew wider and deeper. Joe saw small fish and tadpoles swimming parallel to them. He heard frogs making their dives into the brook. He stared in wonder at other things: monkeys hanging from trees, two lovers having a picnic as they and everything around them floated in the air, a naked woman riding a giant seashell down the flowing creek. ("Lazy bitch," Baker mumbled.)

Distance is a way for the mind to allow the body some breathing space. One does not come upon something, a destination, simply by heading in that direction. For anything of truth, the entire being must be in acceptance, and such was the way with Joe. Though the forest up ahead looked accessible within a day, it was not reached within that timeframe. The entrance seemed to gaze watchfully at Joe and Baker as they made their way, waiting for the journeyman to make himself ready for the things that lay past the trees that would require greater fortitude.

The travelers soon realized they would not reach the forest by nightfall. They would need to wait another day at least. With that realization, they quite suddenly came upon what looked to be a trio of dashing knights, each of them relaxed and seated near the water under a few kind trees. One was a bit older, with a long, thick, white moustache, and the other two looked every bit the part of twins. Their hair was black and swept back from their faces. They stood up immediately as Joe and Baker approached. The armor they wore seemed to cause no discomfort.

"Good evening!" the older fellow bellowed forth. He looked very pleased to have company.

"I guess we've found our spot for the night," Baker whispered over his shoulder at Joe. "How y'all doin'?" he said, turning his attention to the knights. "My name's Baker. This is Joe."

"A pleasure," the older gentleman said, affecting a thick, British accent. "I'm Roderick. Roderick of the Plainsmen." He bowed deeply, as did the twins.

"Cain't say that I'm familiar," Baker said.

"You shouldn't be, though, should you? I made it up," he laughed. "No, I wasn't much of anything in my last life, so in this life I'm an adventurer, and I think I've just decided on my name. These are my two sons."

"Oy!" the two handsome young men yelled in unison.

"That's Basil and John. They've just finished their Journeys, and now we're off to do a little ad-*ven*-turing. Quite lucky they got here at the same time, you know. Isn't that right, boys?"

"Oy, oy!"

"Sounds downright excitin'," Baker complimented in his lazy way.

"Where are you two gentlemen off to?" John the knight asked, looking at Joe with a curl of mischief on his lip. "It's dangerous out there."

"Funny you should mention the Journey, 'cause that's what our friend Joe here is goin' through himself," Baker said, throwing an arm around Joe's shoulders.

"Well, then," Roderick exclaimed, "by all means, come. Sit with us! We'll entertain you with tales of our derring-do!"

"Even if they ain't happened yet?" Baker asked.

"Even so," Roderick said as he gestured the new guests to the ground by the waters. "Better for it, I say. We can come up with the very tales of grandeur that will spell out our days to come. We'll just leave some plot points out. Better to have a few surprises, you know."

"Sir." John the knight brushed away dirt and debris for Joe to take a seat next to him.

"Thank you," Joe nodded with a shy smile.

"Quite handsome, aren't you?" the knight flirted.

"Ah, Sir John has found a worthy gentleman to fight for and woo," the other twin spoke.

"I shall win you a crown," John the knight said as he looked rather dramatically into Joe's eyes. Joe glanced over to Baker, who was grinning widely.

"It's yer heaven," Baker said with a shrug.

"How did you come to this?" Joe asked, trying to find a way out of John's glance. "You said you just arrived?"

"We did! We did!" John boomed. "But that is not such an impressive tale. We were great men, you see. Great men born to average circumstances, that is all."

"We always knew we had the greatness in us," said Basil. "So, we are here to capture it. Maybe take it with us from here on out."

"They were never given the chance to let it out in their previous lives," Roderick defended. "I could tell you of our past, of the deeds we never did. But that would be pointless. We have learned from our mistakes. We know now to take what we can. Squeeze every last drop from the river. It doesn't matter what was done; it only matters what you do."

"And you are the Plainsmen," Joe said with a grin.

"Oy!" the three said in unison.

And so, through the darkening of the sky, Roderick and the Plainsmen told their tales. Horrific battles with seven-headed monster swans; rescuing beautiful ladies and handsome gentlemen from the slime-soaked caverns of some hideous netherworld; and fending off spells from the great sorceress Morgause. It was all extremely bloated but told with such caring and exuberance that Joe and Baker found it quite entertaining.

"All in a day's work," Roderick explained, while all the time John the knight continued his love-struck stare at Joe beneath the moonlight.

Soon Joe found himself moved to sleep, though the tales were animated and boisterous. ("And she came for us with three—" "It was seven!" "Yes! That's what I meant. Seven monstrous trolls!") A strange feeling indeed, since he hadn't really noticed the desire for any rest since he arrived in the barley. Nonetheless, he excused himself and curled up on the ground where he sat.

"Don't you worry, my love," said John the knight in his most heroic tone. "I'll keep an eye out for snakes." He winked again, mischievously.

Joe, then, drifted off into sleep. A rest quilted together with the memories of the past....

HE SAW himself, a child ready to make his first pilgrimage into a world without the constant supervision of his mother. At the end of the hazy, humid summer he would be back in his own place, his own town and county, and attend its school: Kindergarten. The past few weeks he had spent with his grandparents in their over-stuffed house of things that masked deeper needs. He didn't mind it too much but noticed his mother growing ever less robust and sure of herself the longer she stayed with her parents. Grandma was like a withered vampire, sucking out Veronica's soul. Occasionally, Grandma seemed kind, but that would alter, as if she had remembered there were people around and to show heart was weakness.

Joe was in the living room with his quiet, thoughtful grandfather. The man spoke rarely, and then only in carefully selected sentences. He kept to himself and seemed to agree to anything Grandma said just to appease her. But nothing ever really did. She remained ever-spiteful toward him. Yet Joe had seen her once or twice looking at the old man with some kind of affection. Still, she would have denied it. Every so often, Grandpa would smile over at Joe, but there was nothing more between them than that. They could hardly have been referred to as family. Joe sat content, watching a saccharine kids' TV program and hearing the storm that was coming from one side of the house to the other.

Veronica came into the room, her hands up in the air as if trying to bat away a bothersome gnat or fly. Grandma soon followed.

"Veronica, that boy needs a proper upbringing. More than what you could do," the old woman shouted.

"Mom, I don't want to talk about this. Not now."

"Let the girl be," came the kindly voice of Grandpa from the armchair.

Grandma shot him a sour expression. "You stay out of this," she hissed, and she turned back to her daughter. Grandpa pointed the TV remote at her and made a wishful gesture with the mute button.

"Come on, Joe. I think we need to leave," Veronica said as she gently took hold of Joe's hand.

"What about the toys?" Joe asked. He had brought some of his own toys from home. They were in the guest bedroom.

"We'll get new ones. I promise."

"There you go making promises," Grandma said. "You need to

send him to a military school when he gets older. Some place with backbone. Some place they grow men. I'm only thinking of how things could turn out for him if—"

"Mom, that's enough!" Veronica said. "I'll decide what's right for him."

"You have no idea what is right for him. Already I've seen him playing with dolls!" She said the statement in a hushed tone.

"He's a caring individual, and that's all that matters!" Veronica went to her father and kissed him on the forehead. "Goodbye, Dad," she said lovingly.

"See you, hon," he responded, giving her hand a squeeze.

"He's turning into a sissy!" Grandma shot back.

Joe saw the look on his mother's face. He saw the absolute cruelty with which Grandma was able to scratch and wound. Veronica's eyes watered, and Joe decided he couldn't take his grandmother's lashing out, at least not directed at his mother.

"Bitch!" he yelled, grabbing on to one of the numerous naughty words that were swimming around in his head. He pronounced each letter with the loudest and most perfect form he knew. "You're a big, fat bitch!"

The room stopped. The world did, in fact. Grandma's eyes were storms of fury and hurt. Still, Joe swore he heard a chuckle issue forth from the armchair where his grandfather rested. Before the fury broke, Veronica swooped Joe up and carried him outside to the car without a goodbye.

The ride home was quiet. Veronica didn't say anything. She would only smile at Joe on occasion to assure him the world was all right, that Grandma wasn't really all that bad. But Joe knew the truth all too well. He knew, for some reason, Grandma had decided to hate him.

Joe watched out the car window, keeping his mind occupied on other things: passing store signs, red lights, a woman pulling the blinds in an apartment. Just the ordinary things that on the surface seem unremarkable. It was a long trip, so he rested from time to time as well. He dreamed of the fantasy lands he so loved to visit in his imagination, of knights and dragons.

Upon pulling into their own hometown, Joe noticed a familiar face, a little dark-haired boy standing on a corner with his mean-looking mother. The cars stopped at the red light as the few pedestrians quickly made their way across the street. The little boy seemed to notice Joe as well, seemed to be looking right at him through the darkened glass.

"Come along, Louis," the woman said impatiently as the little boy had begun to dawdle behind, to stare at something in one of the cars. He stuck out his little tongue to say hello once again.

MORNING again over the wide plains. The singing creek was a sweet choir to awaken to. Joe breathed in the essence of the world around him. Lovely, lovely, lovely. He saw Baker standing with the Plainsmen by the water, and he rose to join them.

"He wakes," Baker said.

"Ah, sir," John the knight said with a bow. "I was so hoping you might awake so that I could get a proper farewell. My family and I are ready to seek out our adventure. What would you have me bring for you at journey's end?" He took hold of Joe's hand without it being offered.

"Excuse me?" Joe asked.

"I will be fighting for your honor, my love," John explained. "What shall you have?"

Joe had no idea what to say. John the knight held his hand tenderly and with expectation.

"Slay him a dragon. That'll do 'er," Baker said nonchalantly.

"So it shall be!" John exclaimed as he bowed once more.

"Slay your own dragons as well, my good fellow!" Roderick said. "Good luck to you on your Journey!"

Basil bowed, ever the gentleman, and he and his father began walking off onto the plains.

"Until we meet again, sir," John the knight said.

Before he turned away, though, Joe felt a surge of affection for the young knight and gave him a kiss on the cheek.

"You have honored me!" the knight replied excitedly. "I shall slay for you all the dragons in the land."

With a look of infatuation, he quickly ran to catch up to his brother and father, tripping once as he waved goodbye to Joe and cried out his unending devotion.

"Off we go, my sons!" cried Roderick.

"Oy! Oy!"

"Tease," Baker kidded, eyeing Joe playfully. "You ain't nothin' but a tease."

ABOUT THE WAY
HIS RIVER FLOWS

"SO, WHY a tree?" Joe asked, breaking a silence that had ensued since they had left Roderick and the Plainsmen.

"Pardon?" Baker said. He still strode slightly ahead, in the lead. He possessed a languid, almost sleepy way of walking, as if he weren't too interested in getting anywhere in particular and would be arriving there at half past disinterested.

"Why is your heaven a tree?" Joe asked.

"I like trees," Baker said. "Why *not* a tree? You don't like my tree?"

"I like your tree," Joe assured him. "It's a very nice tree. The nicest I've ever seen. I was just wondering why, out of everything, you chose a tree. It seems like here you could pretty much live in a palace if you wanted."

"The palace thing has been done to death, if you'll pardon the expression," he said. "Besides"—he gave a sly glance over his shoulder—"do I look like the palatial type?"

Joe chuckled. "I suppose not. But still, why a tree?"

"Well, you see, Joseph, I built a tree house once. Back when I was...." Baker paused. "I liked it. The best dern tree house ever built, I reckon. Didn't need no Swiss family to do it, either. It was perfect—to my thinking anyway. Never wanted to leave it. But I had to. Life calls, you know. I never got to see it bein' used. Not the way it was intended."

Baker became somber and introspective. It was a strange emotion on him. "Even had a deck," he continued, "that I could play the guitar on when the sun was settin' pretty like. So, when I got here, I built me a better one. Or rather, one was waitin' for me. Weren't no actual constructing involved."

"Why did you want a tree house when you were alive?" Joe asked. "Why not just sit out on a porch and play your music?"

"I didn't say it was for me. Not completely anyway. I built it to share with someone one day." Baker halted at the forest. Joe couldn't tell if he was annoyed by the question or not. Everything that came from Baker's mouth sounded at least a little dismissive.

The creek had gone from shallow stream to shallow river and flowed swiftly into the woods. Tied to a large tree was a small boat, barely big enough for more than a couple of people. A bright red sail flapped with the breeze. On it was written *3P* in scratchy black scrawl like that of a young child who paid no heed the badgering blue lines of notebook paper. The vessel bobbed with the current of the river. The water sang brightly, a winking *ta-dah!*

"This is our ride, chief," Baker said as he approached the small craft. He grabbed the thick rope tied to the tree and jumped into the boat with ease, the guitar sounding a hollow thump on his back. Joe positioned himself in the vessel more carefully, still uncertain of the new place he had suddenly found himself in.

There were no seats in the tiny boat. Joe and Baker were to remain standing. This assumed Joe's balance was functioning properly.

Baker untied the boat from the tree, and the current pushed them onward.

"Looky here," Baker said in dry excitement as he looked over the edge of the boat. "We got critters. Bet you never seen 'em like *this* before."

Joe cautiously peered into the water, careful not to tip the boat. Bright colors were shooting past, swimming with them. Rainbow fish. They leaped into the air through the circled mouths of the singing river spirits, which choked and coughed in displeasure. Joe couldn't help but laugh and swore he saw smiles on the playful little fish as they lingered momentarily in mid-flight.

There were much larger things as well. Otters and beavers and turtles and platypuses. Were they to break out in song, Joe would have thought it none the stranger. After all, the river *did* sing. At one point, a beaver placed its tiny hands on the aft of the boat, as if to aid their speed, using its slight might to push. It stayed there for a while, inquisitive eyes twinkling, then slid back beneath the waters once more with its beaver kin. Joe and Baker were being shown the way, it seemed. Small swimmers of all kinds guided their voyage down the river through the increasingly dense forest.

The trees appeared restless as the boat passed them. They creaked with loud snaps and groans, the sound of bark and wood stretching and twisting. But there was nothing ordinary about these trees. They, too, had faces. Knobby, grumpy-looking faces (*of course* they were grumpy-looking) that eyed the boat with discernable interest. Their eyes were wide, hollow holes, but they were not frightful. Only curiosity could be recognized from their wooden expressions and inquiring moans.

"Baker, *look!*" Joe whispered loudly, caught off guard by the rustic audience.

"Yeah, the trees," Baker said, already past any wonder. "Strange place to call *heaven*, huh?" Baker winked. "And these ain't no special effects. This ain't Oz or Middle-Earth."

The roaring sound of falling water caught Joe's attention. There was a drop-off ahead, a cliff. They had already traveled deep into the forest, and the trees were many.

"Guess we better tie up here," Baker said.

The boat, seeming to obey his wishes, drifted over to a bank, ignoring the strong current effortlessly. The myriad of critters that had accompanied them dispersed in random bursts and splashes. Baker took one long stride off the craft and then turned to help Joe.

"This is your first stop," Baker said. The roar from the falls muffled the other sounds of the forest around them.

"A waterfall?" Joe questioned. "This is our stop? What could be here?"

Before Baker could respond, however, as Joe was stepping from boat to land, something jarred the craft, knocking it from side to side with a grinding wrench. Joe was rendered unbalanced and fell backward into the stream, losing his grip on Baker's hand. The water took him under with a cold and powerful embrace. Submerged in the glassy liquid, he opened his eyes and saw something emerge from the wildest depths, a face-like form glaring at him hungrily in the current. It seemed a transparent visage for the most part, but for eyes made of silver fish that circled in rapid waltzes and a mouth of some golden worm that wriggled around a tongue of writhing three-headed eels. The water that made up the creature was a shade of urine yellow. Somehow it was more polluted than the rest of the river. Remaining fixed as if admiring a meal before devouring it eagerly, the eyes regarded Joe. Then, suddenly, the creature raced for him.

Joe emerged from the depth with a pronounced gasp, struggling to get over to the bank as quickly as he could. Baker was on his knees, holding out a branch into the water for Joe to grasp. "Take hold here," he yelled above the sound of the furious flow.

Joe swam as best he could against the current, away from the watery monster, but he was continuously pushed farther downstream and closer to the falls. All thoughts of this place being heaven had disappeared from his mind altogether.

He felt a tug below him, and he froze in sheer terror. "It's got me, Baker!" he cried. "Something's got me!"

"Keep swimmin', Joe," Baker hollered. "This a-way!"

But all the swimming got him nowhere. Out of the guts of the river rose a figure so large that even the trees seemed dwarfed: a dragon, a demonic waterspout growing high into the forested air. It was of the water, one with it, as if the entire length of the river was its long, sleek body. Joe saw various fish and smaller amphibians swimming around the rank body cavity of the beast in cyclonic twists upward. The liquid features of its face could now be discerned more clearly. The silver fish eyes, the worm lips and eeled tongue, a long snout that dripped river sludge, and small ripples and waves all over its waterscape that echoed the likes of horns and spikes and scales. There were no arms or legs. This was a creature that had no need for those appendages, looming fierce and deadly as a cobra. Its hiss was like that of water shooting into the hull of a sinking ship, only magnified a hundred times.

Joe looked at the river beast in absolute fear as it stood to its full height over the forest and peered down at him in victory. Baker still called from the bank, trying to distract the creature. He threw fallen sticks and large stones, which did nothing but disappear into the stinking serpent-like form and sink to the riverbed.

Without warning, the monster charged down at Joe from its lofty height, head first. Its eeled tongue reached out for him, squirming in greedy anticipation, and Joe screamed in horror. He knew he could not escape this thing, whatever it was. The river held him in its grip. He closed his eyes to the approaching demon and awaited his fate.

But, of course, his fate was not sealed. Not in this life. The story goes on.

From somewhere behind the river monster, Joe heard a challenging yell. More of a squeal, really. A small voice making a mockery of the beast's epic actions.

Joe opened his eyes to see the fiend's attention averted elsewhere, distracted in a moment of greatness by a small figure standing on a boulder on the bank near Baker. The creature juggled its options briefly and then left Joe for the time being to focus on the other completely. It charged at the boulder as it had done Joe. The water around its extended torso splayed up around it in rage. But its intent to cause harm was coolly blunted. As it came within mere feet of the rock, the figure atop it held out a defiant arm, and the transparent lizard fell apart into a million droplets of current with a screeching cry. Its tiny marine prisoners rained back into the place from where they had come with a chorus of splashes. The water calmed then and soon continued on its natural flow over the cliff as if nothing had happened at all, as if the dragon were but a hiccup in an ordinary day, hardly noticed.

Joe, still shaking and frightened, swam to the shore. It was much easier now that the waters were not agitated. The current even seemed to aid him in this, all but stopping in the swim path. Baker gave him a hand and helped him to the safety of solid ground.

"What was that?" Joe trembled.

"Don't really know, chief," Baker said, once again steady and unshaken. "I ain't never been to this area of the forest before. You're all right, though." He helped dry Joe with his own clothes and body. "Where's a giant sponge when you need one, huh?" he joked.

"Whose forest is this?" Joe asked.

But then he heard the voice from the boulder. A tiny thing. Shrill and familiar, yet Joe was unable to place from exactly where he knew it.

"Hi!" said the voice in a loud burst. Joe could see the figure clearly now. It was a little boy with wet, messy blond hair and a toothy grin minus a couple of teeth. He was standing proudly on the boulder, all barefoot and soaked swimming shorts, with two spindly arms resting on his hips. "How d'ya do?" he shouted, though he was no more than a few feet from them. "Thorry about the monthter. I try to keep them under control betht I can." (He spoke with an undeniable, completely likeable, perfectly natural lisp.)

"My name ith Peter! Peter Patrick Pithburgh," he said. The words shot from his mouth, each one like a cannonball of spittle and determination. "But people call me 3P."

Joe stood up from the ground, shaking off his last experience. "You can control that thing?" he asked. "What was it?"

"Jutht a water worm. Ain't nuffin' really. You jutht gotta shthow it who hath control. Can't hurt you if you don't let it. I've been fightin' with that one from the firth day I got here."

Joe looked at Baker in confusion. "Don't ask me, kid."

"It took y'all a while, didn't it," 3P shouted.

"You were expecting us?" Joe asked. He pushed back the wet hair from his forehead.

"Well, yeth. I knew you'd get here thooner or later," 3P hollered. Baker couldn't hide an affectionate smile.

"He's a trip, huh?" Baker said to Joe.

"Come for a thwim?" 3P asked as he jumped down from the rock and hopped up to Joe's side. "A thwim will calm you. The water worm ith thleeping now. I put him in hith playth."

"A swim?" Joe responded incredulously, peering out over the rushing waters of the falls. "I don't think...."

"Yep. Nothin' like a good thwim," 3P said as he grabbed Joe's hand in his own tiny palm and pulled him toward the swift current.

"Wait! We'll be swept over the edge," Joe protested. Though at the moment, he was more concerned about the sleeping habits of the river beast.

"Of courth," 3P said knowingly. "Thath the fun part! C'mon!"

"What?" Joe cried as 3P let go of his hand and rushed at the frenzied stream. "Stop!" Joe screamed. "Baker, stop him!"

"This is his world, Joe. I cain't do a thing. He makes the rules here. He'll be fine."

Baker settled himself against the trunk of a disproportionate climbing tree, unconcerned with the youngster's seemingly dangerous activity.

Seeing that Baker wasn't going to do anything, Joe took off running after the little boy, but it was too late. 3P jumped with a heroic holler into the crystal water. An echoing scream issued forth down the length of the falls. Yet it was not a scream of terror, but a cry of undiluted joy. *Strange thing, that.*

Joe tried to peer over the cliff but could see nothing. The child must have been buried deep beneath the uncaring, pummeling current. Joe's heart was ready to break for him. But to his surprise, he saw the water open like a blooming flower with white petals of foam, and out leaped 3P as if he were a springing trout or salmon. He flew through the air like a puppet on strings and landed safely, almost too carefully, on another large boulder that rested conveniently near the flowing river below. He waited there, looking up at Joe, drenched and smiling with crooked teeth and bright eyes, arms wrapped tightly around his knees as he sat on the boulder. He was calm and steady, not breathless at all. Joe was yet again in a state of disbelief, a state that was becoming more and more common here.

"C'mon down!" 3P shouted, his voice galloping up the falling water with snappy volatility.

"No way!" Joe yelled in return, still unsure as to exactly how 3P came out of the current so unscathed.

"Go on! Have some fun. What are you afraid of?" Baker said from his resting place at the tree. He didn't bother to glance up from his guitar. "Dyin'?" Joe could have sworn there was a trace of a smile with that last word. A little jibe.

Yet Baker was right. If this was an afterlife, if this was a bodiless existence and everything he saw was only his mind's illusion, then leaping from a mountain top was as safe as tripping through a field of daisies. Still, the water was ferocious. It dared the nervous first-timer to swim along with it. The current had stopped singing a ways back. Peculiarly, Joe thought he heard a low chant coming from the river now: *Jump! Jump! Jump!*

"C'mon!" 3P yelled again. He was now standing on the boulder, his arms down at his sides, helping to push out every ounce of vocal encouragement.

"Great courage," a voice said from somewhere near Joe. "Great courage." Baker again, being his helpful self, Joe thought.

Joe took the words to heart, though. He picked up what audacity he could from the surrounding air, closed his eyes, and jumped with a high-pitched yelp back into the rushing stream. The waters crowded over and around him once again, carrying him like a victor to the prize—or a victim to the banquet. The river cheered in approval. Head above water, he opened his eyes to see the great drop of the falls in front of him and felt his bravery ebb.

A mistake! A mistake!

A long tree branch hung low over the waters ahead. Joe grabbed for it, but he was unable to reach it fully. His fingertips barely grazed it. The stream saw to that.

"*Great courage!*" he heard a voice say again. But it couldn't have been Baker. The voice seemed too near, as if it were coming from someone right beside him.

Before he could think of another means of escape, the waters pulled him down the falls. Weightlessness combined with a terrifying, deafening roar. A sense of sublime elation overtook him, and the noise and rumble were silenced as if a glass curtain had closed in around him. He heard only the inner whispers of his excited mind. Rushed whispers whizzing through his head like phantom fireflies. These whispers stirred in Joe a new thing. They were an awakening, the emergence of new memory. In those weightless seconds of unspecified time, he saw faces and matched these faces to names. Suddenly, he remembered places and events of his childhood, of a former self, like he was waking to the reality of the world after a night's restful sleep. It was like the night in the field of barley, only more pronounced and meaningful.

Memories as echoes in visual form:

His mother's gentle face beamed at him from sharp jolts of recall; friends he had known shouted at him through screen doors to come out and play; embarrassing accidents in school plays made him cringe; and the leather from hot car seats stuck to his legs on long rides to his grandmother's house on summer vacation. He was reliving these things. He was able to see every Christmas gift, every birthday party, and every youthful mishap from his childhood in more than a simple snapshot or one-reel film. And it all seemed new and yet done and over with.

And then it stopped. Or at least, the focus shifted to one particular memory....

A LITTLE blond-haired boy with a few missing teeth and wrinkled and torn swimming trunks. Joe remembered him. Why, it was the very same boy! 3P! His name was Peter. Peter Patrick Pittsburgh. He had an unfortunate lisp when he spoke (well, unfortunate to everyone else), and he and Joe were the best of friends. They had been for the majority of their young lives. Eight, almost nine, years. They were captains and knights and astronauts and cowboys. They were Huck Finn and Tom Sawyer. Every day they were some kind of hero. Saviors of a desperate world.

Joe now saw himself as a boy with sandy brown hair looking into a deep stream of water and laughing as 3P goofed and wrestled in the current, pretending to be Aquaman. 3P had loved the water. He loved everything about it. He loved to swim, to swing from ropes and cannonball into it or just float about on his back like a dead goldfish; he loved it all. Joe had fun in lakes and streams, as all young boys do, but for Peter the water was a second home. It was a part of him. He controlled it and never seemed to want to dry off and go back home at the end of the day. A home that Joe never really saw very much of. All he knew of it was that a sense of anger seemed to come from it. Yet once Peter was out the front door, the darkness dared not venture with him. It stayed secret within rigid brick walls.

Joe and 3P had clung to each other's friendship like buoys in a storm at sea. They had been teased mercilessly, both of them. Children are rarely kind when given the opportunity to expose another's weakness. 3P's lisp was a target, as was Joe's tender nature. On the playgrounds they were taunted by those names that children don't really understand but hear their older siblings use as zingers. Even 3P's very own brother and sister would have little to do with him when other eyes were watching, telling those who asked that he was adopted, a poor Romanian baby their family had taken in out of pity. It would have been a terribly lonely thing, that existence, if 3P hadn't had Joe and if Joe had not been supported by the bravery of 3P.

They took the snide grimaces and foul remarks of the day, the shoves in the hallway or laughs on the playground, and turned them into monsters and giant squids they could just as easily vanquish to darkened caves under the earth. They made the bullies' scoffs destructible things.

A large stream flowed behind 3P's house, and every afternoon 3P and Joe would play, just the two of them, fighting the monsters they had coined "Faggo-weasel" or "Ugly Harry" or "Three-headed Tillie." It was a difficult task, saving the world every day, but they were up to the challenge. Even in winter they took to the solid ice with glee and indifference to danger, knowing they could save the day. They were boys, after all. Young boys who were immortal, as impervious to harm as were all the heroes in the legends they had heard or made up. Ice and cold could do them no misfortune. They would slide wildly on the frozen stream wearing worn-down tennis shoes. (Any shoes with traction would only impede the fun.) There was nothing better in all the world than those afternoons. Nothing better than what they had: laughter and joy and the pleasure of young company so splendidly innocent.

But then one day the inevitable heroic tragedy occurred. A ripping and tearing, a great thunderous cracking, dared to intrude. As they played Arthur and Lancelet, the ice unexpectedly moved and gave out. It was a betrayal they could not fathom. 3P was swallowed before Joe could get to him. There were no screams. 3P made no sound whatsoever. He only had a look of incomprehension, of the exposed lie of mortality.

He was lost... he was lost.

The frozen waters of the stream brought him under in a slow, horrific digestion. The tips of his tiny fingers were the last things Joe saw. The ice was too dangerous for Joe to try and save his friend. It began cracking all around him as well. He quickly scampered off the ice and stared to where his friend had just been standing and laughing. The winter land around the stream was as deadly quiet as a prayer from the soul. Trees surrounded the ice like snow-covered statues of mournful saints.

So Joe lay down in heartrending agony on the ice, his hand outstretched to where the mouth of the solid waters had opened, and he wept before finally sleeping until he was awakened in the hospital room by his mother.

It was a silent pit of a room that dripped with somber news and no-good-may-come. In the bed next to him was the young boy he had seen at various times in his life. A young boy named Louis. He thought he heard the name. But Louis was asleep, gauze wrapped about his head.

"He'll be fine," the doctor assured the mean-looking mother. "A fall. Merely a fall."

Veronica cradled Joe tightly, seeing that he had awakened.

"You're going to need strength, my little hero," she said in a concerned whisper. Louis's mean mother gave them a bothered expression. "You're going to have to be braver than you've ever been. Can you do that?"

Joe was unsure as to her meaning, but he shook his head, and then the news broke upon him like ice water.

3P was dead.

JOE hit the water with exceptional speed, feeling the pressured liquid around him and hearing its crystalline chime song in his ears. He was pushed far below the current and yet felt no discomfort or pain. Keeping his eyes closed, he was cleansed. The memory embraced him in warmth. As he surfaced, came back to this strange new world, he didn't know if those were tears dripping from his chin or the drops from the splash and submersion. He only knew something in him had been released. A gate was now opened and ready to accept images from history. His story.

Up he looked to the cliff from which he had just bounded, and there stood 3P staring down at him. How he had gotten to the top of the falls again was a mystery. Joe found he didn't really need to know the answer, though.

3P wore a touching, knowing smile, and his hands were placed proudly on his hips. Joe beamed in sheer joy and laughed, doing backstrokes to the bank of the river. 3P cackled as well, and no sooner had Joe crawled from the current than the young boy on the cliff grabbed his skinny knees and cannonballed down the falls. The water took him in playfully.

Joe felt eight again, and he jumped right back into the singing waters. And thus they played and played tirelessly, reclaiming lost days that, because of an accident, had never happened. There was plenty of roughhousing and horsing around. There were plenty of boyhood shenanigans to last them through the changing colors in the sky and the shifting of the large planets overhead. They were captains and heroes once more. Arthur and Lancelet renewed.

Baker came down from higher ground in his lazy, relaxed stroll and found a tree under which he could watch the playfulness in the stream and strum on his guitar. He played them into the night, a sweet folksy tune.

Once the boys ended their play, once they were ready to be dry again, a strong wooden raft drifted near, and they climbed on. It was then guided to the bank, and Baker joined them. The three of them, content all, lay on their backs and looked at the sparkling lights that speckled a violet sky. They drifted downstream through the curious trees.

Joe thought of his new acquisition of place, his new state of being. He thought of his newfound memories. His sweet mother, his former young life. About the joy and the tragedy. It filled him with the wistfulness of good times long gone. The night sky covered him in its melancholy warmth.

He looked to his side, just over Baker's chest, to the banks that floated past. Lightning bugs blinked, crickets chirped, and night birds sang in the forest. And, through the somber beauty of the quiet evening, Joe thought for certain he caught the silhouette of a broad-shouldered man and a scent of frost.

"Great courage," he heard. *"Great courage, my love."*

THE gentle rocking of the raft nudged Joe slowly back to a state of awareness. The sky was now a clear blue. There was an obvious tinge of morning to its appearance. It was marvelous to wake up to the sunrise. Then it struck him as very odd that he had fallen asleep once again. Was it necessary here? Wasn't sleep a mortal necessity?

"Baker," he mumbled, still staring to the sky, "if I'm dead, I don't need to sleep, do I?"

Baker was fixing a string on his guitar. His legs were crossed in a boyish manner. Between his lips he now chewed on a splinter of wood from the raft. The cigarette had vanished.

"How should I know, Joe? This is your journey. Your creation. Just like in any existence, you make up the rules to yer own world." Baker was dismissive. Nonchalant. He was focusing on the loose string of the instrument on his lap. "If you think you need to sleep, then by all means sleep."

"So, here we make up our own days? Just out of the blue?"

"My friend," Baker said, looking up from his work, "that's the way it is everywhere. We have control of our own *destinies*, if you wanna call it that. Just most people don't realize it. They follow other people's rules. They would rather think about existing (what's called life by some) in less creative terms."

"So I don't need sleep?" Joe reiterated.

"You don't *need* to do anything 'cept learn. But you can *want*, and if you want to sleep, if that's yer idea of bliss, then have at it, son! Close those purty eyes and nod off." Baker finished with the guitar and began strumming it delicately, testing it. A glorious melancholic sound came from the guts of the instrument. Baker grinned around his toothpick and winked at Joe in pride. "Now *that's* music," he said.

As they passed banks crowded with large and not-as-large trees, as boulders and pebbles, bush and forest creatures passed by, Joe suddenly noticed the absence of 3P. A sense of familiar dread overtook him. He jerked around, looking everywhere in panic, trying to peer downstream to see if he could ascertain a small hand retreating beneath the waters, dragged under by an ill-tempered current.

"Relax, Joseph," Baker said. "The li'l runt didn't wanna wake you.

He said to tell you he would catch up with you later."

Joe was relieved but a little angered too. "You should have woken me. How could he just leave? What was so important?"

"Seahorses," Baker said calmly, looking him in the eye.

"What?"

"*Seahorses*," Baker repeated slowly. "Big ones. Apparently li'l ol' 3P had never seen one before. Well, he had seen a seahorse, but none as big as these ones. They were huge. Just came swimmin' right up to us. One of them offered him a ride and, bein' a boy, he took it. Said they were headed out to sea. Some big adventure or whatnot. Sounded kinda silly to me."

"But we weren't through. There's more to do! So much more. Adventures and world-saving to accomplish. I don't understand." Joe was growing a little impatient with Baker's cool demeanor.

"Now, Joe, would *you* pass up the chance to ride a giant seahorse?" Baker looked at him with sly, perceptive eyes. "C'mon. Be honest, my friend."

Joe paused, wanting to argue, and then shrugged in grudging acceptance. "You're right," he conceded as he settled back down. "Wish I had *me* a giant seahorse," he mumbled, looking into the sky. Baker smiled and nodded, not so much in agreement as in understanding. Then he proceeded to play his guitar as they drifted ever downstream in the morning light.

"The days don't end here, Joe. You'll see 3P again," Baker assured him over the chords. "This is the one existence you can be assured of that."

Above the playing of the guitar and the gentle creaking of the wood on water, Joe began to hear the sound of barking. The sound of a dog for certain, and it was getting closer. He rose up and looked around until his eyes caught the golden retriever he had seen upon his first arrival.

"Baker!" Joe said excitedly, pointing to the animal. It raced alongside the raft, barking and causing quite the happy ruckus. "Whose dog, Baker? It's following me. I saw it when I was in the barley field. Does he know me?" Joe inquired under his laughs.

"Yeah," Baker answered. "He knows you. But," he raised his voice at the dog, "*he ain't s'posed to be here yet*. It ain't yer turn, buster. Now you just git for a while. You'll see Joe soon."

With that, the dog stopped running and simply stood and barked as the raft went on, its tail still wagging furiously. It leaped to its hind legs and kicked its front paws as if waving farewell.

"Why'd you have to do that, Baker? Why couldn't he stay with us?" Joe asked.

"Ain't time for that fella yet. You'll see."

Joe waved at the happy old dog until its image faded behind corners and hills and trees of the waterway. He sighed and situated himself again, now too worked-up and excited to simply lay back down and relax. There was so much here. So much that he wanted and needed to see. Being on the raft was now an annoyance. He wanted to go running after the dog or swing from the vines into the river or be riding seahorses with 3P. He wanted to run and scream through the trees like a wild man.

"Calm down, chief," Baker chuckled, sensing the restlessness of his mood.

"Baker, I want to do something! Why are we just floating along the river?"

Without a word, Baker nodded ahead to an approaching bend of bank. At first, Joe could make out nothing but greenery and magnificent growth and was quite ready to say so when a hint of light from the sky caught bare flesh. Joe's eyes followed the light as it spread like the petals of a flower to reveal a young man lounging naked and air-drying from a midday bath. His eyes were closed and his hair swept back in wet locks. Moisture glistened on his fresh, mostly hairless young body. It was as if he had just appeared there, born from the bank and brook. Even the river sang as if awed by his appearance.

Something in Joe placed this image before he even uttered the word *who*.

"I remember this," Joe whispered. "I remember him. His name was Chad."

The young man came clearly into view as Joe spoke, like a memory being carved by word touching air.

"When I would go to my grandparents' farm, he was there working sometimes. He was older, just out of high school, I think. I was only twelve, but I had my first real crush on him." Joe smiled at the sweetness of it.

Chad's strong hands came down along his body, rubbing it softly. He was massaging the sun into himself.

"I was behind some bushes, watching him," Joe said. "Right over there." He pointed off haphazardly.

Chad rubbed himself gently into a lather and let the sun and the cool of the shade mingle. He groaned until he was fully erect and his body arched and shook with pleasure. Such an act of self-love Joe had never seen before that day.

Things now differed somewhat from memory, however. Surreal and real mingled alike as Joe's mind took control of what he was seeing. Flowers from all around Chad's bed of plants sprang to life and bloomed wide as if in ecstasy of their own. Morning glories wrapped themselves around Chad's legs and reached for his penis, wanting to cup it and drink. Stamen thrust into the underside of him, finding their way into his darker regions. Tiny vines curled around his nipples, tugging gently. And then, just as Joe remembered, Chad came in a fierce shot out into the flowing waters. His body bucked in rapturous commotion.

"Me too." Joe smiled as he remembered his hidden theater seat behind the bushes and the sweet stickiness he discovered there.

But as Chad had seemed to suddenly appear, he just as quickly began to vanish. The flowers closed up around him, and the sunlight disappeared from his flesh. Soon he was no longer there at all. Only a healthy spot of fertile plant life on the bank remained.

"I don't understand," Joe remarked. "Was that just my imagination? Did I make that up?"

Baker grinned at him. "Naw. Not really. I mean, some of it happened the way you remember. And you didn't make Chad up."

"He died before me?"

"No. He died quite a bit after you. Many years, in fact. But time don't work the same here. It's what we go through that decides things. When we think we're ready to understand what we went through, that's what decides when we come back. You see?"

"No," Joe answered truthfully. "Makes no sense at all."

"Well then," Baker started strumming his guitar once more, "just sit back and take in the show. Things get explained somehow, but to be honest, I ain't the prophet to do it. All you need to understand, really, is that the difference between one year and a hundred is a wink."

COME TO THE GARDEN

THE river seemed to take them on forever. The forested banks stretched and yawned. Joe tried to see an end to the threading turns and slow curves of the watercourse but was unable. It was like the clown and his trick handkerchief he had seen as a child. The clown pulled and pulled, but the pocket prop kept coming in an endless stream of rainbow silk. How irritating it had been!

Joe's restlessness had not abated. But the river contradicted his mood. It remained smooth and glass-like, unperturbed, as if taunting his vexation. Underneath it teemed with speckled trout, striped herring, golden fish, and silver tadpoles that would always be tadpoles unless they wished otherwise. They swam alongside the raft as if in aquatic procession, a waterway exhibition.

The light grew overhead. Midday. The trees along the banks were now shorter, yet thicker and stouter. More comfortable. They were older than the trees downstream and had lived lives of good feeding and, at least, some purpose. They were of darker, harsher bark, draped in moss, with low-swinging thin branches from which sprouted dark purple blossoms down their whip-like length. Some type of willow, Joe concluded. The curtains of moss and flowered whips swayed peaceably in the cooling breeze. Joe felt a strange chill run through him. It was something similar to sadness or remorse. It grew steadily, this intrusion of grief, and seemed to correspond to the ever more complacent trees along the banks. They began to look more withdrawn and despondent. Their heaviness weighed them down; their limbs were like shoulders and arms beaten by degradation.

"What is this place?" Joe asked. This could be no heaven. There could be no one who would want this. Even the silver song of the water had turned to something more akin to sorrow, and the fish and tadpoles seemed to stick closer to the raft and away from the banks.

"This is someone else's place. Someone you knew." Baker stood at the edge of the raft like a watchful skipper.

"*This*? This is someone's *heaven*? But it's so sad here. So quiet. Where are the crickets and frogs? Where are the birds? There's not a bird anywhere."

"You need to lose that word 'heaven'. It makes no sense here, kiddo. The idea of it limits what this is, what *you* are. This ain't heaven any more than the corner store is a mall. This is existing. It's just another form of being. Beings *be*. And we cannot *not* be."

The raft came near to a rounded turn of ground, a steep bank, over which stood even darker trees of hanging moss and sad flowers. At least they had no faces, Joe thought. At least they could not moan or sing like the river. For if they could, Joe was certain it would be a miserable song.

Before the raft bumped into the hillside, a string of goldfish jumped out of the stream. "*You're here! You're here!*" they shouted at Joe with tiny, high-pitched voices akin to the cartoons he remembered from Saturday mornings as he watched a television that only received three stations. Then they disappeared once more into the flow and completely vanished, swimming away hastily with their silver marine brethren to whatever home or joy awaited them. Joe and Baker were alone now. Even the river whispered past them with caution.

Baker stood on the steep bank with his guitar hoisted over his shoulder. The breeze played with his hair. "C'mon, son," he ushered as Joe climbed up from the wood raft. Baker took him by the hand, and they mounted the hill efficiently and with little effort.

The moss curtain, which glittered and shimmered with dew, parted for them, and the light they had experienced on the river journey faded as they entered someplace new. It was a dim place filled with gardens. Gardens everywhere. Gardens of every variety and form, function, and size. The plants coiled around and hugged one another in such a way that it was noticeably overgrown. Great gargantuan and blighted flowers hung from thick stems as high or higher than the height of a man. Their blooms opened and closed as if they were breathing. As if gasping, taking in oxygen greedily. Their stamens moved about horrifically, searching for some missing nutrient their roots could never find. Joe was struck dumb by their overabundance. And yet, that sense of regret still permeated and negated their sizable growth.

The path Joe and Baker walked was overgrown as well by vines and smaller flowers that seemed to peer up to the larger ones pleading assurance. They were colorless flowers all. There was not a pink or blue or violet to be seen in the gardens. The petals on every blossom were a sickened shade of white. Pale, depressed, and frigid, existing because they had to, their purpose uncertain.

There was chipped and cracked statuary along the route as well. Ancient-looking depictions of wood sprites and sea nymphs and river gods. They seemed alive but trapped and anchored to the spot, dancing with the very vines and tendrils that strangled them.

Disturbingly large ladybugs and beetles crawled here and there, stopping to stare as the new adventurers came upon them. They reminded Joe of the comic books he had become obsessed with as a child. They were comic books about lost worlds, man-eating vegetation, and nightmarish science experiments. They were of less-than-stunning tints, appearing sick and ill due to their very size. As if their growth had drained them of their colors. And their chirps and drones were nothing if not terrifying.

From garden to garden Baker and Joe traveled. Thick, hairy vines reached out for them grotesquely. Limbs scratched at them wantonly. It seemed to grow darker the deeper into the garden paths they trekked. The light from above was blocked. Only the petals of the enormous white flowers glowed with a horrific, unnatural light.

Soon they came upon a forked path with a large chipped stone sundial. (*Strange*, Joe thought, *for a place with no time.*) The garden at the fork was clearly one of vegetables. Legumes, tomatoes, horseradish, peppers, corn, all of them plump, yet faded and less than desirable. The corn stalks in the garden stood even taller than the flowers but were just as lifeless. At the very center, dressed in a plaid shirt and dirty blue jeans, a floppy straw hat and work gloves, was an older woman. She was pulling weeds, as if it would do any good, flinging them into a messy, decaying pile nearby. She stood at once as she noticed the two strangers watching her from the sundial and wiped at her brow with her wrist.

"Howdy," she said in a slight, motherly voice.

She was a small woman, stocky of frame but pleasant of face. Joe could see this as she approached, stepping over the rows of sweet potatoes and onions with an extended gait.

"It's good to see you again," she spoke to Joe. She smiled sweetly as she took off a dirty glove and reached for his hand. Her skin was rough and her grip was loose, almost non-existent. It was as if she were in danger of damaging him if she held too strong a grasp. "How do you like my garden?" she inquired.

"It's very large," Joe said, not wanting to insult her.

"Yes." She laughed. "It is that. You've probably had a long trip. Come on. Let's go get somethin' to eat. The house is just up a ways. Pleasantries are for strangers. There's no need for us to exchange them."

She took him by the arm, sliding hers under his as if she had known him forever, and they walked down one of the crowded paths. Baker followed at a leisurely pace.

"How do you like it so far?" she asked.

"Like what?" Joe wondered, still a bit surprised by her informality. The path they walked on turned mossy and smoother. It felt cool and comfortable under Joe's feet.

"Where you are. This place. It took me some time to get used to it after I died, but you look like the type who can adjust quickly." She pushed a low branch from her headroom as they walked. "From what I remember, you took change better than most."

"I'm not sure yet," Joe answered truthfully. "It's a little scary."

"Agreed." She laughed again. It was a warm laugh, like a thousand bits of scattered sunbeam. What was *that* laugh doing here in this wretched place?

"My name was Abby," she offered. "Abigail Holden, just in case you don't remember me."

"I'll be honest. I don't," he said with relief. "Mostly everything comes in bits and pieces."

"Oh, that's okay, hun. It might be too early for you to recall me, but it'll happen. Something will jar your thoughts and then that ol' memory will belch out of your head like after a good meal." She tightened her grip on his arm. He smiled at her candor and words. There was an edge of worry to her voice.

"You doing okay back there?" Abigail shouted over her shoulder at Baker, finally acknowledging him. She held to her hat as she tilted her head back so it wouldn't fall off her head.

"Just fine, ma'am," Baker answered. Joe looked back and nodded at his guide.

"How long have you been here?" Joe asked, turning his attention again to Abby. They meandered among enormous ferns and exhausted-looking morning glories. Joe thought it resembled more the edges of a jungle than a botanical, vegetable, or any other kind of garden. The humidity in the air was oppressive and as heavy as a wool blanket in the summer.

"Don't really know," she answered. "Can't think of time like that anymore. If I did, I suspect I would have to deal with waiting, and waiting is nothing I need. Can't go crazy here to avoid the waiting, so I'd have to live with it. With time, I mean."

She appeared sad suddenly, and their surroundings darkened ever more, seeming to sense her change in mood.

"But as it is," she lightened up, as did the world, "there *is* no time. Not really. That, thankfully, was someone else's harebrained conception. There's a fool somewhere in the Expanse who came up with time, and we're all the sorrier for it. No. Thank goodness, I have my gardens. They challenge the days with me."

"Do you care for this all by yourself? Is there anyone here with you? This looks like a lot of work."

"My son," she said, looking up at Joe as if that were a secret he should know. Her eyes were proud and sad. "He's in one of the back gardens behind the house. And isn't that why you're here?" It wasn't a question but a statement clarifying Joe's purpose. He glanced back at Baker, bewildered.

Abby fell silent and looked to the mossy ground that stretched before her. Wet, dewy ferns brushed her bare skin and face, and she didn't so much as flinch. It was as if her consciousness had fled out in front and was now leading her by invisible reins. The atmosphere was once again dispirited and ominous. Mournful whispers blew through the air like escaped secrets. Joe saw that it was time to be quiet and inquire no more.

Arm in arm they walked through the large bushes and oversized flora of the gardens until they came to an upturn in the ground. A small mound that revealed, as they ascended it, a quaint, thatch-roofed cottage at the end of the overgrown path. Its windows and doors were squat and round. Anemic white roses sprung from the sides of the pathway leading to the front door. The buds were almost too heavy for the stems to support. Wisteria and blanched flowers, almost florescent, climbed and covered the walls and roof of the little place. They even invaded the chimney, choking it of its purpose, and stifled the hanging wind chimes from making any song. Sunflowers with a sickly yellowish tint guarded the windows, and yet they looked ever upward in hopes of finding their namesake peering down at them through the smothering foliage of the trees, just a glimpse of it. Toadstools larger than Joe could ever have imagined stood like odd, ugly, brown, spongy seats in the front yard of weedy grass. It might have been a charming place at one time, but now it was muffled by its own expectations.

Abby sighed and confirmed what Joe was thinking. "It's excessive, I know. A mess, in fact. But a garden can get away from you. It can grow of its own will if you're not careful or if you're not paying attention… or paying *too* much attention."

In fact, everything seemed to be struggling to breathe, fighting for a proper right to its own existence.

"Come on in," she said as she opened the door to the cottage. It whined woefully.

The cottage, very smallish and reminding Joe of a cloying painting he had seen once hanging in a forgotten living room, had very low ceilings. A chandelier hung from the center of the large front room that served as kitchen, dining area, and living space. But it nearly met the bowl of large, dull fruit that Abby had placed as centerpiece on the short, stubby, wooden eating table. It seemed a whole life was packed into a single space for fear of anything being lost. There was a rocking chair with a quilt naturally draped over its back in one crowded corner. In the opposite corner of the room was a staircase that wound up around a bend in stunted succession. In truth, the entire house was contrary to the gardens. It seemed *under*grown. Everything was of less-than-perfect stature and form. As if, on their way to fruition, all the tables and chairs, even the books and fireplace, had just stopped growing.

Baker and Joe bent their heads as they entered, and Abby led them toward the table, nearly toppling the stumpy furniture as they went. The table's legs seemed to bow from the weight of its own heaviness and that of the large centerpiece. They were seated on backless wood stools, both their knees hiked a bit in the air, and Baker looked especially uncomfortable with his guitar still strapped to his back. Abby set a pair of earthen bowls in front of them and then lovingly ladled a creamy soup of steaming potatoes and carrots from a larger ceramic bowl. Vapor rose from the soup in dancing swirls. Joe was not hungry, but then, he knew here, in this new place, that did not matter. If he wanted to eat and *just* eat, he could without fear of his stomach ripping open from excess.

Abby put the pot down on the stove and pulled up her own stool opposite them. Joe lifted the spoon to his lips and slurped up the hot soup. And it was good despite its off color. It was delicious, in fact. But was there any doubt that it would be, really?

He looked at Abby and smiled. She returned the look with gratitude.

"I can still cook," she said. "Never lost my memory for that. I used to cook all the time for Declan. He was my taste tester for new recipes."

"Declan?" Joe inquired as he continued to eat. Baker was fidgeting uncomfortably on his stool.

"My son... Declan," Abby said somberly, the smile fading from her face and being replaced by a wistful look of far-away.

"But I thought you said he was in the garden out back. You don't cook for him anymore?" Joe felt himself growing tired. Very fatigued suddenly. So drowsy he even swooned a little.

Abby woke from her wistfulness. "Well, I don't need to, do I? I mean, not here. Not anymore." It was a dismissive, if cryptic, statement. "You just eat up," she continued. "It'll help you grow. Maybe not physically, because, well, what's the point in that... but it *will* help you grow. You'll see."

Joe felt an even greater weariness come upon him. And yet, it wasn't like it settled but rather crawled up from the soles of his feet. This strange anemia grew up him like vines, wrapping around every part of him he knew existed. Warming numbness and tingling kisses brushed over his every thought, sweeping them away until his mind was a vacant slate open for new discourse or direction. His vision, too, was caught up by the vines. Light was shielded out until he saw nothing. Everything became a nondescript plane awaiting creation. Baker and Abby had disappeared completely now from any thought or sight. They had seemingly vanished without Joe realizing they were gone at all.

As Joe stood on the wide-open plane of emptiness, he saw something about to appear. Something being born of hidden imagery behind gray curtains....

IT WAS him. Joe as a young man. He was stepping through the void onto a background, a world that was slowly being colored in about him. He was fifteen now, maybe sixteen, coming into his own in looks and a kindling of maturity. He stood naked in a bedroom, not his own, bathed in morning light. It was light that washed away the troubles of the night. The glow from the early dawn cascaded over his young body, so clean and untouched.

Outside the window was a beautiful garden, and there was a woman with a floppy hat bending and tending to its various vegetables and flowers. Joe closed the blinds again so that she could not see. She must be made to think they were just sleeping in, he thought.

In the bed, toward which Joe now looked, was another young man staring at him. His lovely auburn head of hair rested on a folded arm, and a beatific grin lifted up the morning doubt. The young man gestured Joe back to the bed and, a little hesitant, Joe climbed between the sheets, and they fumbled about into new, more adventurous territories.

The Watching Joe, he who was but a presence in the memory, now remembered the sensations. The first hot and cool of it. The prickling of the skin like porcupines in heat. And then that first release of blinding white delight.

Declan. This was Declan. The one to whom he had handed over his first cry of intimate joy. Brothers, they were. Brothers in The Secret. A glorious secret told in wide-eyed wonderment.

Suddenly, even as he sighed in recognition at the scene in front of him, Joe found himself elsewhere. No longer was he in the arms of a first lust. No, now he was sitting quite still beside his mother. His own sweet, kind mother, Veronica, who knew hidden things about him before he could ever figure them out. Who had a knowledge of what made him different from the other boys. She and he were listening to, or hearing, a man lecture in a church. He spoke earnestly. He spoke pleadingly at no one in particular about certain ills. No one in particular, and yet Joe felt all eyes on him as the sermon went on about the evils of homosexuality. Even then the word "evil" sounded to him like a stiff clunker of a word from some antiquarian dictionary. The man lectured endlessly, it seemed. Lessons taken from Biblical stories, warped and twisted beyond any intent. Joe gritted his teeth in discomfort and pain, terrified at the prospect that, at the moment, he was the most hated young man in the world. That even God hated him, and for nothing he ever had any control over. He wanted to cry but could only bite his lip to stifle the ripping emotion.

But then he realized with some relief that he wasn't alone, really. There was at least one other who knew what that layered barrage of resentment felt like. Next to him, in that very church at that very hour, sat his friend Declan, who felt the same reckless hate aimed at him. Hate from God's very own mouth, they were told in more subtle words. They quaked together in their inner nightmares. They held one another with invisible arms to ward off unsavory blows.

Next to Declan sat his mother, Abigail. She looked at them both, stern and disapproving. Had she known what had happened in Declan's room?

Joe sheepishly glanced back to his own mother, who only smiled and took his hand in hers.

"Only ancient opinions," she whispered. "Someone else's laws."

That was all he needed to hear. From that day forward, he was certain he could be completely honest with her. Joe was sure Declan never got the same understanding from Abigail. He wanted to grab Declan's hand in a show of comfort, but it would have served as a spike, a wedge driven between them.

Again, there was a sudden change in location, as if Joe was standing on a rotating stage. He was back in the same house from the morning of firsts. Declan's house, the living room. There was a painting on the wall of a precious little cottage. Too precious. It always made Joe need a dentist, so sugary did it seem. But where was Declan?

Then, a guttural howl made him turn his attention to the sofa, where his mother sat comforting Abigail. A thunderstorm trumpeted outside and jarred the house in sync with Abigail's wails. Joe came closer to his mother and Declan's mother, walking carefully as if he were on hot coals. Veronica comforted Abigail, holding her and hushing her as they both swayed. In her white-knuckled hand Abby held a piece of yellow notepaper. It was balled tight in her fist. It would need to be pried out.

"I take it back! I didn't mean it!" she screamed amid long sobs and gasps. "I take it all back!"

Joe's mother looked to him, great sorrow in her green eyes. "He's dead, Joe," she said, conveying that message to him for the second time in his young life like some beautiful herald of death. "Declan's dead."

It was a familiar moment, familiar words. And yet, somehow, it hit harder than before, throwing him back through the void like an angry catalyst.

"MY FRIEND Declan is dead."

Joe heard a whisper as the fading out began.

"My friend Declan is dead."

The colors bled into one another and then seemed to drain away as a void once again took hold. The Nothing Plane. A now stomach-turning place of directionless confusion.

"My friend Declan is dead."

The vines let go, unwrapping themselves from his body, shrinking back to the Underneath. "My friend Declan is dead," he whispered as he sat at the table on the little wooden stool.

The room came back to him as the words finally took on their relevance and Joe realized he was their speaker. He looked around the darkened room. Only a few candles provided relief from complete mystery. He felt as if he were waking from a deep sleep that was neither restful nor complete.

In the corner, by the low-set fireplace, sat Baker, strumming a quiet, cheerless tune. He watched Joe with a touching concern etched over his stubborn face.

"He's dead," Joe whispered as if it had only just occurred.

"Yeah, buddy," Baker said softly. "He's dead. Was here way before you." The flicker from the firelight highlighted the handsome roughness of his features.

Suddenly, Joe pushed the bowl away with such force it flew across the room and broke into pieces. The uneaten contents spilled out all over the floor.

"*Where is she?*" Joe yelled with anger, jumping to his feet.

"Calm down," Baker suggested as he stood slowly. "There's vengeance in your voice, and there cain't be none of that here. Ain't no need for it. Abigail's suffering for her—"

"Where is she?" Joe yelled again.

"Where do you think? She's out in the garden… with Declan."

Joe's face grew softer. Almost content again. But then the old anger resurfaced and he flew from the cottage, out the back door with wrathful intent and speed. As he raced out, Baker called from behind, "Joe, wait! There's somethin' you should know! Joseph!"

Immediately out the back door, the ground sloped downward. It was an elegant slant of a hill. One might be able to stand at the door and view for miles the surrounding countryside if not for the trees that blocked all but the slightest hint of night sky. A spiraling stone path of stairs led downward to the gardens below. It was lined on both sides by not only trees and enormous flora but also lit torches made from bamboo. Joe raced down them, each step a beat to the cadence of barreling resentment.

As he rounded the final bend at the bottom of the stair, he saw Abby not far off, seated stoically on a stone bench. The firelight quivered and danced about her. Her tired, withered old features were suddenly horrific. Not gentle at all. She now resembled a witch out of a myriad of children's bedtime stories. She sat staring up at a large, moss-draped tree that loomed over a small pond. Night bugs danced over the waters. The moss that hung from the tree was the same silken silver curtain Joe had seen earlier by the bank of the river. It swayed lithely in a somber breeze.

As Joe rushed closer to Abigail he noticed, too, statues. Statues analogous to the kind that were positioned throughout the gardens. Angelic forms with the look of intense innocence. "Where is he?" Joe hissed through gritted teeth as he came upon the bench where Abby sat.

As he approached her, seething, from the corner of his eye he caught a slight movement. A secretive gesture. A smallish statue, that of a child with tiny wings, raised a delicate, chubby stone finger to its lips. The light from the torch nearby danced upon the blameless face. Startled for a second only, Joe returned his attention to Abby on the bench.

"Where is he?" Joe repeated, not as seething now but standing in front of her like an imposing wall of stone. "Where is Declan?"

He heard Baker stroll up behind him, watching.

Abby continued staring ahead at the tree. A tear glistened down her face, sparkling in the sparse light. "He's here," she said quietly. "But he's not really here."

"What?" Joe asked in irritated confusion. The cherub statue continued to look at Joe with a pleading expression.

Abby raised her hand, stretching it out in front of her toward the tree. Her fingers looked as if they ached to touch something. "I didn't mean it," she whispered. "I take it back. I take it all back."

Joe felt the chill of apprehension that those words had incurred in him when he had first heard them. "What?" he stammered out.

"Joe," Baker said, trying to catch his attention from behind. There was anxiety in his voice.

"I didn't mean it. I take it back. I take it all back," Abby repeated, but this time louder and with a certain dire resolve. As if whatever it was she was repentant of would be mended aright by her words' continuous recitation.

Joe followed her outstretched arm, the gently pointing index finger, out and upward. At that moment a stronger wind blew through, snaking through the fortress of inordinate growth. The silver curtain that hung from the tree was pulled up and apart. Joe dropped to the ground in fright and disbelief. His insides froze and melted at once.

The strongest branch of the tree creaked a bitter song, burdened by a body hanging and swaying amidst the crowded, torch-lit garden. The head hung broken, eyes closed. The flesh on the face was drained. Completely colorless. Like a macabre show, Declan hung in the breeze on a sailor's knot until the silver curtain was again brought down. Abby's hand remained out in front of her like that of a soothsayer casting a lot.

Joe tried to rise to his feet. His eyes fixed once again on the lady on the bench. He felt Baker's strong hands grab him under the arms to aid him in standing.

"It's all right," Baker soothed.

"*All right?*" Joe finally stuttered as he made his way over to the child-cherub and leaned against it heavily. "All right?" he repeated. His eyes burned into Abigail. He shook like a rattling leaf in a windstorm.

"Cut him down!" he screamed. "Why don't you cut him down?"

"I didn't mean it. I take it back. I take it all back," Abby said as she slowly turned to face Joe. The lines in her face were taking on the torchlight, soaking it up. Her eyes were black coals. She had said it was impossible to go insane here, but at that moment Joe knew she was wrong, for she *was* mad! Her mind was lost and wandering.

"Stop saying that! Cut him down!" Joe screamed as he ran to Abby, gripping her arms and shaking her violently. Even then she continued to plead her mantra of self-condemnation. Baker grabbed Joe's shoulders and broke him of his grip on Abby.

"I didn't mean it! I take it back! I take it all back," Abby screamed at Joe, her hands twisting into fists of torment. Tears streamed from her eyes. She screamed it over and over, a bitter, high-pitched chant. She was a demon, a banshee. Joe, shaking in rage, covered his ears as Baker held him to his chest. The night was black. Even the torch light shrank in fear from the sound of her dreadful sorrow-song.

Joe broke free of Baker's embrace and ran away from Abby and her gardens. He had to escape her ghastly song and all memory of it. Past the pond, trampling and tripping through the gardens, he fled as Abby screamed after him. Baker called his name, but Joe soon vanished among the trees and hideously disproportionate flowers. He ran frantically, ears covered, his bare feet taking the journey over unfamiliar territory. He paid no heed to his surroundings. The strange woodlands were of no concern.

After a while, when he was sure the shrieks from Abigail could no longer be heard, he lowered his hands and continued to walk without purpose through the forest, stumbling and still gasping through pain, drunk with grief.

It wasn't the same forest any longer. It seemed he was no longer within Abigail's place. Somewhere in his flight it had changed. The growth wasn't as thick. It had lessened in intensity and lightened considerably. No longer did it seem so dank, humid, and oppressive. Joe felt more at ease now. The plants, every kind, had shrunk in size. Indeed, they were very close to the expected heights and normal bounds. And colors began to return to the petals of flowers and wild berries too. Regular-sized animals began to scurry about around him. There were no giant ladybugs here. Things seemed just right: the normal squirrel, the appropriate owl.

There was a light ahead. A light that came from a clearing in the trees. Joe began running again, hurrying to the source of the light for fear that if he waited too long it might vanish. He needed that light like he had once needed oxygen.

As he came upon it, he realized it wasn't a clearing at all but the edge of the woods. Relief washed over him like the waters of the falls. He breathed with sob-laden sighs and then let his legs fold to the ground. His head fell to the softness of woodland grass and leaves with a padded thud. He would stay here, rest here. Here at the edge of the forest, away from Abigail and her haunted mind. Away from Declan. Poor Declan, attached to the branch of a tree forever.

Joe closed his eyes to block out the images. He would hope not to dream. He was already enshrined in a nightmare.

Yet there were memories waiting still....

"LOUIS," Joe whispered up at the young man who was helping him in the store.

He was getting some flowers for Declan's grave, carrying the vase of lilies to the front of the store to pay, when the strength left his arms. A year? Had it been a year since Declan's suicide? The thought had jolted into him at the precise moment he had spied Louis looking over the leaves of an amaryllis. Before he realized the flowers had fallen from his hands to the floor, the glass container shattering everywhere, Louis was below him, collecting the shattered debris into his palm. Joe knelt down slowly, half-paralyzed still by his realization.

"Louis." It was the very same young man he had seen at various strange points in his life. He knew his name and that his mother looked horribly mean, but that was all. How kind of him, *he thought,* to help me.

"Thank you," Joe whispered. He really had no inkling of what else to say. Yet he knew it was one of those moments that life was offering him something, giving him a choice. For some reason, though, Joe was not waking up to grab what was being offered. It petrified him.

"It's okay," the young man said. *"Let me get this for you. Well...* not this one, because it's broken, but...."

Joe heard nothing. He only saw the beautiful blue eyes and those lips and that sweet Louis-ness. He had wanted to believe it was the grief over his friend that caused his clumsiness and made him drop the lilies, that the year's anniversary had just hit him at that particular moment. But he knew deep down it was not so. He realized now the reason for his inability to do much of anything was standing at the cash register buying his flowers... then turning to say goodbye and staring awkwardly as Joe stood silently... then walking out the door until the next odd moment that they would be brought together.

Joe hated himself in that strange, gorgeous moment when a pair of lovely eyes made him forget about his friend Declan.

"Louis," he whispered again.

"C'MON. Get your butt up," said the kindly voice. Baker was helping him again. Waking Joe from his rest on the ground. Light still shone in from between the trees at the edge of the forest. Beyond them was an empty landscape dotted with hills and trees. Farther off, large mountains rose with grace and eloquence into the bluest and clearest of skies.

"Am I gonna have to do all the work here?" Baker inquired, a straw between his teeth and the guitar ever strapped to his back. "Help a brother out."

Joe gained his strength and stood. "I'm okay," he said.

Baker nodded and backed up, scratching his unshaven chin. "Been lookin' for you for a bit," Baker said. "Mind you, I ain't done no runnin'. No need for my handsome ass to do any runnin'. But I've been lookin' for you just the same. You okay, kiddo? You got yourself outta there as if you had wings on your feet."

Joe was drained, his emotions spent and wasted. He stared somberly, sedately, at the ground. "This place," he said. "This place." He shook his head, exhausted.

"Cheer up, chief," Baker said, slugging Joe gently on the shoulder. "Things will get better, and I'm not just sayin' that." He strutted to a fork in a tree and looked out onto the awaiting plains and farther hills.

"How? How does it get better?" Joe asked. "I just saw a man, my young friend, hanging from a tree. I just heard a madwoman screaming. Ranting and raving. How can I forget that? Ever?"

"You're not s'posed to forget, chief. That's the point. These experiences... you keep them. They're part of you now. Always will be, and you'll take them in some form through every incarnation." Baker stood in a relaxed pose, his arms folded over his chest.

"Well, I don't want them," Joe spit out. "How is this heaven? How can a man be dead and hanging from a tree in heaven? How can a woman be as cracked as a broken shell?" He walked toward Baker with a demanding glare.

"There you go again," Baker replied. "Kid, this *ain't* heaven. Ain't no such place, at least not the way anyone thinks of. We exist. That's all. I keep tellin' you. We go from one place to another. We exist and we learn. Sometimes when we cain't take it all in, we go a bit bonkers." Baker spit the straw from his mouth and faced Joe, leaning on one shoulder against the tree. "Abby couldn't deal with what she had done. Who knows if she'll ever get over it in this place. She hangs on to the guilt. It's what feeds her thoughts, and so that's what she sees all around her. You gotta let go of things, Joe. Else it'll eat at ya."

"But what about Declan?" Joe whispered emotionally.

Baker put his hand on Joe's shoulder. "Declan ain't there. That weren't him. He's not hangin' from a tree. That's her image of him. Nothin' more. She grew it like she did all those other trees and flowers. It's an overgrown guilt like those overgrown vegetables."

"So, he's somewhere else?"

"Oh yeah. Declan's around," Baker said, pushing himself away from the tree with his shoulder. "He just ain't been back to see his ma yet. It's just not the right time, I guess."

Baker walked out beyond the shade of the forest. "You ready to git now?" he yelled back over his shoulder, looking out onto the plains.

Joe felt a calm return to his being. He could at least take some solace in the knowledge that Declan was not, in truth, hanging in the gardens. "I think so," he said, walking to meet up with Baker. "Are we walking again? Going by foot?"

"Naw. We got a ride comin'," Baker answered. "You're gonna be okay, son. I promise you are." Baker grinned and tousled Joe's hair.

"Yeah. I got you looking after me." Joe smiled lightly in return.

"You got more people'n you realize lookin' after you."

Before Joe could question the folkie, Baker's attention was caught up by something approaching. "Our ride's here," he said.

Coming toward them across the sea of grass were two rather beautiful stallions, their coats shining in the bright sunlight, one black, one white. They did not run but gracefully lifted their legs in almost matching strides, like show horses. Their manes and tails were long and lustrous.

"Are these for us?" Joe asked.

"Yep," Baker said. "You know, this'll be my first time on a steed. At least, my first time in the last two lives." He winked. "But my daddy used to work horses back in the day. These two... lookin' at 'em, they remind me of the studs he used to care for."

"Very good," came a deep, resounding voice from the direction of the stallions. Joe stared at the stallions in amazement. "We *are* studs," the voice said. It issued forth from the black horse, which now stared directly at Baker with its large, round eyes. It stopped with its companion in front of them. They were both large, muscular, and imposing animals.

"At least, we were back on Earth," said the white horse. They both whinnied at this apparent inside joke.

"Fantastic," Baker grumbled, his brow arched in a show of sarcasm. "They send us talkin' ponies."

"We're stallions!" the white horse leered at Baker with big unforgiving eyes. He huffed and snorted disagreeably, stomping a hoof to get the point across.

"Okay, okay." Baker retreated, holding up his hands.

"You're here for us?" Joe asked, still confounded and giddy from the sight.

"Yes, sir," the black stallion affirmed. "My name is Buck. This is Phil. You must be Joe."

Joe nodded and bit his lip as he smiled. "3P sure would love this!" he exclaimed to Baker.

"Well, get your bony asses up here," Phil said and again stomped a hoof. "We haven't got the *whole* day."

"Don't mind him. He's a harmless old ninny," Buck said as Baker climbed atop him. "You know, we've been together since God was a boy, and I don't think a day goes by when Phil's not grumpy most of it."

Phil looked over to Buck sharply. "You're sleeping alone tonight," he said briskly as they rode off onto the plains.

Baker looked at Joe and chuckled beneath his breath.

"We didn't mean to start a squabble," Joe said kindly. The appearance of talking horses had nearly made him forget about Abigail's gardens.

"Yeah," Baker interjected. "Sorry about the pony comment." Though his apology didn't sound completely heartfelt, and he could never altogether wipe the smirk from his face.

"He'll get over it," Buck assured him. "He can't spend a minute without me."

"You conceited, carrot-eating, fat-hipped...." The insults streamed from Phil like running water. But it was a warm kind of insulting. Like a dance between the two of them that was as old as the mountains ahead.

And so Joe and his guide Baker set off again on the way to their next destination on the strong backs of a couple of argumentative stallions. The memory of the gardens faded, if just for a brief time. The moons and heavenly bodies in the blue sky hung like guardians over the ground as Joe was taken onward.

ONE OF THESE THINGS FIRST

The horse-borne jaunt through the wide-open plains was a mixed array of dazzlement and sometimes boredom. When Phil and Buck rode slow and yapped and hawed, it was interesting and, at times, very entertaining. Yet when they did not talk at all due to Phil's short temper, the time on horseback seemed to trickle by, as they passed very little else but lovely landscape.

"The Eternal Second is a very large place, isn't it?" Joe pondered, finding heaven at that moment rather dull.

"As large as every imagination's grandest invention," Baker replied.

And it was constantly changing and reinventing itself. Before their eyes a hill would rise or a lake would drop from the sky in a sudden roar. But Joe found even the circling moons and blue vistas could become tedious after a while. The novelty of magic was wearing off quickly. Still, there were mountains forming in the distance and forests sprouting from dry creek beds like poetic verse come to life.

In the slower instances, Baker would start strumming his guitar to alleviate the stillness as they rode slowly. Buck seemed to enjoy the music. He even whistled to it on occasion and shook his haunches in rhythm. But Phil was, of course, stubborn and obstinate, having already taken a dislike to Baker. More than once he made mocking whinnies, snorts, and neighs.

Every so often they would stop riding, and Joe and Baker would climb down to feel the freshness of a creek or walk barefoot in the soft grasses. Baker would find a spot under a tree, as would the horses, and they would watch as Joe admired his new body in the reflecting water. The sunlight bronzed his bare chest and back.

When it was time to get going once again, Phil and Buck usually started with a swift gallop. The countryside flew past like smeared paint on a discarded canvas. Joe loved this. He loved the feel of the wind as it swept over his chest and whooshed over his shoulders. Baker was less enthusiastic about it, concerned more with his guitar than anything. Because, while it could be easily and quickly replaced, a musician grows very fond of a particular instrument when it plays his or her soul song. And that particular instrument is hard to find, even after death. When Buck suggested they take it slower for Baker's sake, Phil grunted and huffed but finally agreed to the request.

"We're not so different from him," Buck argued for Baker. "We race through the air, the wind; Baker gleans music from it."

Soon after, the foursome came to a patch of thick, strong, and awkwardly tall olive trees. They were lined as if they were part of an orchard. Interspersed with them were fig and date trees. They were all knotted and leaning at varying angles, as if pushed by a cyclone or at least a very agitated wind. The bark at the base of the trees had been scratched or worn away. Chips lay on the ground, scattered over the trampled grass. Countless pixies and hummingbirds flew about nervously, darting past the heads of the four travelers.

A trail led them over a small stone bridge that overlaid a mere trickle of a stream. On the other side were more trees, worn and rubbed, and then a sudden end to the orchard.

"He's around here somewhere. Be careful," Buck warned. The stallions had slowed down considerably. "The great ass!" And those words were not meant in a complimentary manner.

"Who?" Joe inquired through hushed breath.

Pixies giggled in his face as if they knew a secret. Joe swatted them away, and they dispersed with irritated squeals.

"We should have gone around," Phil said.

"It would have taken too long," Buck said. "The boy needs to get this over with."

"Who lives here?" Joe asked again. He was getting somewhat uneasy now.

There was no need for a reply to Joe's question, though. On the other side of the bridge—though how or where he had hidden was a mystery—stood an enormous centaur. Joe's mouth dropped in awe at mythology taking form yet again. The creature was larger than any horse or man put together and was shaded a curious blue, as if he had been holding his breath for too long. Muscles striated from equine tail to the cords in his human-like neck, and he had his long hair twisted up and fastened into a bun behind his head. The annoying little pixies had placed clovers and fruits in his hair. His enormous square jaw was set with large, perfectly square teeth, and his brooding eyes glared intently at the four of them.

"You will not slip by so easily this time!" the centaur proclaimed to the two horses with a voice that nearly uprooted a small fig tree nearby.

"We just need to get through, Chiron," Phil said. "Isn't there some hero you could be training? Some half-naked hero who is destined to save his village or something?"

"Oh, my lovely one, my fight is not with you, but with your *friend.*"

"You're not getting it!" Buck growled at Chiron. It was the first time Joe had heard Buck raise his voice even a bit.

"I will get my payment!" Chiron yelled, stomping and quaking the already petrified land around him.

"What is it?" Joe asked quietly into Phil's ear. "What does he want?"

"'Tis not much," Chiron said, coming closer over the bridge to speak directly to Joe. The stones barely withstood his weight. "I just want a kiss. One lovely, lonely kiss from this beautiful steed as payment for crossing my bridge some time ago." He cast his eyes longingly upon Phil. "Of course, now the fee is twofold."

"Never!" Buck cried as he jumped in the way, forcing Phil backward a few steps. "You'll not get it, you old troll!"

"Fine then," Chiron roared. Figs, dates, and olives fell from the trees—his rude loss of self-control. "I shall have it the old-fashioned way."

His tantrum frightened the pixies and birds into the nooks of the trees.

"Baker, if you wouldn't mind," Buck said, still staring down the centaur.

Baker did not need to be asked again, though the question had not been asked outright. He slid down from Buck slowly and walked to the sidelines where Phil and Joe waited.

"Buck," Phil said, "this is not necessary. I should just give him a kiss and then—"

"Don't you dare!" Buck warned.

"I have fought and won a kiss from many a hero since my training days were over—Alexander, David, Achilles—but none of them have been as foul-tempered about it as you!" Chiron bellowed.

"Pussies! Every one of them!" Buck shot back vehemently. "Tonight I call an end to your tyranny of flirtation!"

Phil rolled his eyes and shook his head in embarrassment.

Suddenly, Chiron reared up on his hind legs, showing his true strength and mass, the hard muscle and thick veins. Before Buck could do the same (though, it would have been, admittedly, less impressive), Chiron used his massive arms and threw the stallion up against a tree with one sweep. The tree cracked like a ginger snap, the pixies and birds fled as if under attack, and Buck went down to the ground with a painful, "Oomph!"

"So easily undone," Chiron said as he walked over to the fallen stallion. "If only you—"

But Buck caught him under his great equine chest with his own head and strength of neck and hoisted the centaur with all his might into the air. Chiron, though, immediately regained his footing and took Buck by the neck. Again the gallant horse was swung against a tree, and again, pixies fled from it with tiny screams.

"Poor Buck!" Joe exclaimed.

"He's a fool!" Phil replied, though his worry was apparent. "A prideful fool!" There was an overwhelming pride and love for his champion in his own voice as he said this.

The fighting went on like this for a bit, though, to say "for a while" would be a great overstatement. Buck was getting the Buckness beat out of him. Still, he would not give up. He was completely prepared to fight into his next lifetime if need be.

Just as it seemed lost, as Chiron stood over the rickety and befuddled Buck, ready to pound him into submission, Phil put an end to the wrestling match.

"Stop!" he yelled. "I'll do it! You can have your damn kiss."

Joe looked at Baker in shock.

"Phil, no," Buck said with a slight, beaten voice.

"It's just a kiss, Buck. Then we can pass. Stop playing the damn hero! You're worse than this big oaf is."

"Ah, a smart stallion indeed," said Chiron, readying for his prize.

Baker walked over to Buck, compassionately helping the brave stallion to his hooves. "Sorry, ol' fella," Baker said. "You did yer best. But that thing's a monster."

Buck watched helpless and dismayed as Chiron leaned in for his payment, his kiss. This would surely be the worst defeat for Buck in any lifetime. Both Baker and Joe felt for the old steed.

But then, just as Chiron closed his eyes in expectant glee, Phil brought his own head back quickly and gave the giant centaur a massive head-knock. One so loud that it surely caused a great deal of vertigo to Phil as well. The centaur collapsed with a thunderous boom to the wooded ground. There he lay with his tongue unattractively hanging out.

Phil wobbled and swerved from the head knock but soon regained his balance.

"Phil!" Buck perked up excitedly, not quite understanding what had just occurred. "*You devil!*"

"Hush up!" Phil replied contentiously. "Now let's get out of here before he wakes up! I don't want him angry at me too. Can you ride? How do you feel?"

"Hell, yes, I can!" the rejuvenated black stallion said.

Baker climbed onto his back hurriedly just as mumbles of coherence began to issue forth from Chiron. Pixies whispered and poked at him to awaken him. A few of them dived for the victorious steeds as they prepared to depart.

Soon, however, the foursome was on its way, galloping faster than they ever had. Joe and Baker held tight to the manes of their steeds as they cleared the bridge and the wood fast as lightning, out into new-forming landscapes. Not even Baker complained about their velocity.

"You love me," Buck teased his sardonic partner as they sped through a sudden birth of caves on either side of them.

"Shut up."

AS THE sky turned a deeper blue and lights began to twinkle in the skyfield, the foursome arrived at their destination after a hastened rush through the plains. They had come upon a smallish, circular patch of woods sprouting up from the otherwise flat surroundings. The trees here had an importance to them, an air of intoxicated regality. These were not the straight up-and-down trees of any old forest, not the puff-and-blow-down variety of Chiron's orchard nor the over-fed giants of Abigail's gardens. No, these were vigorous-looking, white-barked arbors, and they seemed to twist, bow, and dance as the riders approached. Their limbs grew out in such lines of beauty one was tempted to grasp at them and play and dance along. They curled and twirled, gliding through the air. Still, they did not dance to the wind alone but to a music that came from deeper within the wooded circle, the sounds of drums and flutes and cymbals playing an catchy ditty that made the trees woozy with queer and sensuous oscillations. It was infectious. The music reached out for the riders and their steeds. Phil and Buck walked slowly through the music as it graced the evening air.

As they ventured inward, the leaves of the trees began to change into a multitude of shades. Blues, greens, and bright reds; yellows, pinks, and purples.

"So many colors!" Joe gasped.

The leaves from the playful trees seemed a symbol of their ecstasy. There were more colors and shades of colors and descendants of colors than Joe could have ever dreamed existed. They fell ceaselessly from the limbs to the ground in soft, lilting rainbow showers like confetti. Whenever one leaf would fall from a limb, another would grow in its place immediately, and always of another shade. The ground Phil and Buck tread upon was a carpet of impressionistic beauty. The leafy confetti lavished over the travelers as well, getting caught in their hair, tails, and manes.

"Where are we?" Joe asked, catching a palm full of confetti to examine it more closely.

"It's a party," Buck replied. "Don't you just love a good party?"

"Be careful, though," warned Phil. "They probably won't like you." He shook his mane and tail, shaking off the colorful leaves.

"Phil!" Buck chided with his deep voice. "They'll like them just fine. Claire likes everyone."

"Claire?" Joe inquired.

"You'll see soon enough," Phil grumbled as they came nearer the music and heard the unmistakable sound of laughter and singing.

"Do you live here?" Joe asked, still looking around the vibrant patch of forest in wide-eyed curiosity.

"Nope," Buck said. "Our place is in the Meadowlands. We were just asked to bring you here. This is Claire's place. We're guests, you see. Everyone you meet here is a guest of our friend—of your friend—Claire."

They came to a vast, spanning, multi-colored fern that was as huge as anything Abigail grew in her gardens but pulsating like the beat of a heart (*thump, thump, thump*) with vibrant hues of individual colors. It stood before them like a happy, gorgeous gateway.

"You ready for this?" Buck asked. "Because you're going to love it!"

He did not wait for a reply. Buck followed his companion Phil through the organic entryway before them and into the midst of music.

Joe could not believe the nursery rhyme spectacle that met his eyes as he was carried into the inner circle of the wood. The music—that swift, kicky jive—was issuing forth from instruments played by a menagerie of animals. A small calico cat played a wood flute; a large gorilla pounded on two heavy drums; and a very happy penguin brought its short wings together to play the cymbals. There were other instruments as well, and the creatures playing them chimed in at various times, each instinctively knowing their place. A raccoon strumming a harp here, a blue jay whistling a tune there. But they all added to the joyous raucousness of the wood. There was no melancholy melody here. All the band players and the assorted guests danced about and shouted in playful abandon as the colored leaves fell all around them.

A large tower of animals sitting atop one another's shoulders like a living totem pole—the base of which was an adolescent hippo—began to teeter in the direction of the new arrivals. Others scurried and cavorted about the pile of hoisted creatures, cheering them on in some contest of fortitude. None of them seemed to notice Joe and Baker on horseback until a voice called from the top:

"New friends! You've brought us new friends!"

It was a squeaky voice, hyper and energetic. The source of that eager holler began to climb down the five other animals it had been lifted upon with ardent glee. A small, squat black bear now leaped from the hippo's haunches to the ground. Plumes of rainbow confetti lifted all around as it landed. The little bear wore a bright orange flower fixed aesthetically to one side of its head, behind an ear. Its little eyes looked at the new arrivals jubilantly.

"You've brought them!" she (for there was no doubt now it was a *she*) repeated.

The party slowed a bit, though the mood remained ever gleeful. The music softened as the other creatures crowded near to see who the new revelers were, and they spoke in excited, hushed mumbles.

"Yes, yes," Phil muttered, somewhat annoyed. "We brought them. Though this one," he said, nodding in Baker's direction, "is a real piece of work."

"Phil!" Buck chided once again.

"Well, welcome to the party!" said the bear. "Welcome to my home, Joe." She held out her furry arms in an extravagant gesture. "My name is Claire. You'll know all about me when the time's right. That's why you're here, right?" she winked. "Hiya, Baker!" she waved excitedly.

"Claire," Baker nodded in amused acknowledgment at the very popular bear.

"Everyone," she squeaked as she turned to face the crowd and raised her stubby arms to the sky, "Phil and Buck have brought us new friends. This is Baker and Joe!"

A noisy hoopla that sounded much like a dangerous stampede, only happier, arose from the animals.

"Let's make them feel welcome," Claire continued. "Phil, if you would, carry our friend through the welcome parade."

Another loud roar of approval. It was an amazing thing to see non-humans smile. It wasn't just the shadows of smiles Joe had seen in life from dogs he had played with, but real-life, happy, toothy, eye-shining smiles.

"I hate parades," Phil grumbled as the band struck up a zippy revelry at Claire's behest.

The mass of animal guests parted as Claire joyfully led the way, pumping her arms, one then the other, in rhythm with the carefree music. The little bear was nothing if not a leader. Phil followed suit through the confetti leaves, though a bit grudgingly. In fact, Buck had to prod Phil's rear with his nose to get him to take the first resentful step. Joe waved in sheer enjoyment of the moment. The animals to the side, as well as those in the band, waved and cheered in response like the spectators to a hero's homecoming.

"Hooray, Joe!"

"Welcome, friends!"

"Tickle Phil's ribs. Cheer him up, Joe!"

After Phil and Joe came Buck and Baker. And then, one by one, all the animals and birds made their way into the procession until only the band was left playing on the inside of a living carousel. Soon, the musicians, too, joined the merry-go-round and played as they went. The littlest critters whose instruments were too large for them to carry were lifted to the backs of the larger beasts. Joe found himself almost as lighthearted as a kid. He was almost as happy as when he had been with 3P. This rowdy, stinky, magical procession led by a round little black bear was just the sort of thing 3P would have loved.

Joe, caught up in a great fit of laughter, looked back to Baker, who seemed to be enjoying himself as well. Yet there was a different sort of joy on his face as he watched Joe. He wore a relieved and caring expression of guidance. He enjoyed seeing Joe's enjoyment more than the actual proceedings that were causing it.

The circular parade went on until Claire thought the welcome had been sufficiently relayed. But still, after the procession had ceased, the party continued beneath the canopy of trees that let in only glimmers of the night sky. Laughter streamed out of the Circle Wood on all sides, catching every creature not at the party in its wake. There was quite a lot of drinking, though whether or not there was any real intoxication Joe could only guess, because *everything* here felt like it was at least mildly inebriated. Everything had that lazy twist, that blurred fluorescence. Seeing a pug dog drinking rum from a wooden goblet alone gave Joe the feeling of giddy dislocation and disbelief. And when the dog realized he was being watched by Joe, he smiled with delirious content. This only made Joe giggle the more.

A bonfire was lit in the center of the wood, and Joe was dragged giggling into the happy whirl of creatures. Claire clasped at his hands with her tiny paws, and they went round and round the fire, prancing and skipping and singing ditties made up on the spot. The cinders flew high into the night, enfolding the laughter and merriment that were then carried off by the music and a higher air to some place where joy might be needed. For there was plenty of joy in the Circle Wood.

Baker had joined in the fun as well. The drum-playing gorilla (who politely introduced himself as Sam) saw Baker's guitar upon his entrance into the wood and, as there was no guitar-player in their band and to have one would be most agreeable, asked if Baker might care to play.

"Well, it'd be right dumb of me to turn down a drum-poundin' gorilla, wouldn't it?" Baker answered as he stared up at the mighty Kong.

However, Joe could tell Baker had been itching to play since he first heard the music upon their ingress, so for the time being, he seemed to forget his melancholy manner of song and do his best to join in the more upbeat festivities.

Buck also managed to break Phil of his foulness, and the two of them galloped and trotted like young colts all about the forest, kicking up the rainbow leaves in colored plumes of vibrant dust. Both horses were very careful not to step on any drunken chipmunks or crush any carousing field mice by mistake.

The flamboyant spontaneity of the moment so caught Joe that he found there was nothing else on his mind, only the flow, just the natural go of things. It was the circular motion of all things living and dead and in between. He was in the moment, as he should have been.

The tongues of the flames from the bonfire licked and played with the wooded area, casting beautiful, elegant shadows over the ground before and around the dancers. Everything and everyone glowed. All this was gorgeous, and Joe would have been quite taken with it but for one thing: he found himself more interested in the fire itself. He was enthralled by the beauty of its golden heart. And it was that—the inviting warmth of heart—that took his hand and led him down another forgotten path. A new former truth revealed by an element….

HE WAS on a couch now, surrounded by young people. They were talking and laughing profanely, though none of their comments were directly aimed at him. Some were dancing to music turned up to its maximum level on a large stereo in a corner. He was at a party just as boisterous as the one he had left on the other side of the flames. He was younger here. Like the others at the party, he was about eighteen and ready to leave high school, ready for college. But he was alone even here. Though he was friendly and smiled and conversed pleasantly, he was left always the solitary man. So he had found the couch after a few minutes of asocial ambling and nursed his plastic cup of rum punch.

He stared at another young fellow across the room. A young man involved with the party, enjoying it, not a classmate nor anyone Joe had ever seen before. Joe thought him the most attractive man he had laid eyes upon in quite some time. Brown hair clipped short and neat, broad sportsman-like shoulders, a tapered waist and a well-defined chest that could be seen through the white T-shirt he wore. Such a handsome guy. Joe sighed just staring at him. If the music weren't so loud, everyone would have heard that sigh.

Chidingly, Joe forced himself to look away, to stop gawking. Nobody could catch him. He was always so fearful of the obvious signs of secret lives. Especially his secret life. His feelings were to be hidden. They had already caused the death of Declan. So Joe had decided to suppress... repress... those dangerous emotions and longings. That was the way it had to be now, he explained to himself, as if in a melodramatic television film or some well-intentioned "message" flick.

And his phantom friend, that Louis who used to show up at strange and difficult times, hadn't been seen for a long while. Not since that day in the flower shop. Louis was the only image that made loving seem like everyone else's notion of loving.

Still, despite his prohibitions, Joe's true feelings swam through the moat of denial he had built around his mind, around his actions. Curiosity forced him to glance over once again to the young man in the white T-shirt. Then, in a quick, decisive manner, he closed his eyes. He would sit still on the couch and pray no one had noticed his eyes studying the guy's ass. He realized they had lingered there for a few seconds too long.

Yes. Joe would simply sit here for a few minutes more, then get up and find a ride home. Deny... deny... deny.

But then there was an applied pressure to the back of the couch. Joe opened his eyes to see a girl with a bright orange flower stuck in her stringy black hair leaning toward him. She smiled broadly and innocently and smelled of tangerines and wine coolers. She wore thick-rimmed glasses that were much too large for her face, and from her ears hung earrings in the likeness of bushels of assorted fruits.

"Whatchya lookin' at?" she questioned as her shoulders convulsed to the music.

Joe was taken aback. "Uh, nothing," he said with apparent annoyance on his face.

"I think you were looking at that hot guy over there," she charged. "At his ass."

Joe was immediately humiliated. She was so loud and vocally careless.

She flung herself over the back of the couch to sit beside him. The word "tacky" came to Joe's mind as he caught a glimpse of her whole costume. She appeared to be going for the layered effect. Brightly colored tops—first an orange T-shirt, then a long-sleeved button-up of blue, and over that a pink shawl—mismatched with her green-and-yellow striped skirt, hot pink socks, and black heels. Added to this, she had a mess of bracelets on each arm that jangled more than jingled at the slightest movement of her wrists.

"I was not looking at his ass!" Joe defended himself in an angry whisper.

"You were too. But it's cool. And I don't blame you. It's a nice ass... I mean, as far as asses go." She spoke with no hesitation, saying whatever slipped from her thoughts. Apparently she had no internal filter. It all simply gushed out, be it treasure or sewage—mostly, in Joe's opinion, the latter.

"Who are you? What the hell do you mean by sitting by me and accusing me—"

"It's not an accusation. It's a truth. You should embrace all the things that make you just a little different than everyone around you. There's nothing wrong with it. In fact, that's why I like you. I might like you better than anyone in this room right now." She looked about, as if making certain she had not overstated. "Seriously, do you really want to be like all these people?" she said with a wide, sweeping gesture. Her bracelets clamored in appeal.

"They look happy to me," Joe said. He smiled at a school acquaintance as they passed him.

"Is that how they look?" the tacky girl asked, the earrings dangling fiercely. "Do I look happy?"

"You look like you're trying to cover your unhappiness with the pretense of being different. I see it all the time. The whole nonconformist thing."

"Maybe I am." She smiled with crooked teeth. "But then, maybe this is just me, and I'm okay with it. Maybe I know I'll never be prom queen, and I'm okay with it. Maybe life is short and I'm trying to suck up as much flavor as I can."

"Maybe," Joe said. "Or maybe you'll never know who you are

because it's masked beneath all this." He made frantic movements with his hands to encompass her extravagant ensemble. His resentment toward her was ruffling his calm.

"I know who I am," she said, still grinning. "Claire. And the hot guy you've been staring at? His name is Ben. He's my gay cousin."

Joe looked at her, dumbfounded.

"When you think you might like to get to know him, get hold of me. He's a real nice guy. He thinks you're cute too. Told me so earlier when he saw you walking around."

And then, just as unexpectedly as she had sat down, the tacky girl named Claire rose with a silly leap off the cushions of the couch, as if the backsides of her legs had springs.

Joe looked in the direction of Ben, who was indeed looking at him, and there was the slightest hint of understanding. Of mutual interest. Claire ran up to Ben, wrapping her arms around him. He chuckled and hugged her in return.

What a wonderful smile he has! *Joe thought.* Like an "all clear!" Like a call out of hiding.

WITH that, the tug of careful flames gently pulled him in from the past, ending the lesson. He ventured through the warmth of the heart and was soon in front of the bonfire again.

The party, the animal revelry, had died down, and Joe was now the only being still standing. The fire faded to tiny, whispering embers that were then carried away by a light breeze. Warmth was everywhere still. Joe felt the kindness of fur touching his hand and looked to see the little black bear gazing up at him tenderly with enormous brown eyes. The night wrapped itself about the wood like great enfolding wings.

"You remember me now, don't you?" Claire said softly.

Joe nodded and grinned. "Yeah, Claire. I remember you now.

Thank you," he whispered, and he squeezed her paw.

"Eh," she shrugged. "Ain't no big thing."

"Claire," Joe said quietly, again looking toward the dying embers. "If I can ask, why are you here? How did it happen?"

"How did I bite it?" she said bluntly, with no change in voice or demeanor. "Well, after high school I got a gig at a zoo, one of those poorly kept ones. It was struggling to stay afloat and had a real hard time getting and keeping any exhibits. My job was taking care of the animals there. I would feed them and sometimes hose them down. I loved my job. I loved animals. They were always so much more interesting to me than people. And nicer to me too. I never met an animal who cared what I looked like. Well, one day I was helping just outside the elephant compound, and somehow one of the boogers got loose. Imagine that! All the visitors and staff got out of the way—all but me."

"You were…," Joe was trying to say it delicately.

"Squashed," Claire completed his statement. "Guts and everything squished right out of me. Didn't even see it coming. Damn pachyderm fell right on top of me! Didn't hurt, though. I don't recall feeling a thing at all. Just woke up here next."

"Not a thing? Well… that's good," Joe said matter-of-factly as he continued to watch the used pyre.

"Yeah," Claire agreed just as matter-of-factly.

Around them, sleeping or resting or just remaining quiet, were the other animals, the other guests. There were Phil and Buck sleeping in snugglement despite Phil's earlier threat. There was Baker stretched out on a pile of rainbow leaves with his guitar to his side and his hands under his head. There was that little drunken pug dog, resting in his goblet like a poster Joe remembered from his second grade English class. The confetti of the trees had stopped descending, and the wooded circle was still.

Joe and the bear stood for a while, the two of them hand in paw in silence and nostalgia. As the last spark of fire was lifted up to the sky, Joe saw, in the serenity of the wood, a figure in shadow watching him.

By second glance, the figure was gone again. *The Stranger.*

WHEN the moment came, the colors folded back into the sky like waves in a great ocean. Joe lay with his eyes wide in amazement at the continual changing of the horizon as he watched it perform just past the trees. It was like the Aurora Borealis every night, but sharper and slower so that one could see the complexity of it all. It was heartbreak and its mending in one experience.

Claire was nowhere in sight. In fact, most all the other animals had gone sometime in the very early morning. They could be heard trafficking lightly out through the arbors. Joe only saw Baker in the wood now, still resting with his guitar.

The new light called to Joe, and he answered. Slowly, he rose and waded through the fallen debris of colors toward Baker.

"I hear you, kid," Baker said with his eyes closed. He sighed, getting a good morning stretch on the ground, and opened his eyelids. He took hold of the neck of the guitar and came to his feet.

"Another day, another adventure," he said with a smile, brushing the confetti from his clothes.

"Hey, you two!" the tiny, shrill voice of Claire called to them from beyond the perimeter of the wood.

Joe and Baker walked in the direction of the call, out through an elegant brachial archway. They came upon Claire sitting with her chubby legs crossed on the grass just outside the circle of trees. Phil and Buck grazed on the plains, and beyond them was a sea of rolling hills. Then, farther off, hazed by the distance and the humidity, was a massive range of mountains. A flock of silver birds flew up from somewhere behind the two stallions.

"How goes it, Claire-Bear?" Baker kidded as he and Joe took to ground near her.

"Ready for my new day!" she answered. She shot her arm out in front of her, pointing with a tiny claw to the rising landmasses that lay ahead. "There's where you're off to next." She was as jovial as ever.

"Jeez, this place is like a living map," Joe said. "No one could ever get lost here, I swear. Everyone seems to know where I'm headed but me."

"It's the same for all of us in the beginning," Claire squeaked cheerfully. "You can get lost, though. There are lost souls here too. They just wander and stumble about, sad and incomplete. They look real tired all the time. But most of us find our way okay. Then, when we know our way well enough, we can help others out. Others who don't know their way so well. Some lost ones maybe. But the truth is, we never stop discovering new things. There's always more."

"Well said, li'l bear," Baker chimed in.

"You ready for what's ahead?" Phil inquired as he and Buck drew closer in graceful strides. Joe didn't realize they had stopped grazing. His voice now sounded more concerned, less sarcastic.

"Yeah. I think I am," Joe answered.

"Then we better git," Baker said as he stood and then gave Joe an unnecessary hand.

"You be careful, young man," Phil said. There was absolute gentility in his eyes now. The grumpiness had all but disappeared. "There are gonna be tough times ahead. You'll need your wits and strength."

"Don't scare the boy!" Buck huffed. "You'll do just fine, Joe. You'll make it to the end just fine. You've got a great guide. Some here aren't as lucky to have someone like Baker at their side."

"Thanks," Joe replied. "I know I'll make it through. It was nice meeting you both." His voice betrayed his wariness the tiniest bit. "And it was wonderful seeing you, Claire," he said, looking down fondly at the little black bear.

She sprung at once to her back paws and wrapped her arms tightly around his waist.

"You too," she said. Joe heard a little sob. "You've got a lot to do. But remember, it'll all be worth it."

Joe bent to her height and gave her a proper hug. Yes. Definitely sobs.

"We'll see you," Buck said as the two wanderers began to head toward the mountains on foot.

"Joe!" Phil shouted after some distance. "Don't let *that* one boss you around!" he hollered, referring, of course, to Baker.

Joe smiled, then turned and waved a final farewell to the stallions and the bear.

"That pony's a damn pain in my ass," Baker mumbled as the two refreshed travelers made their journey onward to the core of the massive stone giants that lay before them.

MOUNTAINS 'TWEEN ME AND THE SUN

THE traverse to the hard stone of the mountains was slow in passing. Gentle hills rose from the plains as Joe and Baker journeyed forward. That is to say, they did not form spontaneously as other land features were apt to do in this place. No, they had been there all along. Only the light play made them seem like mere waves of grain and grass, a delicate deception of diminutive disappointment. From the vantage point of Claire's forest, the mountains looked but a half-day away. (A "day" being an aging measurement that Joe was finding very difficult to discard, having yet to distinguish between growth and time.) The distance, however, was even more deceptive than the hills. Land and yards seemed to stretch and grow ahead here, waiting for a time that *it* thought was appropriate. Joe could almost hear the yawning growth spurts.

The sky soon grew dark—Night's great mantle thrown overhead—and Baker thought it best they camp on a sloping patch of ground without making much headway.

"Sometimes," Baker explained, "getting anywhere here can be downright irritating. Eternity's slow in going."

Baker played his guitar by an easily set campfire, and the chords bounced and echoed off the trees and the night. He sang with his scratchy voice anything Joe could come up with. "Tower of Song," "You Ain't Goin' Nowhere," "A Case of You."

When the dawn came again, they continued on, but still the mountains never seemed to come any closer. They remained immense, unattainable and aloof, clouded by the haze of the ether. They could not decipher from their position on the ground how high the mountains heaved into the atmosphere, but Joe could not remember seeing anything so majestic and stirring. It was as if great stones poured endlessly from the sky like formed magma right out of the thick clouds.

As they went on, something not as inspiring caught their attention. Seeping into the air around them, Joe and Baker perceived a putrid stench of sulfur and ash. It leaked out over the hills, which grew smaller in height and less vegetative as the stink became more pronounced. Joe grimaced and pinched his nose, making a sound of disgust.

"We must have wandered into a bog or mire, Baker," he said, not expecting a reply.

From where the offending odor permeated, they could not yet tell. The hills, though not stately or too terribly high, were many and acted as shields and guardians of the myriad small valleys between them. The true source of the acrid, putrid odor might have been anywhere.

Soon, however, the sound of fevered, tormented voices could be heard. The voices crawled through the stench as if it were a thick mud. They were almost inaudible at first, muffled by the heaviness of the atmosphere. But very soon they could be heard quite clearly. They became screams and high-pitched cries of agony and terror. They darkened the world. Joe slowed his pace, but Baker urged him on with care.

"Ain't nothin' to do with us," he said. "We just gotta pass it, 's all."

"Pass what?" Joe had to strengthen his voice to be heard above the terrifying cries.

Baker never answered. Instead, Joe saw with his own eyes the obstacle they were to ignore. They were nearly on top of it. The gentle hills, now barren of most of their vegetation (only what looked like dead grass and tumble weeds remained), surrounded a vast circular area. It seemed a wide, gaping mouth in the earth, the jagged rocks around its lip like monstrous canines and incisors. This was the origin of not only the abhorrent stench but also the curdling screams that now threatened to deafen. In the middle of the circle, the ground gave way as if impacted by a large meteor or asteroid. From the gaping hole that had sunk into the dirt and rock came the offenders of Joe's senses, the smell and sound.

The air around them was a revolting yellowish mist that Joe feared to walk through.

"C'mon," Baker urged again. "Cain't hurt you unless you ask it to."

Joe held his nose tighter as he and Baker made their way along the edges of the crater through the dry, dead landscape. He wished he possessed another pair of hands so he might have been able to plug up his ears as well. Joe wanted to vomit from not only the reeking air but also the cries of pain. It was a nauseating bombardment of the senses.

The chasm was a wide and hungry thing that plummeted into solid darkness, into pitch and unsettling black. Every so often, a hateful, hot, red glow would burst momentarily at the blackened depths of the pit, like an exploded land mine or a blast from a nighttime bombing during some useless war. These flashes would be preceded by a wave of heightened howls and pitches.

"How far down does it go?" Joe asked above the screams. He was trembling. How does one calm nerves when they don't truly exist?

"Who knows?" Baker replied. He seemed disinterested in it and kept walking at a steady pace, looking only at the ground that offered his next footstep. "Never been down there myself. You won't need ever to go down there either."

"What is it?" Joe waved a plume of yellow from his face.

"It's a silly place. That's all."

"Hell. It's hell, isn't it?" Joe's voice shook at his sudden realization. "Pitchforks and fire and demons?"

Baker stopped and turned, looking at him somewhat disappointedly. It was a look Joe was becoming increasingly familiar with. "Now, chief, if there ain't no heaven, would there be a hell? Think on it. I know you're smarter than that, more logical. I guess I'll play preacher and teacher here. Those souls down there," he said, lazily swaggering to the edge of the pit, "they were misled. They're regular folks like you and me. Only they believed too easily what they were told. They're followers who didn't question."

"Just regular folk?"

"They believed they were condemned. Believed it full force because they was told to. They didn't even look for balance. And they was scared ever to question those that told 'em that. So there they are. They could have saved themselves from a lot of shit. If they had just looked around for different ideas, for their own personal—"

"So they believed what their preachers told them and now they're being punished for it? That's not fair. That doesn't sound right at all, Baker."

"They're only being punished by themselves. There ain't no higher power doin' it. Not like you're thinking. As I said, there ain't no hell. You keep makin' me repeat myself, boy. There ain't no heaven, God, devil—none of it. Only the mind makes it so. 'S'a powerful thing, the mind. We can create somethin' outta nothin'." He paused. "Are we done with today's sermon?"

"Those poor people," Joe whispered down into the foul darkness. He thought of shedding tears for them, but the moisture would be licked away by the flames before it ever reached them.

"Naw, Joe," Baker comforted him, putting a strong hand on his shoulder. "There's hope yet. Look yonder," he said, nodding to the far end of the crater.

Rising up from the depths of the black pit, Joe could just make out the top steps of an ancient stone stairway. They were obscured by yellow mist and jagged rock. If Baker hadn't pointed them out, he would have missed them completely. They were well-traveled steps. And what was more, Joe could just make out people dressed in burned rags, three of them, ascending the stairs. They trudged, tired and worn, but up they came to the flat land that Joe and Baker stood on. Waiting for them eagerly were three other souls. Guides like Baker. Each guide embraced his or her charge, and the joy that shone on the weary face of each soul from below was enough to make Joe cry. He could almost forget about the stench and the screams that spoiled the air.

There were other guides too, waiting near the edge, peering into the pit. Some patiently holding, others more anxious.

Joe noticed an old woman with gray, frizzled hair. She called down into the darkness with great zest and spirit: "Jolene! Jolene, you knock that nonsense from your head and get up here to your momma!"

Who knew how long she had been standing there.

"They can escape it. They can get out of it," Joe whispered hopefully.

"Yep," Baker said. "There's always a way out. Those fellas over there climbin' the stairs... well, they finally woke up. Happens all the time. Sooner or later the realization kicks in and they can rescue themselves from their own stubborn attitudes. Don't need anyone's help. They just come climbing up outta that pit and git on their ways, start their journeys. Yay for them, right?"

"It's sad what they have to go through 'til then, though."

"Well, human beings have always done one thing very well, and that is create their own hells and bask in their own misery. They complain about what they create for themselves; they relish the pain. What they don't do so well most of the time is find a way out of it. Now, c'mon," Baker said, squeezing Joe's shoulder. "Let's get a move on."

The stench of sulfur and ash slowly dissipated as the two travelers made their way once again into the hills and beyond, leaving the hell of others behind. Joe couldn't help but look over his shoulder, hoping to see more awakeners climbing their way up from the pit.

THE gateway at the base of the great mountains was an uninspiring thing, nothing to base ballads or folk tales upon. There were no shrouding folds of mist. There were no monstrous trolls ready to devour those entering, nor was there a riddling sphinx. The passage was simply there, located between two large boulders. A small, dull pathway into the stone. The mountain itself was jagged and haggard-looking up close, splintered and uneven. No longer did it seem so majestic. Even the ground before the gateway was mute and inauspicious. It faded blandly from the lively grass of the plains to dirt and gray earth scattered with pebbles and rocks here and there, which grew in size and numbers as Baker and Joe approached the mountains.

"This is it?" Joe asked in doubt as he stood with Baker at the passage. A dull wind whistled through the gateway.

"This is it, chief," Baker confirmed. He waited until Joe was ready to walk through the boulders and then followed. "You're always looking for that dramatic edge, ain't ya?"

"This isn't going to be the best thing for our bare feet, is it?" Joe commented, ignoring Baker's playful jab.

Yet as he spoke these words, he saw in front of him, hidden by the boulders, very smooth and neatly carved stone steps that went up the mountain as far as Joe could see. But there wasn't just one set of stairs offering a single alternative to travel. No, others branched off from the first set of steps at a well and went spiraling and meandering this way and that. And those steps, too, had branches reaching and then breaking off into another flight. Joe could now see what he could not just moments earlier when he was on the outside looking in. The jagged cracks and slants were not malformations of stone at all but ascending steps all headed, in some distant and distinct way, to the very top of the mountain. The summit, if there was one, if in fact the mountain didn't continue upward forever, encroached too high in the sky to be seen, buried deep in pink and white clouds. Joe was once again in awe, and he gazed up for so long he began to think at any moment the stairwork might all come crumbling down upon him, exhausted by the sheer intricate nature and power of itself.

"Which one should we take?" Joe asked, looking with puzzlement at the steps, at the utter multitude of choices.

"Don't matter none," Baker replied. "Whichever way we take, we'll get to where we're s'posed to be… eventually. Kinda like that old saying 'all roads lead to Rome'."

"I suppose you know what you're talking about," Joe agreed, and he gave a sigh signaling commencement, a "here goes nothing" gesture.

He proceeded to climb the root stairway to the stairwell, at which point he turned slightly, with a sly grin at Baker, and took the flight just beside the center route. Just that wee bit off-kilter.

"You're a sneaky booger," Baker kidded. "Can't call you predictable."

The climb went along unencumbered for the most part. The steps seemed surprisingly easy to navigate, as if there were a caretaker sweeping off fallen rocks and rubble every day. Joe named this make-believe person the Stair Keeper. He kept an eye on the world below him as it lessened in size but lengthened in expanse at every stride upward.

After what seemed an acceptable day's travel, Joe and Baker settled on another stairwell at a much higher altitude for the night. As Joe looked out over the vastness of the landscape, he was satisfied by their progress. Everything below now seemed diminutive. From their vantage point they could see ever-changing sky, the wide plains, the rolling hills, and a steadily flowing river off to the east. If Joe squinted his eyes in the growing dark around him, he thought he might even be able to make out the tiny patch of wood where Claire held her nightly soirees. He smiled at the thought of the frivolity taking place there as he and Baker now sat on the side of a hard stone mountain. He wished he were there instead. And though he couldn't see it, he knew beyond that was the miserable cottage of Abigail and her mournful gardens. With that bleak thought, Joe turned his attention back to Baker, who sat on one of the branches of the stairs, playing his doleful folkie heart out.

"How did you get here, Baker?" Joe asked, finally comfortable with their relationship. "How did you die?" He was on the edge of the well with his legs hanging off the side.

"Was wonderin' when you would finally get around to askin' me that," Baker said. He stopped playing the guitar, and the last chord of music drifted out over the plains in a lonely echo. His eyes followed its invisible journey. Higher above, a single bird sailed elegantly through the nightening sky.

"Like I said before, I was a musician—or I wanted to be. Never really got too much notice, but I loved doin' it. Everybody has a passion, and that was mine. Doesn't really matter how good you are at something as long as it gives you some kind of happiness, you know.

"One night I had this gig in Fishkill, New York, of all places, playin' at this dive. Now, understand that 'dive' is a matter of opinion. I'm sure some poor folk thought this place was a palace, but not me." He paused. "Anyway, wasn't for much money, this gig, but I was young and wanted the experience. And they threw in a free meal. Was all I could ask for at the time. I knew I was never gonna be a Townes van Zandt, so I took what I saw comin' to me and shut up about the rest.

"Well, the set went well I guess. About as well as could be expected, anyway. It was real loud in the bar, so I don't suspect anyone actually heard my playin'. Noisy waitresses and drunk truck drivers mostly. Not the kind of place record producers frequent. At least, none I ever heard of. Afterwards the manager paid me my measly allowance and gave me my dinner. Tuna on rye! *Can you believe that?* That was my dinner!"

He chuckled, remembering the tiny bits of occurrences and faded memories only the participant in such events can find humorous. "Well, as luck would have it, the tuna was spoilt. I got me a bad case of food poisoning from it. Real bad. It was the most painful physical experience I guess I ever had. Died at the hospital the next day after they found me face down in my motel parkin' lot. Still had my guitar in my hands too. They was good enough to bury it with me." He tapped lovingly at his instrument. "This ain't the same guitar, though," he continued. "Music has soul, but instruments don't. That's the one thing about being here that chafes my hide. That guitar had more spirit than most of the folk I ever met."

"Wow," Joe said in a quiet whisper. There was a gleam of surprise and revelation in his eyes. He had turned his gaze from across the plains and now looked at Baker with a curious heartbreak.

"Yeah. Not a very glamorous death, huh?" He plucked haphazardly at the strings.

"You got food poisoning from eating fish in *Fishkill, New York?*" Joe almost laughed, yet the look of revelation was still in his glance. His breathing had also quickened. Something in Baker's tale had caught him off-guard, but he did his best to hide it. Baker was still dreaming of his life and did not see Joe's reaction. Still, there was something that transpired in the air between them, a question and an answer. To decorate the silent understanding with words would have been redundant.

"The damn cook was the one who done it," Baker reasoned. "When I see that cook here," he said, pointing his index finger knowingly, "I'm gonna give him a piece o' my mind. Yes, sir!"

Joe was silent for a moment, eyeing the vastness around him again, stilled beneath the sky. "Baker," he finally said, "do you miss people? Did you have anyone to miss you?"

"Sure I do," Baker answered. "Don't everybody? I had me a damn pretty wife. We just got hitched, too, not two weeks before. When I first got here, after I remembered her, I missed her somethin' awful. She would sing with me sometimes. Sing as pretty as any damn bird you ever heard. She even got up on stage with me some." He grew wistful and even more melancholy. "I miss her singin' at me. I truly do."

"I miss my mom," Joe said. "I miss her so much, and I think it's all beginning to dawn on me what all this means, that I'll not see her for a long, long time. Now that I'm remembering it more and more, there was nobody who was there for me like she was." Tears wet his eyes. "She could sing, too, my mom. She sang so nice. I wonder if, after I remember everything, she died before me?" He shook that thought, too, from his mind. "But then, I hope not. I hope she's still there, singing away."

"But you sure would love to see her, wouldn't you?" Baker said in hushed tone.

Joe sighed. "I sure would, Baker," he said. "I sure would."

Above them, in the night sky, the silhouette of a great bird glided in elegant turns. Had Joe looked up, he would have seen a giant winged creature that seemed to hover for an instant and then retreat higher into the shadows and heights of the mountain.

"...PLEASE GIVE ME A SECOND GRACE..."

UPON new light, Joe and Baker set outward and upward once more to obtain greater distance from the ground below. They chose a flight of stairs at random and went. Joe was finding the air of the mountainside agreed with him; it rejuvenated him like the first whiff of spring. He ascended the mountain with a pleasant face.

"Looky there at that goofy grin," Baker prodded.

They had climbed an admirable amount of steps when they came upon an area of the mountain that seemed a long stretch of hall compared to the stairs. They walked along a wide area of flat ground that appeared as if it had been blasted out by dynamite. Here and there grew a resolute bush or a small, lonely tree. Both sides of the stretch were lined by the walls of the mountain. A quiet roar of wind echoed off the rock. Joe and Baker were in a deep canyon, like a fold in the mountain. Far above they could see the stairs continuing to sneak in and out of cliff sides and caves. That was the journey yet to come. But here, on the floor of the canyon, there was nothing. Not a single acclivitous step. There was only a long trough of dust.

They walked on, down the stretch of the stone vale, until their attentions were simultaneously grasped. Ahead was a strange and eerie glow in the air. The heaviness of a fog had assembled in the canyon. A thick, clustering mist crawled ever closer like a crippled animal. It stretched from one side of the canyon to the other, clinging to the walls, a fog with fingers, inching forward as if in fear and dread. Upon sight of it, Joe began to clutch at his own chest. The air seemed harder to breathe.

"Dammit!" Baker said. "I was hopin' we wouldn't have to come across one of these."

"What? What is it?" Joe asked, suddenly alarmed. He wanted to run from it, to tell Baker to do something to keep it away.

"A creepin' mist," Baker replied, putting a hand on Joe's back. "Prepare yourself, kiddo. What you see in there ain't gonna be any fun, and there ain't no way around it." He set his concerned eyes upon Joe.

Joe was therefore hesitant to venture any farther, but then he really didn't need to move at all. There was no avoiding the mist. It came at them, groveling along the ground with vapor-like roots, overtaking them quickly, a swirling mass of white and dampness that reached for them, sliding its pleading, moist fingers along their bare skin. Joe instinctively held his breath and was at once in the midst of it. It pulled on him with a persuasive grip.

"Keep goin'!" Baker shouted as it engulfed him as well. He spoke with more verve, because the mist had begun to muffle everything. It drank up sound like water. "Just keep walkin'."

To Joe's horror, he could make out faces in the containment of the surroundings, faces molded from the very vaporous air. The faces' mouths contorted and stretched in such ways that it made Joe step back in fright more than once. The eyes sagged and melted in wretched frowns with pupils as black as scorched sun.

These were the anguished. These were the sad and desperate. Howls and cries of the most piteous kind came from the nothingness of the moisture composing the faces. They appeared on all sides of Joe, crying out, pleading for help, for some sort of resolution. But resolution of what?

"What the hell is this?" Joe whispered above the screaming mist. His voice shook with terror.

"Nothin' but sadness," Baker replied. "These are the faces of people—beings—caught in between points of existing."

"What do you mean?" Joe gasped at the ghostly horror that surrounded him. He still clutched at his chest as he struggled forward.

"They're not dead, really," Baker screamed through the vapors. "They're not wholly here either. These are ones who should be here, who should have passed, but have been kept in their previous states, immobile. Hangin' there. They've been hooked up to machines so their bodies are still alive, even when their consciousness and self is ready to leave." Baker huffed, "And they call it life-support!"

"That's terrible," Joe whispered, jerking away as a writhing tentacle of mist tried to secure a grip about his arm.

"People do strange and terrible things to keep their lives and all of its pieces together. They don't realize, though, that when it's over—well, it's over. To force someone to hold on like this…."

"Heartless," Joe finished the sentence.

"I was gonna say ignorant," Baker corrected.

"I don't want this anymore. I can't stand it!" Joe said as he started running through the suffocating mist. "I'm sorry, Baker. It's too much!" He felt as if his chest were about to implode.

He did not look to see if Baker was behind him. He knew he was there. Baker could barrel through mountainsides with his nonchalance as his only tool.

Faces screamed past Joe, howling for his attention. Joe swatted and struck at them, feeling shame at doing so. They evaporated from the air only to reappear elsewhere. He found himself yelling, cursing at these lost beings to leave him alone and find their peace somewhere else. He commanded them to haunt the living, or wake up. Yet they continued to stalk him, to try to bring *him* into their misery and torment. They wrapped their sorrow around him, and he struggled to break loose. He had the terrifying feeling that he was losing the fight. He was beginning to feel numb, as if he were being reached into and emptied in scoops. His fingers tingled; his mind froze with painful white flashes. The mist was ganging up on him, surrounding him. Scream upon scream for attention. He found he was unable even to cry out.

Joe did not realize when he finally emerged from the great fog. He had closed his eyes to the world, only hearing the dreadful moans. But he came through, and it was his own doing. Somehow, he had summoned the strength and forced the creeping mist off his flesh. When he burst from its last hungry fingers into the canyon, into the sun once again, he inhaled with the strength of a small cyclone and then crumpled to the ground.

It was not until Baker made it through as well and grabbed him by the shoulders that Joe opened his eyes to a clearer view. He breathed heavily and deeply as Baker held on to him, cradling him in his strong arms.

"It's all right," Baker whispered in his ears. "It's okay, son. We're through it. We're through the mist. You're out now."

High above, a winged creature watched, engrossed, from a stone perch. Then it flew off in a parallel direction to Joe and Baker's intended path.

BAKER trailed behind Joe as the younger man trudged up various sets of stairs. Joe was silent, and his ambition was seemingly gone. All the wonder with which he had first embraced the mountain had evaporated, sucked dry by the grieving mist. Baker tried some words of comfort: "It's part of your journey. I don't know why you had to see a creeping mist, but, for some reason, you did. It'll make sense in the end." Joe did not reply.

They at last came upon a much grander staircase than any they had previously encountered. This one was very wide and the steps much steeper. There were ten steps, then a well, ten more steps, then a well, and so on up. There were no forks breaking away from this stairway as far as either of them could tell, just a single large pathway stretching up the mountainside and disappearing into the cloud cover. It was exhausting to look upon.

"Best get on up," Baker urged kindly.

They only made it a few staircases, though, before Joe decided it was enough. Emotionally fatigued, they rested for the night on a stairwell. Baker held Joe's head in his lap, stroking and brushing his hair tenderly, until the light of the new moon shone. The sound of the wind in the mountains was all that could be heard.

"YOU'LL want to get higher today," a strong voice called from above Baker and Joe as they both lay on the stone stairwell. The voice echoed off the rock walls like a claxon warning. "The mists have been creeping about a lot lately. You'll want to get higher."

Joe rose with a start and a shudder at the mention of the creeping mists.

Baker stood slowly and looked upward and around. "Who's there?" he shouted. This once he stood to his full height, back straight and shoulders broad, as if ready to defend his emotionally fragile charge.

"Up here," the voice called back from some altitude.

The travelers were then able to pinpoint its issuance. It was the massive winged thing that had been spying on them from the start of their climb up the mountain. They had thought it was a large bird and nothing to do with them. It was perched on a ledge, and Joe thought it looked ready to pounce. The pinnacles of its wings sprung like symmetrical blades behind it.

"There's a city up farther," the voice with wings continued. "That's where you want to go. That's where I would head if I were you. You might find someone you know there. Souls are always finding others they know there."

"Who are you?" Baker yelled. His question bounced and ricocheted off the rock, then floated away unanswered.

"Follow me," the voice ignored the query. "I'll be up here. Keep looking to the sky, and follow me. I'll keep you safe from the mists."

"Another talkin' critter," he mumbled to Joe with a roll of the eyes.

"Just so's you know, I could keep you plenty safe."

"I know," Joe said, hoping to alleviate Baker's guilt.

The creature, bird or demon, spread its large wings and took to the air with a resounding cacophonic crack as air was whipped and sliced around it. Joe thought it a strange-looking bird. And even though he was viewing it from very far off, it appeared to him to be too slim to be the body of a bird. Something wasn't right about it. But he tried not to let Baker see his misgivings.

The two land-bound travelers watched the sky and followed the bird's flight. It did make things go faster. The climb seemed less tedious as they watched the feathered guide circle and swoop in elegant tricks and fancies of flight. It helped lessen Joe's anxiety. On more than one occasion, the bird perched on a cliff and waited for them to catch up. It would then take off again, shattering sound with its expansive wings. The stops and starts didn't appear to bother it at all.

At last, nearing the end of their arduous climb, Joe and Baker lost sight of the bird as it flew into thick pink clouds overhead. A thin layer of pink also rolled and settled on the steps ahead, causing Joe some concern.

"Don't worry," Baker soothed him. "These aren't creepers. We're safe."

With that reassurance, Joe took a deep breath and forged ahead through the sweet-smelling air. At once, the cloud haze parted and Joe saw a large, gleaming, white stone arch—a true gateway reminiscent of what he had expected to see at the base of the mountain. It was enwrapped with vines of pink and white roses. Beyond it was the city that the bird had promised. A bustling metropolis built from and into the mountain itself. The city shone a brilliant white, as if every structure were coated with polished pearl. Joe thought of every history course he had ever taken. The edifices were that of a Classical Roman style. Ancient Earth stuff. Eminent columns and lovely statuary laced with an air of contentment.

In the center of the main plaza, which Joe and Baker had entered, was a fountain in the design of Bernini's Fountain of the Four Rivers whose water shot high into the air in a myriad of directions. Children played about, running circular games of tag around the fountain's base as birds perched on the river gods and the obelisk.

The dress of the city's inhabitants was very subdued and undramatic. All around were robes and gowns of white and brown with the occasional blue or purple. People were jovial and welcoming, though they did not notice the new visitors in unison. It was a gradual acknowledgment, almost as if they were invited guests to a Sunday picnic. They were greeted warmly by the citizens, like residents of the mountain who had merely returned from a night out.

Though they had lost sight of it for a bit, Joe and Baker kept their eyes on the winged creature when it came back through the clouds where it had been gliding. Being attentive to the creature's directions was hard, however, due to the merriment and beauty, the sheer warmth, emanating from the mountain city around them. One thing was apparent now, though: their aerial guide was not a bird at all.

It flew high above, almost touching the pink clouds that hung heavy and swollen. There was a tinge of orange to them now. As it flew, the creature's broad wings dragged along bits and pieces of cloud like cotton. It led Joe and Baker down streets and busy thoroughfares, past the markets and schools. Always the people were kind and never once angry or perturbed by the commotion among them or the intrusion of the two strangers. Children ran past them, giggling and carefree, offering picked flowers and happy grins.

Finally, the flying thing made its rest on the balcony of an elegant structure built into the rock face. The structure stood a bit larger than the other buildings, with more levels. The creature waited for Joe and Baker to approach, making their way through the lighthearted populace.

When, after gentle nudging through the streets, Joe and Baker stood under the balcony, they saw the creature was much more familiar than a bird. Nor was it a gryphon or Pegasus or anything resembling ancient myth, as Joe expected. No, the creature was simply a man—a man with wings. Wings of the whitest and most pure color Joe had ever seen. They arched up behind him in majesty and splendor. Yet the man himself, the actual body, was not so different than any of the others down on the streets. Nor was he any different from Joe. The truth was Joe saw more than a little resemblance to his own facial features in the winged man.

"Oh," Joe heard Baker say, as if understanding the answer to a riddle.

The man spread his wings with a special sort of pride radiating from his handsome face and glided down to meet them on the stone steps of the building. He wore a brown beret of the kind Joe had seen in old photos from the early days of the twentieth century. His shirt was a common light brown with suspenders that held up darker brown pants, and his feet were shod in black boots with thick, masculine heels.

He tipped the brim of his hat and gave a faint smile of recognition, looking from Baker to Joe for a few moments of registering silence.

"Don't get any weird ideas, Joe," Baker finally spoke. "This *still* ain't heaven, and he ain't no angel."

"Hush, Baker," the winged man said briskly, clearly familiar with the folkie. "If he wants to think this is heaven, he can go right ahead. It's as close to the idea as one can get, I suppose. But as far as me being an angel... well, Baker's right about that." He chuckled. "I'm no angel. That's not to say they don't exist, as Baker has probably told you. They're very much real, but I'm not of their ilk."

Joe grinned in much the same manner as the winged man. They could have been doppelgangers, reflections of one another but for a few minute differences in height and hair color.

"You don't recognize me, huh?" the man asked. "It's okay. The last time you saw me, I was an old man. Though before that I can't say we saw very much of one another, and that's a shame."

"That's your namesake, Joseph," Baker interrupted. "That's your momma's daddy. Grandpa Joe."

The elder Joe smiled with kindness at his young relation, a big smile now, prideful and chilling.

"Ah," Joe gasped. "I do remember seeing you some, but there was something… some reason that I didn't get to see that much of you. You certainly didn't look like this, like me."

He tried hard to remember this man who was barely a footnote in his earthly existence. The citizens of the busy stone city went on around the threesome. Their voices flowed like river water, in the background and non-intrusive.

"You'll get it. Don't stress yourself. You know by now how these things come back to you here," Joe Sr. said. "I'm just glad I got the chance to see you before—" He stopped there, as if frightened he was going to give some great secret away.

"Why this place?" Joe inquired. "Why do you live here in this crowded place with all of these people? From what I remember of you, you liked your space, your solitude."

"Reminds me of the Mediterranean here," Grandpa said, looking around. "One of my favorite places in all the world was Italy. I loved its art, its culture, the history. I was over there during the War. Met the love of my life there." He said it with a sad twinkle in his eye, revisiting a memory. He had the same reflection in his eye that the Stranger had had while looking at Joe in the barley field.

"Grandma?" Joe asked.

Grandpa simply looked at him, tilting his head as if Joe's question made no sense. "No," he said. "I never much cared for her. It's a sad truth."

Baker chuckled and cast his gaze to the ground, shuffling dirt and pebbles with his feet.

"But you married her," Joe said in confusion.

"Yeah, I did," Grandpa Joe agreed. "But then, we all make mistakes."

"But do you see her? Is she here?"

"She's here. I know that for certain. But I've not seen her since I passed," Grandpa said as he came over and put an arm around Joe's shoulder. His wings unfolded behind him just a little. Joe felt the touch of silky feathers on his bare skin. "This will all be explained. All this stuff about your grandmother. Besides, why all the concern for her? As I recall, she wasn't exactly a favorite of yours."

"She wasn't?" Joe questioned as the three of them walked down the street. Joe did remember a certain bitterness toward the old woman for the way she had treated Veronica. But was there something else? Something still in the memories to come?

"I don't think he's got to that memory yet," Baker announced, answering Joe's questions.

"Oh, I see," Grandpa said, and he looked at Joe's face, his own face, with love. "Maybe that's why you're here with me then."

They continued walking, passing the monuments and museums, admiring everything that came into sight.

"You want to see where I live?" Grandpa Joe asked.

"Sure," Joe answered. He was still astonished by the youthfulness of the being in front of him, by the absolute vitality and beauty of someone who had been but a wrinkled, frail thing in every memory he had.

Without the slightest warning, Grandpa Joe wrapped an arm around Joe the younger. "Hold on tight," he said, ready to take off. "I'll be back for you in a bit, Baker."

"I'll be here," Baker assured him.

The crowd dispersed as Grandpa unfolded his strong wings and caught the air. Children cheered at the sight. Joe felt the quickening of excitement as the ground left from beneath him and the city became smaller and smaller. Baker's face stared up at them from below. He gave a quick thumbs up to Joe.

Soon they broke above the sweet cloud barrier. The pink and orange billows cushioned them on all sides and muffled all sound as they flew into and out of it. And Joe found his suspicions confirmed—the colored clouds did indeed taste of candy. He licked the sweetness from his lips as they rose even farther. The feel of the air around him was like the cool side of a pillow, refreshing.

The clouds were below them now. Here and there mountaintops and ranges jutted up through the foamy sea. Joe felt he could walk on these clouds, jump onto a mountain range then leap back onto the fluffy pinkness and not be the worse for it. It would absolutely support his weight. The wind, the sweet candy, the sensation of flight, were mesmerizing and freeing.

They came at last to a mountaintop that was lined on the outside with a portico and a veranda like a landing pad. Grandpa flew in through the small columns, each carved in the forms of golden muses, and set Joe softly on the marble floor.

He folded his wings, ornamented with cloud. "Welcome to my villa," he said.

"A villa above the clouds," Joe marveled as he looked out onto the hilly clouds of pink and orange.

He stared in wonderment at the view, leaning on one of the gold columns, as Grandpa Joe took flight once more to retrieve Baker from the bustling city streets below. Stars were beginning to shine and twinkle in the sky overhead. The horizon was the convergence of the darker starred sky and the soft colored clouds. Soon Joe the elder came again through the clouds, his great wings whooshing and dripping with atmosphere, Baker and his guitar in his arms.

TOGETHER on the veranda they passed the pressing of the dusk. Serenity and calm soothed away what anxiety Joe still held from the encounter with the creeping mists. The air was sweetly scented and tasted like sugar on the lips. Baker strummed light lullabies into the evolving sky as he sat against one of the golden muses. Joe the elder had gone inside the mountain villa for a moment only to come out again with a tray of drinks colored like sunsets in lovely slim flutes and delicate china bowls filled with the most perfect, airiest chocolate ever moussed.

Above the night clouds, which took on the subtler colors of blue and violet, whisked and darted night beetles and glowflies.

Joe felt at ease and comforted by the discovery of family. He was in his own grandfather's care now. He felt a connection forming between them, like a bridge being built quickly with invisible but sturdy stones.

Joe and his earthly grandfather talked as Baker, who would occasionally join in the dialogue with wry comments and sardonic observations, played the troubadour with equanimity. As is the course with most conversations at dusk on verandas or balconies, they talked about everything and nothing—seemingly important things from the life they knew, excursions into the mundane, and the randomness of death. They spoke of people: of the mutual acquaintances they had shared and of the deeper loves of a mother and daughter. Their thoughts grazed over the few moments they had spent with one another, and they felt sorrow for the missed opportunities for further interaction. Unable to help himself, Joe asked his older counterpart of his adventures, of his life story.

"You'll know what you knew soon," he was promised compassionately, if cryptically.

But the elder did tell him he had been a fighter pilot in the Second World War. That he had fallen in love while in Italy, and it was the most beautiful time of his life. As he was speaking, his eyes once again twinkled with a peaking sadness, making Joe remember the Stranger. That was all, though. No more.

"Despite the fact there are no rules here, no laws, it's an unspoken agreement to not reveal what's still to come," Grandpa explained. "It's good to have some secrets. They make you want to journey on, and you *need* to journey on. So I will tell you nothing else of that life."

Of his existence in his present form, however, Grandpa Joe was more forthcoming. He told of many an adventure and romance with his love. ("Oh, yes! We found one another here almost immediately.") Again, though, he never gave any hint of his love's identity. He told of meetings with heroes and saints, villains and thieves, legends and housewives.

"All of them," he said, "very interesting. All of them with a story to tell."

Of course, his heart was in the air, blowing about with the winds. He was a flying man, a gliding spirit, a trapeze artist with wings. So it was with those same types with whom he spent most of this existence: Amelia Earhart, Charles Lindbergh, the Wright Brothers, and others Joe had never heard of with more ancient-sounding names. Grandpa had sought them out in this form when he knew they were here and could be sought out. Some, he explained, had left anew. Gone on when they had heard the call to seek new experiences in other forms.

"Some time or other," he explained, "we all want to return, to have new adventures in another existence. Some want to return sooner than others. I think it's the soul's desire for boundaries. You grow the most, you see, when there are boundaries, when there are things to climb over."

But Joe the younger couldn't imagine ever leaving now. He was becoming enamored with this place. With the villa itself. And, most of all, with Grandpa Joe. The idea that he was part of the winged man, that they were kindred spirits, made Joe sigh with pride.

In the course of the night, after thousands of words had been spoken, Joe began to fidget. To feel restless. He wanted dearly to explore the mountain home. His curiosity to go inside was overwhelming, so he asked permission of his earthly grandfather and walked into the villa's interior through a large arched doorway as Baker played on behind him.

What he saw was, like so many things here, not what he had expected. That was to say, Joe thought he would be greeted by a vast many-chambered abode, that he would walk down long corridors dimly lit by candles, scattered with brooding furniture, and other such romantic notions of a villa. He had imagined a Gothic romance novel brought true. What he saw instead was one very large vaulted and coffered room. The only light came from lanterns that drifted about the space like orbs of magic at varying heights.

The chamber was filled with comfortable furniture, not the stuffiness that would possibly have suited it better. Scattered throughout the chamber were tables that looked used, yet elegant; sofas that were lounge-worthy, yet still held an aura of grandeur and class; and carpets woven from fine materials, yet aware of their natural use. There was a golden harp in the form of an angel and a black piano draped with a cloth of the finest silk. Interspersed among the finery was statuary. Among these were renditions of the Angel Gabriel, the goddess Nike, and the foolish mortal Icarus. Also decked throughout were vases that held beautiful orchestrations of plant life. Lilies, morning glories, and babies' breath scented the room, which also smelled of freshness and crisp air mingling with the cool sweetness from outside. It was the scent of exhilarating freedom.

The walls were no less breathtaking. Hung floor to ceiling were elaborate frames with the most gorgeous, if stock, of painted scenes. There were many that concerned the sky and flight, angels and doves, eagles and stars, but some, too, that delved into other themes: into landscapes and tragedies, histories and myths. Even the coffers above were filled with a colored story, each one of them detailing specific chapters of a tale. The floating lanterns drifted by them as if knowing where he was looking and upon which painting or fresco he was turning his gaze, so Joe could see clearly.

Joe began following the paintings like a patron in an art gallery. He wanted to see them all, but there were so many. The room was so large. So he determined to start at the end of the great chamber where he had entered and begin a slow and studious examination of each work of art. The lanterns floated near him as he examined each piece. The art his grandfather must have created.

The paintings were precise. Every blade of grass seemed to wave softly in the breeze, every muscle seemed to flex and striate. The colors were vibrant and full of buoyancy. It was as if the art had a pulse, as if it breathed in and out. The subjects in these paintings appeared to be regarding Joe in return. Their eyes were fixed on him.

Slowly, as Joe made his way through the works, they began to take on a more familiar aspect. Faces began to change to recognizable expressions, to forms he knew. To memories....

THERE he was, at a painted dinner table in the center of a painted dinner scene. He recognized it as his grandparents' home. And the family he could now remember, the mass of distant biological relations who were never more than strangers, was all around. The food was served and placed skillfully and with care and design across the surface of the large table. An enormous turkey was the centerpiece of the meal, and it was surrounded by cranberries, sweet potatoes, stuffing, and other such items.

Joe sighted himself standing at the center of the table with a look of fright and concern on his face, deftly rouged. Beside him sat Ben, his boyfriend, looking up at him with a similar expression of jittering disaster. Ben was the first boyfriend Joe had ever really acknowledged as such. His conversation with Claire at the party where he'd met Ben had opened him up to his true self. Joe took a drink from the wine glass and sat waiting for a response—any response—from those seated around him at the table. A response to something he had just said, words already spoken.

Ah, yes! Now he remembered this long, dry, painful moment.

His mother sat beside him and covered his hand with hers, shielding his trembling from the others' eyes. Then the levee broke, and Grandma stood, nearly kicking her chair from beneath her. Though the painting moved, it did not speak. There was no sound in this memory. Joe, however, heard the words clearly enough. They had been branded in his mind.

"Disgraceful.... You should be ashamed!" Grandma railed on and on. "This is how you raise your son?"

And the feeling of hate for her came to him. Grandpa had been right. He didn't much care for the old woman. Not so much for attacking him, but for attacking his mother.

He watched as his painted self stood once again and defended his mother against the bitter old woman's tirade. Then, after a barrage of insults from the hag, Joe took his mother and boyfriend by the hands, and they left. But not before he saw the glance. Grandma shot a sharpened arrow of accusation and pleading down the long, crowded dinner table to the old man who sat opposite her. The old man now looked at his grandson, Joe, with understanding and pride as he left the room. It was a look that had not registered with Joe at the time. All he was concerned with was getting his family, the only family that mattered, out of Grandma's firing range.

"See this? See this?" he heard the old woman shout at Grandpa as they were leaving. But what did that mean?

Then the colors of the frescos and murals mixed and ran as another canvas came into sight. In fact, the paint seemed to run from canvas to canvas, wall to wall, a continuous, thick, liquid river bringing to the surface things that were.

Just a month, a mere month later, and the old man lay dying in his bed. Joe went to see him not because he knew his grandfather terribly well, but because they were family by worldly definition and he owed him that respect. Grandma stood trembling in the corner of the bedroom. Her eyes of accusation and pleading had not changed much, though now they were mingled with sorrow. Joe and his mother were there to see the passing as well.

The old man's eyes lit up with joy and gratitude when he caught sight of Joe. His dry lips moved in speech as Joe sat down beside him and Grandpa took his hands.

Again, the words played like a recorder over a silent film.

"Don't worry about Grandma," the old man comforted. He glanced at Grandma, who didn't seem to hear him. His face was wrinkled and dry, his skin thin and defenseless. "She doesn't understand."

Echoes. Untamed echoes.

"Do you?" Joe asked. "Does anyone else, really? I feel alone." A bitterness was creeping into him, replacing the loving boy he had once been.

The old man squeezed his young hand. "You are not alone in this." His voice was as adamant as he could make it. "I had a friend," he explained. "I had a friend in the war. Do you see? He was a pilot as well. Another American. It was he, not your grandma, to whom I gave my heart all those years ago. And she knows it."

Grandma whimpered and covered her mouth, stifling a cry.

Joe's eyes wetted with tears. His surprise could not be hidden. "Where is he now?" he choked out.

"Waiting for me someplace else. He died in the war," the old man said, choking back tears of his own. "Since then I've just been waiting and existing until we're together again." He coughed, a dry and brittle noise.

"Oh, Grandpa," Joe gasped as he fell onto his namesake's chest with loud sobs.

"You are not alone," Grandpa said. "Don't let the world make you angry. Angry is too easy."

At the door, with the face of an awaiting angel, stood Joe's compassionate mother, Veronica. She walked over and put her hand on Joe's back and her own father's face. She connected them, became a lovely link across ages.

As Joe watched this show of tenderness, the lesson done, the paint began to fade once more, to run and mix until the figures were not known to him at all. It was not the image of him and his grandfather on a bed with Veronica standing over them, but that of two angels embracing and being fed by the light and love of God.

The painted world changed to someplace he had never been but existed only in his grandfather's adventurous world and creative imagination.

JOE stood motionless, taking in the memory like blood, as if it were a needed transfusion. The lanterns stayed with him, casting shadows on the walls. All was quiet and respectful, prayerful.

Finally, Joe walked slowly toward the large arched doorway he had entered. There sat Baker, fast asleep on the marble floor, the guitar leaning up against him to his side. And in the sky, above the blue clouds and below the twinkling stars, flew the free and exhilarated silhouette of Grandpa Joe, somersaulting and swooping through the darkness as if it were a refreshing dip in a cool creek. Joe leaned against the side of the doorway and watched, a tear and a smile on his face. The continual circle of things was finally becoming evident.

JOE and Baker stayed longer at the villa than they had at their previous stops. The sky changed its shade and hue so many times that Joe began to lose track. Yet he realized far too soon that things would have to change. He and Baker would need to move on to the next destination of his soul journey. They spent the allotted time they had, though, in the comfort and relaxation of each other's company.

They soaked up as much as they could of Grandpa Joe's good fellowship. There were trips down to the city and midnight flights over lazuli clouds. They chased curtains of rain and connected the stars dot-to-dot. Joe thought it the most magical time of any existence he could remember.

IT WAS an early dawn. A new dayspring came upon the villa and its field of clouds. Joe awoke on a plush red sofa in the inner chamber. Light slid in through the windows like promenading beings made of sunbeams. Baker was up and trying his hand at the piano in the corner and doing very well at it; he was a consummate musician. The folkie on the guitar had a jazzy sound at the piano.

Out on the veranda, Grandpa Joe stood in between a pair of muses, his tremendous wings arched in their restive position. Their feathered tips were so long they curved at the bottom to the will of the stone floor. He stared out onto the breaking horizon. Joe walked quietly up behind him and stood beside him at the edge of the veranda. His eyes cast out over the rolling sweetness. The colors of the clouds were especially bright this morning, pinker than Joe could remember seeing them on any other morning. Off in the distance, there was a shape like a giant light bulb coming toward the villa. It was an indication of change.

"What is that?" Joe questioned, looking to his grandfather.

Joe the elder peered ahead in yearning, a slight touch of bittersweetness on his youthful face. The small bill of the beret cast a shadow over his brow.

"It's time for me to leave," said the older man. Baker continued to play the piano lightly in the chamber.

"You mean us. It's time for Baker and me to leave," Joe corrected, saddened by the abruptness of the disclosure.

"No," Grandpa Joe restated. "While this balloon is your ride, it's time for me to leave as well. My time here is through."

"I—I don't understand."

"My pilot friend, my love, my companion, has gone on ahead of me, into the next existence. I must follow. He's waiting there for me."

"You're leaving?" Joe exclaimed. "You can't leave! I just got here!"

Joe the elder looked at the younger with compassion. "He is my soul mate. I have to find him again. We both decided to go on to the next existence. But then I got word you were coming, and I stayed my leave. He went on ahead, and I promised him we would meet again. I promised him I would find him."

The balloon edged ever closer. Its dark red color was reflected on the clouds.

"Can you understand that?" Grandpa asked.

Grandpa was right, of course. Joe was coming to the realization of how things worked. It would be selfish to ask him to stay behind. Still....

"We'll meet again." Grandpa held a hand to Joe's face. "We're always together," he said. "Every new existence is a reunion of souls."

Joe wanted to object more, but Grandpa silenced him with a gentle headshake.

"It's interesting," Joe said, "how a heart can break just as easily in heaven as it can on Earth." He wiped away tears with his palms.

Baker had stopped playing the piano and now stood at the door with the guitar strapped to his back. Joe the elder turned to him and nodded. "It was good seeing you again, Baker," he said with a wink.

"You too, Gramps," Baker nodded back. "Catch ya next go round."

The hot air balloon was nearly at the veranda. It was a strange-looking thing. On board, manning the contraption, was a thin woman in a striped suit of yellow, orange, and red. Her long hair was swept up beneath a red hat with a large ruby brooch and a white feather. Ahead of the basket, pulling it like a horse does a carriage, was another similarly dressed woman on a bicycle. Instead of a hat, though, she wore a pilot's cap and goggles.

"All aboard," the woman in the basket said too loudly for the moment.

"This is your ride," Joe the elder turned to the younger and said. A gathering mist was in his eyes.

"Do you have to leave?" Joe asked his grandfather even as he knew the answer. Even as his bottom lip quivered.

"I have to. You'll understand why. You will. I promise. And very soon. Someone waits for you as well." He winked.

The balloonist tapped her nails on the basket impatiently, and the bicyclist revved herself as if preparing for a race.

Baker climbed on board and waited for the younger of the two Joes.

Grandpa Joe swooped up his grandson in his arms, wrapped him in his wings, and gave him a breathless hug. "It was good to finally know you, Joe," he whispered under tears. Joe could say nothing. He was stifled by his own emotions. "I'm so proud of you," Grandpa went on. "I've always been so proud of you."

Slowly, Joe backed into the basket. "I'll miss you," he choked out. "Why is it I'm always arriving when you're leaving?"

Grandpa smiled and waved as the balloon drifted away from the villa, being steered by the balloonist and propelled against the wind by the cyclist. Joe watched with an aching heart as his grandfather all but disappeared once again behind the clouds. When the villa was out of sight, Joe bowed his head in heavy thought and cried.

"Joe," a hushed Baker said. "Look there. *Look, Joe!*"

Joe raised his chin. In the sky, riding the clouds alongside the balloon, was Grandpa Joe whooshing his massive wings, scattering the pink all over the expanse. He did somersaults and tricks in the wind. Joe laughed in delight even as the tears of farewell clung to his cheeks. Grandpa flew with the balloon for a bit, keeping them company, passing Joe a final smile. Then, with a tip of his beret, he departed, splitting through the clouds and out of another existence.

"Is he gone?" Joe sniffed.

"Ah, no, Joseph. He ain't never gone. Just changed, is all."

"...THAT WILL NOW BLACK THE SKY..."

THEY sailed smooth and sure above the clouds. The cyclist propelled the balloon with hunch-shouldered conviction. She hadn't seemed to notice the new passengers in the basket at all. The air was blessed with the same sweet, clear scent that Joe and Baker had woken to every morning since they had come above the clouds. A refreshing breeze brushed their faces. Nothing but the balloonist's lighting of the burner could be heard as they made their way thenceforth, casting an oblong shadow on the blushing billows below.

Joe leaned over the edge of the basket, contemplating a *last* goodbye. He had thought he was through with farewells. Joe thought waking up in heaven (for he still thought of it as such, no matter how much Baker objected) should be a jubilant parade of rapturous greetings. He had thought goodbyes were an earthly thing. But they existed here as well. Sad partings and breaking hearts were waiting in the shadows of every incarnation, it appeared.

They floated ever farther away from the mountain and the villa in the clouds. Soon it was no longer in sight, shrouded behind the atmosphere altogether. The balloon ride was quiet, undisturbed by word or breath. The operator of the vessel was not talkative. She had a stern, serious face and a committed stare, which was fine with Joe. He was in no mood to befriend or be befriended. For the time being, he was content to be asocial and let his eyes see the shapes in clouds.

Nothing much happened. A flock of geese flew along with the balloon for a while, ducking in and out of clouds. They honked greetings, but Joe did not reply, and the birds sailed away into another patch of sky.

Baker leaned against the back of the basket, watching the stoic driver with mild interest. She and her cyclist partner seemed to have an unspoken way of communicating. Either that or perhaps they had taken this exact route so many times that they didn't need to converse for directions. Were the cloud shields and clusters static? Was it always "take a right at the cloud shaped like a turtle"? Or "drop ten feet at the cloud shaped like Indiana"?

When, on one occasion, the balloonist did glance around at her passengers, Baker was sure to give her a flirtatious wink. She looked away without responding. She wasn't embarrassed or shocked, but it was as if she were tossing the gesture over the side of the carriage. Baker grinned despite her reaction.

"So this is it, huh?" Joe asked in a deflated huff, finally interrupting the silence. The wind whistled by his ears.

"What's that, kiddo?" Baker said, ambling to Joe's side of the basket with unease.

"We just float around here in heaven too? As aimless and directionless as when we were down on Earth? When we were alive?"

"Now, Joe," Baker comforted softly. "There's a point to it. You might not be able to see it very well right now, but it'll pop up. You'll find it on your journey, somewhere down the way."

"Why does there need to be a journey, anyway? I mean, wasn't life hard enough? We should just be able to imagine ourselves anywhere we want. We've earned it!"

"Maybe we have," Baker replied. "Maybe *you* have. And when you're here longer, you will be able to do just that. You'll be like that damn genie in the bottle on that TV show. Point at something, think of something, and make it be. Personally, though, I think that would take the fun outta any experience. You appreciate things more when you gotta fight for 'em. You know that. There are lessons to learn from the Journey, Joe. Reasons we gotta see."

"Ah. Lessons to be learned. That old standard." Joe sighed. "What about you? What did you learn, Baker?" Joe gazed at the folkie, wanting an answer—pleading for one.

Baker was silent for a moment, simply staring back at Joe. "I had to learn to forgive, like everybody," he finally said.

There was something deeper in Baker's glance. As if there were something more he wanted to tell Joe, but he couldn't summon the courage yet.

"Forgive who?"

"Well," Baker sighed, coming closer to Joe, "I had to forgive my daddy for bein' a drunk; I had to forgive my momma for never standin' up to him; and I had to forgive myself." He paused and brought a hand up to massage Joe's shoulders. "I had to forgive myself for lettin' certain things slip away, you know."

"Everything slips away, though, doesn't it? There's no keeping anything, as hard as we try. So what's to forgive?"

"Some things do slip away, yes. Some things can't be helped. But they are never truly lost. We find 'em again. They're merely tucked away in closets or hidden in dusty corners. Then there are other things we lose through our own shortsightedness or, as in my case, longsightedness. That is, I was so concerned about the future that the present just…. Those ones are harder to get back."

"But can they be found? Can we get them back?"

"Hell, yeah," Baker assured him, his voice lifting from gravity to hope. "Wait long enough, and it all comes back to you. And believe me, son, I know what I'm talking about." He gave Joe's shoulder a playful slap. "You're just fine, Joseph. Just fine."

Joe smiled, sensing the affection in Baker's voice, hearing the concern. "I'm fine, Baker. You're right. I'm just fine."

AS THE air began to moisten and it seemed dusk was about to settle (for it had been a long ride), the sky began to fill with traffic. At first, there were only one or two more cyclist-drawn balloons in the vicinity. But then more and more could be seen drifting or being led in an orderly fashion down some invisible skyway. It wasn't long before Joe's own balloon joined the aerial freeway. Every one of them headed in the same direction. Occasionally, another balloon would join or one would break off, as if taking an off-ramp. The balloons were colored a uniform yellow like the brightness of a sun, and the balloonists and cyclists wore the same outfit as that of Joe and Baker's balloonist and cyclist.

As the balloons streamed along the celestial highway, Joe could see something appearing on the clouds, a destination, perhaps. At first glance, there was only the tiniest hint of it. It was impossible to know exactly what it was. But as the balloon floated ever nearer, Joe's eyes made out the distinctions of the place. It was another city. This many-structured city had bell towers and domes right in the midst of the clouds. In fact, the clouds were the foundations for the architecture, which gleamed with silver and glass. The buildings sparkled and shone with brilliant reflections of light that bounced continuously, unendingly, from one glass spire to another. The effect was one of clarity and prisms. Of clear sight and refracted light.

The balloons were trafficking the people in the other balloons this way and that, bringing visitors and taking them away as if they were pilgrims to some sort of Mecca. The brightness of the colored envelopes of the balloons contrasted with the darkening mixed hues of the sky's blues and oranges; this in turn created a fabulous wealth of colors within the silver glass city itself.

The bright balloons weren't the only form of transport to and fro. There were also great sailboats with their massive sails gliding over the pink clouds and parting them like surging waves. There were smaller boats as well, schooners and skiffs and canoes, some of which carried only one or two passengers. And every so often, a boatman would throw out a glittering net from his place in the cloud sea as if to catch a great haul.

On the glimmering docks sat men and women and children with long crystal fishing poles, the strings sunk into the cotton softness. What were they fishing for? What mysterious bounty existed in the clouds? In the very vapors? And would not the weight of the catch, whatever it was, break the crystal pole in two?

Joe's balloon drifted on into the middle of the activity, casting its shady plumpness over the glassy facade of the metropolis. Citizens and visitors walked below along the busy silver streets. Rainbows and prisms danced all around them.

Then Joe noticed another peculiarity as the balloon settled above the heart of the city. Down on the glimmering steps of a large academic-looking structure, citizenry were scattered about, reading from books as if it were a public library. Other people came in and out of the massive doorway of the building in streams, every one of them with a book or more in hand. And up from the domed silver manse, the largest in all the city, floated words. Words in letters and sentences, even entire paragraphs. They were a bit transparent, yet they were there, swimming in the air alongside the balloon. Physical manifestations of phrases drifted upward, far higher into the atmosphere than any balloon might dare. Some were thin and wiry-looking, while others were plump and full. There were ancient words, definitions, and hieroglyphs, and script, lyrics, and languages not even discovered yet. They whirled in gentle cyclones higher and higher. One could read an entire book or love letter or training manual in the air if one stayed in the same position long enough. It seemed as if words from every type of written work ever created were there dancing around the balloon.

"What the hell is this?" Baker mumbled, swatting at a sentence as if it were a pesky bee or a mosquito. The letters scattered from the disturbance but kept climbing all the same. A capital O got caught on his ring finger, and he shook it loose frantically.

"It's the City of Thought," their balloonist said, still staring straight, still committed to her job. "Be careful of your thoughts here. They're not your own. Once you think them, they belong to everyone. Somebody will most likely read them and write them down for posterity."

"What are they doing down there?" Joe asked, peering over the side, still interested in the sailing vessels and fisherfolk. "What are they fishing for in the clouds?"

"Dreams. Ideas. Thoughts. It's what they do. Thoughts, after all, have to come from somewhere." She said it all indifferently, like a bored tour-guide.

"They come from here? Dreams come from here? From the clouds?"

The great silver netting he had seen thrown in was now being pulled up from the clouds. A wriggling mass of white fluffiness was contained therein. Was that what thoughts looked like?

"They come from everywhere. They glide into us from the air. Rain down with a summer cloudburst or a winter's first snowfall. They seep in through our ears and sink into our skin."

"I'll keep my thoughts to myself, thank you," Baker said, a bit testy as he shooed away another set of words—big, long, multi-syllable words.

"Well, then you should never come here," the pilot said.

"Well, I ain't got a choice, do I?" Baker shot back.

"This isn't your stop," she corrected him. "We're just passing through."

"Where are we headed, then?" Joe asked, as his question physically passed before his eyes and drifted up. He smiled at this newfound form of creation.

"I am taking you to the ground," she answered. "Back down to solid. But to a specific spot. That's why you needed to fly a little first. The flight will get you there faster, without having to traverse the mountains. From there, you are on your own. I am not part of your particular journey."

"Don't worry, kid," Baker assured him. "I know where we're headed next." He looked at the pilot, who still had her back to him. "And it ain't in the darned blasted sky!" he yelled. "Besides, like I told you before, chief, you'll get there eventually anyway. This is your path, no matter the bumps along the way."

"Still, I would have liked to have seen the City of Thought," Joe gently moaned. "To walk along its streets. I liked school very much. The learning part of it, anyway."

Baker came to his side. "We'll come back sometime. How's that? And without company." He smirked at the balloonist, who paid him no mind. "It'll just be me and you."

Joe smiled at him. "But you wouldn't like it. You said so yourself. You want to keep your thoughts to yourself."

"Well, maybe I can rig up some contraption, ya know? Put some ingenious helmet on my noggin made from a thick kinda metal so's my thoughts cain't get away from me." Baker squeezed Joe's shoulders tight. "I'm a clever grunt when I have to be."

Soon, the balloon flew on, and the City of Thought faded from view, its captured thoughts and dreams floating into the ether like backward rain. The cyclist never tired or asked for a rest as she continued to pedal furiously.

Wafting upon the clouds, there was really nothing much to do. Joe found himself bored and almost lulled to sleep by the gentle rocking of the basket and the whistle of the wind. Occasionally, he would skim his fingers along a close-streaming cloud, pulling it a bit along with the balloon. Then he would put his fingertips to his lips and taste the sticky sweetness. The taste reminded him of pleasant things: eating the sticky candy at summer fairs in Augusts with his mother and then Declan too when they were old enough to go alone: bumper cars, whack-a-moles, fake tats, and farm shows. Once, Declan had put his hand on Joe's knee on the Ferris Wheel when they were high in the air, away from care. Oh, the excitement of that moment! The freedom! The touch lingered on Joe's knee for weeks after. He could still feel the flush.

At last, after some time of nothing but clouds and birds, the balloon carried them past a large, too fluffy, generic white cloud on which was positioned a gateway of gigantic golden arches and bars surrounded with ridiculously large pearls. The gate was unpolished and somewhat forgotten. For Joe, though, it was a welcomed sight. Finally, there was something to look at. Adhered to the front of the locked gate was a sign that read:

CLOSED

DUE TO INFREQUENT USE

The lettering was big, bold, and gold, not to be missed, written in a refined manner. Through the bars of the golden gate Joe could just make out a white, empty area of mist and large pillared sanctuaries, like temples to ancient gods—or if not, at least very important gazebos. There were also sets of stands made from marble that looked very much like the kind Joe could remember standing on for choir in elementary school. But there was not a soul to be seen anywhere.

"There's yer heaven, chief," Baker answered Joe's curiosity. "You see, it existed, I suppose, at one time. Back when people thought that's what the afterlife was. Looks kinda like a ghost town now, huh?"

"Heaven is *closed*?" Joe said incredulously.

"It's been out of business for a while," said the disinterested balloonist. "I saw the last of its citizens go myself. They walked out of the pearly gates like curious children venturing someplace they thought they might get in trouble for being."

"Where did they go?" Joe asked.

"Who knows," she replied. "Back to Earth, over to some other existence, or maybe they got a good look at how the rest of us were going about and decided we were having a better time of it. But they left, and in enthusiastic hurry."

"Saint Peter done shut the door, eh?" Baker chimed in.

The balloonist muffled an irritated huff. "He never much liked the job or the costume. Sandals and robes are so out of date. He was waiting for everyone to wake up from their stagnant, unbending ideas. He only took the job because everyone—every single Christian on earth—expected him to be there, waiting for them. Towards the end he got plain moody. It *was* a job that everyone else put upon him, after all. He never asked to be the Gatekeeper."

"Where is he now?" Joe asked.

"Went back to another life on Earth. Wanted to do it all over again, but this time with less responsibility. He was up here for Earth ages. He was hoping to hook up with those other eleven fools that ran in his gang. I say 'fools' with affection, of course." She said the last bit rather like a dead weight.

"You mean the apostles?"

"Whatever," she said, still staring ahead.

"So what caused everyone to finally wake up?"

"What causes any of us to finally understand something that's been staring us in the face? Again, who knows? I couldn't tell you. They just had an epiphany, I suppose. They realized there had to be more to death than floating around on fluffy clouds and singing in choirs. Probably got very boring."

"But—"

"Listen, hon," the balloonist cut him off, "you're sweet, and your curiosity is endearing. Really, it is. But I got a job to do, so do you mind?"

Baker looked at Joe with a shrug and a smile, and Joe decided to hang back with Baker so he would not irritate their chauffeur any longer.

"Heaven is closed," Joe repeated to himself.

Joe wondered if there was anyone who still believed in the afterlife as harps and angel choirs and Saint Peter at the pearly gates. What would they do when they got here? Would they simply float around its perimeter, waiting for it to reopen like some theme park, thinking perhaps it was simply closed for the season or repairs?

The sky darkened into more somber colors as they made their way past Old Heaven. It no longer looked as cheerful as it had. The balloon took a descent into the clouds, looking for a landing spot.

"Hold on," the balloonist said. "I don't like the look of those clouds."

As they drifted lower, there was a quick flash of electricity striking out in their balloon's direct path. It blinded the sky with hot white. In its flash, Joe saw what looked like a giant hound take form from the angry atmospheric gloom and rip out a thunderous bellow. Its eyes flared bolts as it snarled madly.

"What is that?" Joe asked. He came and stood next to the pilot, clutching tightly to the basket. The beast stared down the balloon, roaring and relentless. Lightning shot from its mouth and eyes like warning.

"Gabriel Ratchet. A hound of storms and fury," she said in her emotionless manner, though louder so Joe and Baker could hear over the roar. "We'll have to try and go through it, most likely. He will not be friendly."

"You cain't avoid it?" Baker asked from behind, more for Joe's sake than his own.

She didn't answer but kept her eyes ever watchful as they made their way down through the thick ceiling of cloud. She was right. There did not seem a way to escape the storm. It was a wall extending from the highest high to the lowest low of sky.

Below, Joe could finally see ground, an earthy patchwork of fields, streams, mountains, and plains. Still, there was going to be no escaping the mad-dog storm. It would be upon them before they could land. Looking up again, Joe saw the sky was no longer the candy color it had been for so long anywhere. Even in their wake, the sky had darkened. Now everything around them looked threatening. Gray, black, and dark blue swirled in an ominous portent of things to come. The howling wind began to rock the basket, to batter the balloon from side to side.

Gabriel Ratchet reached out his giant paws to swat at them. Lightning tore through the air.

"Hold tight," the pilot yelled over the racket.

The wind wailed past as Gabriel Ratchet tossed them about like play toys. Lightning lit up the heavy, bruised clouds, and a hard rain began to pelt them, blowing sideways into the basket. They were pummeled and stung by small wet fists, it seemed. The cyclist kept her speed, battling against the sky beast as the balloon continued on its descent.

Baker did his best to shield both Joe and his beloved guitar while still trying to retain his own balance. It was an impossible task. The hound's vicious roar came at them from all sides as they were thrown this way, then that. Joe did not know where to look.

Suddenly, a blast of wind stronger than Joe had ever felt blew against the balloon, jarring everything. The hound's paw struck with fury. Baker and Joe were both knocked to the floor. When they regained their composure, they saw the pilot hanging on the outside of the basket, trying to pull herself in again. Quickly, Baker and Joe rose and aided her. Once they were all three again in the basket, they noticed the cyclist and her bike were gone, torn from the basket. But they had no time to wonder about her, for Gabriel Ratchet was coming back for another swipe, ready to pounce on the balloon.

Another tidal wave of wind knocked the balloon around. The hound howled so widely and loudly Joe could see deep into its jaws, where there was nothing but twisted debris and broken things. The balloon twisted in such a way Joe feared it might never stop turning. The ropes were being wound too tight. Gabriel Ratchet was through playing with his toy. There was a ripping, a tearing through seams. The snap of ropes could barely be heard above the roar of the storm. But the look on the balloonist's face brought the terror of the situation home.

Before he realized anything had happened, Joe felt himself weightless, but this time without the aid of another's arms about him, without the help of a winged man. This was not a comfortable feeling at all. This was a rattling descent, not a sublime ascent. He was falling through the storm. He had fallen over the edge of the basket, rocked out by the storm, and was now hurtling toward the ground with the hard rain.

Baker reached for Joe in a last feeble attempt of rescue, but there was nothing that could be done. The envelope had been completely severed from the basket, and Baker and the pilot were pulled away into the feverish, hellish jaws of Gabriel Ratchet, the hound.

And as Joe fell, he knew it was all swept away. That it was all for naught, and he would end his new existence without knowing fully who he had been.

Somewhere on his spiral downward, Joe lost grip on the moment. Overtaken by the blinding grief of losing both Grandpa Joe and Baker, he gave himself up once more to the consciousness of memory….

JOE was a folklore and mythology major. He and Ben had been dating a while now. They were a known couple at college. Ben reveled in that fact. Joe knew it made him feel the groundbreaker, the trailblazer, the (intentional) unintentional activist. Ben had started a campus organization for gay kids. Joe wouldn't have minded a little more discretion. Why did everybody need to know? Why was it everybody's business? It irritated Joe a bit, and there were arguments aplenty. In the end, though, Ben would win out. There were times Joe didn't even think he really liked Ben very much. His attitude could border on stereotypical and snippy. Their arguments were easily fixed, however. A quickie in between classes would usually do it.

Ben was a planner. He planned their weekends months in advance and stuck to his plans despite the weather—or because of it. He had also accumulated quite a mass of moderate-to-very swooshy gay companions, shopping partners and catty cohorts that seemed unhappy most of the time if they did not have a drink in hand or some other queen to tear down. These were the types Ben liked. These were the types Joe detested. Everything they said seemed to come from some old Bette Davis or Tallulah Bankhead film. They were masters of the clever jibe followed by a flick of an inconspicuous cigarette.

It was an October Saturday when things finally ended. That last inch, or the proverbial straw, that finally made Joe look at his life and want change. Long ago Ben had ceased to be the hot guy he had met at the party. He was now something completely different.

Joe, along with Ben and an assortment of Ben's flouncy friends, was at a festival a few miles down the road from their college, a good private school with a solid academic reputation. They would spend the day, Ben had decided, walking around the booths of handicrafts and "hill-jack" delicacies, trying them out and gagging ostentatiously no matter what they truly thought of the taste. It was, for Ben, a parade of pretentious play-acting. Truthfully, Joe never found anything wrong with the food and so never played their game. It was all very agreeable to him. Deep-fried Ding Dongs weren't that bad at all.

Joe was standing alone near an unpatronized booth as the "Ben Friends" were off getting their pictures taken in some outfits they would later swear the locals truly wore—which, of course, would be a lie. He watched Ben with disinterest. He was a fatiguing young man. What had Joe seen in him aside from big arms and a round butt?

Ben had helped him. That was true. Without Ben, there would have never been a "coming out," as it were. But why was he still with him? Ben had indeed become a stereotype... or had he always been that way? Joe didn't even know. He just knew Ben wasn't what he wanted. Not truly. Not anymore. Joe had even taken to looking at other colleges for the following semester. Maybe, he thought, time away from Ben would strengthen their relationship. Possibly that was all that was needed. There was that old adage about distance making the heart grow fonder, or was that time?

As he was digesting these thoughts, trying to make sense of where he was and how he might get to someplace else, a figure passed in front of the yappy, embarrassing group getting their photos taken and receiving stares because of their obnoxiousness. It was like a vision, a phantom, but it was indeed a real person. Joe woke up immediately from his misery. His decision on what to do was made at that moment, and he knew it.

It wasn't just any passing figure that had eclipsed the sight of Ben. It was Louis! Joe knew it. When he looked again, though—when he had collected himself from the epiphany—Louis was gone.

Joe felt a panic and an excitement build in him. He hadn't seen or heard of Louis for so long. He had nearly forgotten him. Why now? There had to be a reason. He left his place across from the photomat and began quickly walking about the festival in a distracted daze, searching like the hungry soul he was for this person he had known in some manner his entire life. He nearly toppled people over. He ran into children and senior citizens alike without regret or apology. "Asshole!" came calls from around him as he searched. But he paid no heed to anyone. His only thought was of finding Louis.

Every now and then he would catch the top of a head of beautiful black hair through the crowd or the kindness of blue eyes glimpsing around, but nothing ever certain or near. The crowd grew denser, busier, and more hateful as Joe continued his search. He wanted to be able to toss everyone out of the way, simply pick them up and hurl them for being such grand nuisances. How could so many people be here? What was so special about this? Have a corn dog and move on!

He nearly collapsed under the weight of his search, so hopeless did it seem. He was dizzy and sick from the smell of cotton candy, fried foods, and cigarettes. People were looking at him strangely now as his breathing took on panicked rhythms and his eyes glared with anger and fear.

"Joe!" a voice called from behind.

Louis? Was it Louis?

Joe wheeled around in excitement but was met with a disappointment, which soon turned to anger. It was only Ben with his "Ben Friends."

"Joe, where the hell have you been?" Ben yelled. "What's wrong with you? Are you sick? Should we go home?"

The "Ben Friends" rolled their eyes in impatience as Joe simply stared, getting angrier by the minute.

"Say something, my God!" Ben cried in annoyance. "You're so embarrassing!"

"I think," Joe began, "I think... I'm going to transfer. Yeah. I think that would be for the best."

EVERYBODY HERE WANTS YOU

THE first thought Joe had upon waking (aside from the immediate realization of being unharmed) was that he was alone now. Baker had been taken into the jaws of the hound along with the basket and the not-so-friendly balloonist. There was no soft guitar playing to greet him as he awoke. No soothing melancholy strings. Just the hushed sound of an expectant world.

Joe opened his eyes to see above him a roof made from fallen and flung fern leaves and other similar debris from the storm. He had slept the storm away on plant rubble, having been hurled into slumber before his body was laid down by the strong arms of Zephyr. He pushed back the leaves of his atmospherically constructed bedchamber, letting the droplets that had accumulated on them fall and trickle all about him. In soaking wet jeans, he stood, gathering the information on his new surroundings. The hill of debris that had been his bed was a small mound deposited in a perfect pallet-like manner. It had been comfortable enough. Joe had not awakened once before the morn.

He pushed the damp hair from his eyes. Around him was assembled a bleak, wasted landscape, mostly jagged rocks and large boulders of dark gray or sooty black, all of it thriving apocalyptic and desperately biblical. It appeared as if an atomic bomb had annihilated anything that grew for kilometers around. The only other plant material that could be seen was the scattered remnants that had been carried there with Joe and tossed carelessly by the storm.

"Baker!" Joe cried, his eyes searching the farthest horizon.

He knew in his gut it was a useless plea, that he was nowhere near. Yet he still felt the need to try. He had grown accustomed to the folkie's moodless mood.

"Baker!" he yelled again. His own voice answered him in redundant waves.

Joe climbed down from his bed of ferns and brush and called once more. The wind whistled a lonesome melody over the desolate terrain. He felt as if he were alone, the last man in the afterlife. He had been left behind.

He walked to the gloomy purview in front of him. The ground was rough and dusty beneath his feet. The moisture from the storm had long since soaked into the starving earth. The presumptuous blackened rocks peered stalwartly over a steep bluff. As Joe approached and saw what lay down the pitch, he felt at once a stomach-churning dread. Drowning the lowlands and stretching onward was a heavy, whirling mist. An occasional leafless treetop jutted up helplessly from the mist bed. The tree limbs were like crippled fingers reaching out for pardon from some perdition. Joe listened hard. He could hear no howls of torment, no entreaties for mercy. But all he could think of upon seeing the great sea of fog was the creeping mist he and Baker had encountered in the mountains. The memory reached out for him, threatening to stop him cold.

"Baker, where are you?" he whispered to himself, his voice quivering in newborn fear at the abysmal sight in front of him.

Near him, high and ominous, stood a scorched pillar that overlooked the misty lowlands like a watchman. Joe imagined human attributes on the thick column of rock: crippled arms and legs and a twisted face of sorrow and pain. A forgotten guardian turned to stone by the very thought of the creeping mists that now also stalled Joe. Forcing himself to grasp the deformed leg of the pillar, Joe began to ascend it in order to see across the lowlands. He had to find another way so the trapped souls he assumed were hidden therein would not harass him with their heart-rending appeals. He had to prevent them from dragging him under their horrific swamp of sadness, where he would remain forever with no hope of recovery or rescue—like Prometheus, forever tortured. Joe was uncertain whether the lowlands were even the right way. He had lost his guide, after all. Maybe, after studying the horizon from the tip of the pillar, he would be able to see a more welcoming route.

At the top, Joe wrapped his arms around the pointed head of the pillar. The column was strong and sturdy. He saw, to his relief, that the mists did not go on forever. There was an eventual fading away farther off, but it was still quite a distance. Nevertheless, Joe did not want to even set one toenail into the mist, be it creeping or standing. He did not know this place. He was a newbie to heaven. There could be worse horrors still hidden in this murk.

So he twisted about on the pillar head to see his other options. As he did so, the strength of the column of rock was called into question by the strangest thing. A moth, a tiny thing with drab brown wings, alighted on the very tip of the pillar. There was a crackling of stone, a sudden loosening. The moth at once fluttered away, but the damage was done. Joe cried in terror as the pillar broke in two. He let go of the tip, leaving it to tumble downhill alone, but that did not save him his own fall. Losing his balance and grip, down he went, sliding along the cliff wall into the deep mist. His screams were soon muffled by the thickness of the fog.

When he landed at the base of the bluff, Joe leaped to his feet at once. He prepared himself for the horrors to come. He was expecting mournful half-souls, swamp things, or hounds. But there was nothing to be seen. This was by far the most fear-inducing aspect of the situation. The mist was too thick for him to see even his own hand in front of his face as he waved it through the heavy moisture trying to find a safe path. His only relief came—and it came immediately—in the fact that this was not a prison of souls after all. This was not a creeping mist as he had feared. In truth, there were no external sounds at all. He could hear only his feet sloshing over saturated ground and his breathing, erratic and edged.

"Baker, where are you?" he begged again, if only to cut through the blanketing silence.

He felt the wet ground squish up between his toes. Grass and mud and twigs covered his feet. His guiding hands occasionally found a slippery tree he could navigate himself around and then lean against for a momentary respite. After a bit, the trees seemed to come in a fairly predictable rhythm, every six or seven steps. He could do nothing but follow the rows of trees.

It went on like this for a while. Joe's confusion of time and place grew with each step. He lost his bearings and began to run into the trees and falter as if they had pushed him and bullied him. He struggled to keep his equilibrium. Low-hanging tree branches would graze his face from time to time, startling him, causing him to curse in surprise.

So discombobulated was Joe that, upon tripping on a large, unearthed root, he fell face-first to the marshy ground and remained there with nary an attempt to rise. He decided he could go no farther. Not even if all the lost and trapped souls in this world and the former came down upon him at once in a deadening horde of inexorable agony. This was where he would stay and end his journey.

If he were a young boy, if it were he and 3P, this would be an adventure like none other. He would have loved it. And the adventurer in him, that little boy, still found some intrigue in his situation. But he needed rest, just a little rest. Then perhaps he could walk on.

"Just rest and get your bearings," he said to himself as he lay facedown, drinking in muddy water. Yet the notion of getting any kind of bearing in this thick condensation was laughable. Destination had no place in his thoughts now. He lay in the mud and soggy grass, unaware of the passing of time. Mucky amphibians and filthy swamp rats were Joe's only company. They slithered up beside him or crawled and hopped over him on their ways to other places.

"Get up," a gentle voice said, the words clearing the mists, coming from them as if formed from their dense but airy consistency. Like a hushed whisper and echo. It was a familiar, welcome voice.

"Get up, Joe," it repeated.

Joe raised his head slowly from the wet ground but still could see nothing through the haze. "Baker?" Joe asked sluggishly, wiping the mud from his mouth.

"No, Joe," came the reply. "But you'll see him again. Don't be concerned. First, though, you've got to get up. Things to do, Joe."

It was the Stranger. Joe was sure of it. The feeling of warmth and love, of home, swept over him. It was that sweet feeling he had known when he had first awakened in the field of barley. A gracious warmth spread through his being. With that warmth, however, was a stab of remorse. He remembered the frostbitten barley stalks. Then, quite naturally, as if it were something he had known all along, Joe realized who the Stranger was. A thrill burst inside him.

Joe stood, wobbling a bit in the disorienting fog. "Why are you here with me?" he asked. "Did I find you? Did I ever find you after the festival? Are you going to stay with me?"

"Not now, Joe," came the gentle response. The elegance and tone bounced and vibrated like a ballet through the mist. "Not just yet. You've got to continue. You've got to keep going. You're so near, Joe. You're so near."

"To what? Near to what?" He searched through the mist impatiently, unconcerned if he tripped on a root or ran into a tree.

"Keep going. Great courage, Joe. See! The mist is lifting."

And just as the Stranger said those words, the curtain of confusion was cleared. First, there was the slightest hint of light, a discoloring like a cleansing of the fog. Then, as if taking form from a wish, came clearer surroundings. In the beginning, everything was in silhouettes, and then the true forms of their nature appeared. Joe stood now amidst a sparsely forested area. It was a butterfly-spotted meadow with high, green grass. The trees stood alone but not lonely at intervals scattered over the meadow. Joe was relieved to see that the sky had returned to a lovely shade of blue. There was no threat left in it, not a streak of gray. Behind him, the mist had brightened to reveal an orchard extending back to the base of the cliff.

Joe searched for the speaker in the mist, though he knew he had already gone away. The feeling of warmth and unconditional acceptance had vanished, leaving Joe alone again in this new and unfamiliar place. The mist had completely disappeared now, as if it had never been there at all.

Joe wiped the mud and muck from his face and body with a maple leaf plucked from a tree and then continued walking. It was all he could do.

His walk was long and uneventful. Yet he enjoyed the solace. There was a simple pleasure in meandering through the tall grass of the meadow. Leaving the meadow and the orchard behind, he began to walk with more purpose. His footfalls were solid and his path set. After all, he had someone waiting for him—the Stranger.

He walked dirt roads that passed small cottages and fields of cattle and sheep. He passed picturesque images as sublime as anything ever put to canvas by a Dutch master. On a whim, feeling brave and dangerous (for what could be worse than what he had already encountered?), he jumped a stone fence and made his way through a herd of bison that grazed, completely oblivious to him, even as he stretched forth his hands to feel their hides.

As the evening approached, Joe decided to find an area to rest. It was becoming deathly dark around him. The night clouds obstructed any hint of moonlight. They were not harbingers of storm, however, so Joe relaxed. He was cautious as he stumbled at last upon a tree that overlooked a soft, trickling stream in a ravine. He tripped over something—most likely a soft patch of mossy ground or a small furry creature that wasn't quick enough to scurry out of the way—and almost fell headfirst into the trunk of the tree, catching himself just in time. He settled into the hollowed-out tree base quite comfortably and was soon carried off to sleep by the sounds of the water in the creek and the rustle of the leaves that sounded like breathing.

AS THE morning haziness faded from his head and the country surrounding him, Joe awoke and became gradually aware of a slight soft touch on his wrist. Nothing grabbed at him, but rather something gently grazed his flesh, paralleling the gentle trickling of the stream nearby. He realized, his eyes flashing open in alarm, that the touch was the feel of skin. He jumped to his feet, swiping his wrist as if he were skittering away from some spider or thousand-legged millipede. At the base of the tree, right next to him in fact, lay a young woman with her back resting against the trunk and her arms and legs spread out at varying angles. She rested naked and calm.

"Has she been here the whole time?" he wondered aloud.

She couldn't be dead, could she? This wasn't a growth of form that belonged to someone's feverish guilt, as in Abigail's garden, was it? A hundred rushed nightmares and wonders crowded his mind.

He bent to inspect her more carefully. She seemed very real, her flesh pink, her lips soft and new, her hair fiery and red. But what was she doing here? And why had he not sensed her there earlier?

And then, from the corner of his eyes, he saw the fingertips of yet another hand lightly placed on her ankle. Not grabbing at the girl's ankle but palm up and fingers loose and relaxed. The hand was connected to another body—that of a young man. Another human form draped over the young man's legs. That body was, in turn, touched by another resting form, and another after that. Joe gasped and stepped back as he saw, stretched out before him, a long, heavy field of motionless, sleeping, naked bodies. They lay peacefully in the grass, neither tossing nor turning. The bodies stretched for miles all around. Rolls and mounds of flesh, like some macabre crop. They looked as if they could have been dead but for their healthy complexions.

Joe stepped back again, reeling from what he was seeing before him, and, as he did, he fell backward over something. The very same something from the night before that had caused him to nearly crack his skull on the tree. It was an old man, his long gray hair the fur or moss Joe thought he had felt.

"Sorry," Joe whispered out of habit.

The old man didn't stir. He remained as placid as the other living dead in the field.

In his position on the ground beside the old man, Joe glanced up and caught a glimpse of the limbs of the tree he had slept beneath. They, too, were strewn with sleeping people, their arms and legs dangling like fleshy willows. Quickly, he rose and carefully stepped over the bodies that slept, doing his utmost not to trample on any fingers.

Some great battle, he thought. *Could that be what this is? A great war in the afterlife?*

To his surprise, as he straddled the bodies, some larger than others, he noticed he was not the only one wandering about. There were quite a few, actually, as he made his way into the midst of the field. Some of these wanderers seemed to just stand around the outer edges, waiting in the paths between adjoining fields, while others were in with the dormant crowd, helping them as they awoke in confusion and wonder. The people awakening always wore the same expression of epiphany. Joe recognized their look of contentment and joy. It was the same look he had had in the barley field before his journey got under way.

"Excuse me," Joe said, approaching one of the many watchers on the outside of the garden of men and women. He nearly fell over the form of a very heavy-set man as he came to the clear path. "Excuse me. Could you tell me where I am? I've lost my guide, and I'm a bit confused."

"Certainly," the young Asian woman said. She had a radiant smile, and her eyes held the wisdom of an old soul. "This is the Garden of Disbelief. It's what everyone's called it as long as anyone can remember. But even here, we still like our theatrics, don't we?"

Joe looked at her, hoping she would explain.

"These are atheists, honey," she said bluntly, gesturing to the mass of sleepers. "They didn't believe in an afterlife. Nothing at all. So when they die, that belief of disbelief manifests itself… well, they end up here, lying around oblivious to their existence until…."

"Until they wake up," Joe finished her statement. "Interesting," he said, looking about. He was relieved it had nothing to do with overwrought guilt or repressed pain. He was relieved he would not have to endure the same kind of horror he had witnessed upon seeing Declan in the tree.

"I'm here waiting for my son," the woman offered with a smile. "You try to raise your kids to stand for something, huh?" she joked.

"Have you gone to look for him? This field is so big."

"No. There's no need. He'll find me. I'll wait here as long as need be. Others go and look for their loved ones, but my son was always very independent. He'll find his way."

"You're a good mother."

She smiled at him pleasantly, the look of secrets. "I always told him to believe in something. It didn't matter what, so long as it nourished his soul. But as I said, he was independent. Always so independent."

Joe thought deeply for a moment. "I don't recall ever believing in God or an afterlife, not whole-heartedly anyway. Why didn't I wake up here?"

"But you did believe in something, right? Some entity? Some macrocosm?"

"I guess so. I mean, I didn't *not* believe."

"Well, there you have it," she gleamed. "You trusted in the *possibility* of some otherness. Your mind was more open to new ideas. You didn't let preconceived notions get in the way of your spiritual growth one way or the other. But whether you knew it or not, your spirit did indeed grow."

Joe smiled at this. He liked the sound of it. "Well," he said, "I'd best be going. I've got a journey to complete."

He watched as the fingers of a woman lying nearby in the fields wriggled in pre-awakening awareness.

"Good luck to you," the kindly Asian woman said.

"And to you," Joe replied. "I hope you find your son. Or rather, I hope he finds you."

"Oh, he will." She winked.

So Joe walked out of the field of human forms headed toward some unknown but preordained meeting with other unknown but previously met souls. He was beginning to appreciate the answers to the riddles of life and how the mystery resolved itself. Explanations abounded around him to enigmas pondered upon for lifetimes.

BEFORE too very long, he rejoined the dirt road. It was there waiting for him patiently, ready to lead him on. He walked a while, not venturing off as he had done previously. He journeyed forward, happy to feel bare feet on soft, fine dirt. The road snaked and ebbed and proceeded.

Soon, in the near far-off, the road passed by a tree-lined avenue that led to a massive Greek-styled house. Columns lined its very large front porch, and wisteria climbed its pristine white walls. The place called to Joe; the trees beckoned him to enter with their branches. As he waded through an army of bright, perfect dandelions under the canopy of the trees, a sizable lawn fleshed out in front of him with dozens of young men. It was a giddy sight, and Joe stood rooted in the dandelion path. Handsome young men, all of them laughing and having fun, most of them barely clothed at all, played at Frisbee; they lay about on blankets, tanning; they gave definition to "horsing around." Many of the young men were on the porch, hanging off the columns with languid ease and seeping sensuality, throwing coquettish glances at one another as they drank from dewy glasses of some kind of sweet tea. It was a very loud, lusty gathering of youthful beauty.

Upon surveying the scantily clad group, Joe at once felt over-dressed. The warmth of the sky beat down on their tanned, well-built bodies as they dallied about without care or worry for modesty. Theirs were bodies to adorn the friezes of temples, showcases for rigorous training, dedication, and athletic superiority.

Various activities were pursued in separate areas around the outside of the manse. A small crowd had assembled in the center of the lawn as two nude young men went at each other in a classic wrestling match. Joe noticed the ridiculous size of their penises. In fact, even those wearing clothes had cartoonish bulges in their short shorts or tight jeans. The surrounding crowd cheered and hollered in excitement at each pin or successful point. On yet other parts of the lawn, some played at naked football, while still others improved their accuracy skills by way of a very interesting type of ring-toss. The competitive spirit was high, but not angry in any of the games. It was quite like courting, Joe thought. A tug-of-war between pursuer and pursued. That was what all sports seemed to be anyway: a homoerotic race to the end. But exactly *whose* end was a mystery until the game had finished. With penises the size of these, "sore loser" was an understatement.

Yet not all of them were being athletic. Aside from those lounging on the lawn on small blankets and towels, sipping their teas or the flirtatious fellows on the porch between the columns, there were also those who courted other young men up against tree trunks or the wisteria-blanketed sides of the house as their erect penises rubbed against one another in fleshy snuggling. Then there were those who were more constructive in their frivolity, painting up on the large balcony or learning to play guitar on the grass, gathering inspiration from those around them. But however they enjoyed themselves, it was clear to Joe this was a place for men to be men and be with men. It was a celebration of masculinity and praise for the force of nature or divine power (if there was one) that had caused it to be.

Slowly and inquisitively, the beautiful inhabitants of the manse lawn began to take notice of the new arrival. A quiet came over the crowd, causing even the wrestlers to stop mid-straddle. The guitar stopped; the flirting hushed. Only the settling of ice in glasses of tea could be heard. Whispers came from the lips of the men, curious smiles and friendly nods. One of the group—he stood near the columns on the porch—breached the frozen moment and ran inside, his well-toned butt striating as he went.

Joe stood motionless, befuddled. He was uncertain if he was even supposed to be there or, indeed, was welcome. Perhaps he had crashed a very private party.

Some of the crowd stepped closer to him, grinning. Joe did not know what to make of it. They all wore very pleasant expressions. There was no hint of hostility directed toward him nor irritation that he was there. He was surrounded now by more carnal beauty than he had ever known. He could hardly concentrate because of it.

"*Welcome, Brother Joe!*" came an emphatic, booming voice from the doorway of the mansion. The young men, every one of them, turned their attention thereto.

Out of the house and onto the porch came the finest looking man, if in fact he was a man, Joe reasoned could have ever existed. He was a giant, standing taller than all the others, and tanned, with thick black hair that hung below his ears. His chin was perfectly square, and his nose and brow were strong and Romanesque. His body was a rippling display of muscles, devoid of any fat. He possessed arms that surely contained more than one set of biceps and triceps; an enormous chest that could double as pillows with large brown, round nipples; abs that rippled like waves; legs as big in size as some of the other guys' entire bodies—and then there was the penis. Yet again, Joe had never seen anything like it. It was large and dangerous, with an intrusive head and aesthetically perfect vascular lines. Everything about the man screamed impossibility. Joe felt his own cock stiffen even more at the sight and appreciated his jeans for the small amount of modesty they allowed him. He could not help the sigh that escaped him as he eyed the giant on the porch.

"Hi," Joe swallowed out, still staring in amazement. His eyes could barely take in this new figure. He was just literally too much. The other men chuckled as Joe ogled.

"You're late," the gorgeous giant said as he came down the steps of the porch and nearer to Joe. The steps barely supported him. His huge member bounced and swung from leg to leg, hitting each muscled thigh with a loud smack.

"We were expecting you sooner. But then, I suppose the storm had something to do with that, huh? Ol' Gabriel Ratchet trying to snuff out the Flame of Life."

"Y-yes," Joe stammered out as the behemoth stood in front of him, towering over him, all muscles, pectorals, and penis. Like Penis Tits, the God of Sex come to life.

"This is the Brotherhood," the man said with a wide, sweeping gesture. His pectorals twitched and flexed involuntarily, his arms Braille maps of blue veins. "Which you are now an honorary member of." He looked around for a moment in confusion. "Where is your friend? Your guide? Has he not come?"

"Baker. We were separated in the storm." It made him sad to say the words. "I don't know where he is."

"That's too bad," the man consoled. "Well, no worries. You'll most likely see him again. That's how it works here. We'll take good care of you in the meanwhile." He put a thick arm around Joe's shoulders and walked him to the porch.

"My name is Guy," he said by way of introduction. "You know me, but I didn't exactly look like this when we met. When we had our nasty fun." There was mischief in Guy's grin and a sly reflection of excitement in his eyes.

"No kidding," Joe said. "I think I would have remembered someone who looked like you. Even over Death's amnesia." The other brothers laughed at this as they walked along with Guy and Joe in a flesh-muscled crowd. Joe jerked in surprise and some longing as Guy's long, flaccid penis swung over and hit his arm.

"We've got a lot to catch up on, Joe," Guy said as Joe was led indoors past those brothers waiting on the porch. Though curious of Joe, they all looked at Guy as if he were some naked Messiah. "You should stay a while. There's no rush. Not here. You can stay a while, right?"

"I don't know. I suppose. But I do need to find Baker, if he still...."

"And you will. Or he'll find you. But he wouldn't have too much fun here, I'm afraid. I don't think we're his type. Maybe it's a good thing you're here without him." Joe was led into the foyer. "For tonight, my old friend, it's all about us, all about boozing and amusement!"

The others cheered in agreement around them. Hoots and hollers and window-jarring *yee-haws*.

"Get Brother Joe cleaned up. Then let's get some food and wine," Guy shouted, raising his arms in proclamation. "I'll be back in a few, Joe. There's something waiting for you here. Has been for many days now." He said this last bit more quietly as he turned and walked through the throng of admiring on-lookers.

Joe couldn't help but watch Guy's huge, muscular ass as he walked away. He was too enamored by the giant to even ponder on what it was that was waiting here for him. He swallowed hard, thinking on the prize hidden between the two globular slabs of brawn. Again, he felt the prickly heat of lust and did his best to shake it off.

It was only then, after Guy had walked away, that Joe noticed the house. On the inside it was like a thousand other fraternity houses. Messy. Hung with art that made no sense in any context. Furnished with items that were scarred, scratched, and stained in stereotype. The rooms were of no particular importance for any particular function. They simply existed for the pursuit of pleasure and pleasure alone. The large staircase was a jumbled fall of tossed clothes. At this, Joe wondered, since all he really saw most of the brothers actually wearing was an occasional bandana around the neck or a pair of boots for the hell of it.

Yes, the house was a complete mess, but then, who would expect otherwise? For they were, after all, boys. And naked, fun-loving boys at that. This was how they existed. This was how they wanted to be. Lost Boys, and happy for it.

The mass of young men pushed Joe by sheer numbers into one of the various functionless rooms in the house. They shouted and called out their names in introduction, held out their hands to give strong, solid handshakes, and patted Joe on the back as they went. Joe had never felt more popular—or more in heaven. Their bloated, trunk-like penises rubbed against him as they walked.

"We've heard a lot about you," said Brian, a tousle-haired soccer player type.

Joe sat on a cushiony but patched-up faded blue couch. Foam snuck out in tufts from pillow edges. Empty paper cups were littered around the room on tables and in corners. Overhead, a large chandelier hung from the ceiling; torn streamers and articles of clothing dangled from it like spontaneous ornaments. Stuffy old paintings hung crooked on the walls of the room. They were mostly portraits of handsome athletes on which the boys had drawn moustaches, glasses, and buck teeth. Clearly, these were not brethren.

"About me?" Joe asked, bringing his attention back to Brian. "You've heard about me?" He tried to keep his eyes from glancing downward at Brian's well-coiffed, erect penis as it pointed strenuously, attentively at him; it seemed to eye him. "How in heaven do you know about me?"

"Well, Guy told us some of your story when he first got here," Brian answered blithely. He drank a thick beer from a paper cup. "And then, more recently—"

"Not long ago at all," another interrupted. Others concurred in murmurs.

"Not long ago at all, we got someone else here that knew you. He's not a full-timer like most of us, though. Not alumni, neither. He's just passing through. An honorary bro like you." Brian took another swig from his cup and held it up high in the air.

"Refill!" one of the brothers announced as a third took the cup and passed it around until it was magically brought back to Brian refilled.

"You know somebody else who knew me here?" Joe inquired. "Who?"

There was a tussle behind the boys who crowded around the couch. Someone was pushing their way into the room from the doorway.

"Declan," Brian said, as if Joe should already know the answer.

Joe's mouth fell agape. "Where is he?" he exclaimed as he stood up.

"Calm down, bro. He's right here. Just walked in."

Brian gestured to the crowd. The mass of naked young men parted, and there, in front of a large bay window with a few broken panes, stood the only fully clothed individual in the house. He looked at Joe with nervous anticipation, wearing a suit and tie.

"Declan!" Joe cried as he leaped over the back of the couch and all but flew past the brothers. The two embraced in an elated tackle, both awash in tears.

"Hey, Joey," Declan choked out. "How have you been?" He still looked young, still the sixteen-year-old boy with the auburn hair.

"Declan, how long have you been here?" Joe asked, cupping the boy's face.

"Don't really know. I've been traveling around since I got here. Couldn't go through with it all yet, you know? My journey scares me sometimes. I couldn't force myself to see my mom."

"So you know she's here?" Joe sniffed.

"Yeah, she died pretty soon after me," Declan said. "My journey isn't complete until I see her. But it's a difficult thing, forgiving. Even harder through love."

"You need to see her, Declan," Joe said softly. "She needs you now. She needs you to come. She's sorry. She's so sorry. You wouldn't believe the things she—"

Declan looked at him, begging him not to go on. Guy walked back into the room at that moment, sparing them the pain and averting the brethren's eyes from their reunion.

"Where's the party?" Guy boomed out.

The brothers cheered in a roar of agreement, their engorged penises bobbing as they jumped in excitement.

"What do you think of *that*?" Declan said with an impish grin as he gestured at Guy's massive organ and his athletic disciples.

Joe whistled lightly and shook his head while clicking his tongue. "That's something else!"

"I think our guests need some libations!" Guy proclaimed to the group.

At that, the nude brethren rushed Joe and Declan with cheers, hoisting them in the air like football heroes.

"To the drink and revelry!" cried Guy as the crowd surged out of the room in intoxicated joy. Joe and Declan surfed hands with laughter and ticklish pleasure.

What followed was nothing more than the excess of delight. There was drinking and food, of course—pizza, hamburgers, hot dogs, and beer—but afterwards and more importantly there were the games. Games for bliss played throughout the house as one brother sought out another. Hide-and-seek, pin-the-tail, roughside bowling, and the same prize every time went to the victor. Joe watched with enchantment as the brethren gave in to their desires, creating their heavens in a dirty frat house.

Joe himself abstained for the moment, preferring instead to be a spectator. His modesty would not let him do more, and he cursed it. Brian was the brother most intent on bedding Joe; he was irrepressible. But when Joe refused for the final time, it was not as if it were a crushing blow to the soccer boy. No sooner had Joe declined the offer than another brother took the erect organ that had stared up at Joe earlier wholly into his mouth, whipping it frantically with his tongue. Brian moaned with hedonistic pleasure. Right there in front of Joe, on the very same couch. Joe could only stare in amusement and try to move his attention elsewhere.

Guy sat in the corner of the main room on a creaky love chair. Its legs bowed at his enormity, but oh, what happy cushions! He smiled rapturously across the gang of frolicking bodies at Joe as a sinewy wrestler bounced up and down on Guy's thick cock. The wrestler was trying to take every bit of the organ in but could only manage a third of it. Still, he hollered and groaned like a man impaled, throwing himself onto the penis harder and harder. Guy leaned his head back as the wrestler massaged the giant's huge chest and tweaked his erect nipples.

Declan was nowhere in the room. He had ejected himself from the orgiastic feast and gone out to welcome dusk on the porch. Joe thought this might be a good idea for him as well. He could hardly take the sight of Guy without desiring him violently. And he hadn't the nerve to proposition his new "old friend."

Taking his leave of Brian, who was otherwise involved, he snuck out the door and found Declan sitting on the steps. The brethren's grunts of ecstasy could still be heard as Joe found a seat next to his friend. The evening was layered—dewy grass, thin mist, the scent of wisteria and magnolia, lightning bugs, and somber, easy sky.

"Not into that tonight?" Joe asked, folding his arms around his knees.

"It's not really my thing. All that grunting and groaning. But the guys are nice," Declan answered. "It's like this every night here. Wild, huh?"

"Oh my God!" Joe laughed in agreement. He grew solemn after a heavy pause. Dusk light poured over the trees and dandelions. Cicadas chirped in the distance. "I missed you, Declan. Why'd you leave like that? Why'd you have to go without even saying goodbye?"

"I couldn't see a way out. You were the only other guy like me I knew. I thought we were alone. I was so sure it would never get any better. That life would never change and I would always be hated. The perils of being raised in a small town, you know. Only, I never believed I would ever get out. You had your mom. She was so great. But me... my mom...." He halted, taking a deep breath. "You know what she said to me?"

"I can guess," Joe said quietly. The sky was just beginning to darken into its magnificent blue coat hung with twinkling lights.

"Does she remember me? How was she when you saw her?"

"Not good," Joe replied truthfully. "She needs you. She has this garden and, man, let me tell you, it's out of control. You need to go help her care for it. She's lost without you."

"Yeah. We always did that together. Tended the garden. But then...." He swallowed the hurt. "I'll never understand why we can still hurt here. I sometimes wish we were ignorant of everything but the present. Things wouldn't hurt so. Heaven sure isn't like they told us it would be."

"Well, *they* didn't know everything."

"Seems to me they didn't know *anything*."

"Hey fellas! The party's inside," Guy loudly proclaimed as he came out onto the porch, casting a mountainous shadow over them.

"We were just talking," Joe said. "Catching up. We'll get back in there."

"You better," Guy warned jokingly. "There are some brothers in there who are all about you, Joe. How long has it been since you got your rocks off and didn't have to worry about the consequences?" He squatted down beside Joe, his huge, just-used member lying flaccid against the stone steps.

"Yeah, it's time for me to rejoin the party too," Declan said as he rose. "I know romance isn't exactly their thing, but maybe I can find somebody to court me without strings."

"That won't be an easy task, Declan," Guy agreed. "They're a pretty debauched gang. Guess I'm a bad influence."

"I think I'll stay out here for a bit longer," Joe informed him. "It's nice here."

Declan leaned down and kissed Joe on the top of the head and then went in through the large doors.

"Good friend you got there," Guy said.

"Yeah. I missed him," Joe replied. The sky was beginning to make shadows of the large lines of trees that paralleled the dandelion road. Dusk was settling. Crickets were out in battalions, singing with the cicadas.

"Let's go for a walk," Guy nudged. "It's a nice night for it."

Joe was hesitant at first. He was falling in love with the lonesome sky. "Why not?" he persuaded himself, and they both rose to walk into the evening.

The humid night air made the fragrance of the dandelions and the grass more fresh and the aroma from the wisteria and the trees more lovely. The lightning bugs began to appear in greater numbers under the trees. Joe and Guy kicked through the tall dandelions like lovers on a first walk under the moon.

"So, you live here?" Joe asked, not really knowing what to say, yet feeling the need to say something.

"Yeah, I like it. Truthfully, I love it. I travel now and then, but mostly I'm here." His voice was so deep and heavy it seemed to have its own echo in the night. He looked at Joe with familiarity. "You still can't place me, huh?"

"No. Sorry," Joe said, looking at him softly. Their walk was slow and leisurely. The smell of honeysuckles wafted about on a barely there breeze.

"I want that to change," Guy said as he suddenly pushed Joe against the side of a tree and pulled down his jeans in one quick movement.

"What are you doing?" Joe exclaimed, reaching for his pants. He was already hardening, though, from the eroticism of the moment.

"I want you to know who I am," Guy explained. He pinned Joe's arms against the tree. "Don't fight this, Joe. I promise you want it."

And there was truth in that.

Guy turned Joe around gently so he faced the tree and lovingly caressed his shoulders as the two of them found familiar ways to know each other. Such gentle kisses from such a large man, such tender hands.

Joe gasped in an intoxicated mix of fear and incredulous excitement. The moment he had fantasized about since seeing Guy that very day on the porch in all his masculine splendor—was there any other being or spirit in existence who could possibly be *more* masculine—had arrived so soon. He felt Guy move into him, and Joe could sense the cascade of self-knowledge as it was about to come cresting on pleasure.

"I want you to know me," Guy whispered in his ear. His strong arms of brawn and veins held tight to Joe, and his flesh burned from desire and need.

Joe felt Guy's muscles ripple and flex all around him like a coat of protection and admiration. He felt sedated. As if it were, in fact, all right. As if this were part of the plan, and he would not be rent apart by Guy's organ. He was open to it.

And then, in a flash of ripping hot steam, Joe felt the gush inside his being. The flooding of every vein and passage with a burst of intense pleasure as Guy screamed victorious at the dusk-light sky. In the midst of that blinding, ecstatic inner light, Joe remembered....

JOE had transferred to a new college farther away from home—one of the few that had a folklore and mythology department. Ben had ended things in an angry huffing fit complete with slammed doors and vicious rumors. This had left Joe weakened. Though he was somewhat relieved to be single, it made him feel alone and at a loss once again. Maybe he would never find anyone else. Maybe his stormy relationship with Ben had been the best he could have hoped for. Maybe transferring to the new school was a mistake and he would be alone for it. Maybe he should crawl back to Ben. Maybe God was laughing at him. Melodramatic possibilities abounded.

The first few weeks at the new school were trying. Everyone around him knew one another, and Joe didn't feel up to negotiating into their lives. He wasn't sure he was up to letting them know him. Mostly he kept to himself, studying in the college library Friday and Saturday nights when the rest of the campus was celebrating the weekend. He had fallen once more into his solitary habits, chased there by his own inner discomfort. The boy adventurer hushed into a corner.

It was in the library one Friday evening that Joe met Guy. An upperclassman, Guy was a well-liked man about campus. Joe had, of course, seen him before, but he had never thought anything of getting to know him. Guy was an athletic type in one of the fraternities at the college. Not the football stud or basketball star, but popular and very attractive nonetheless.

Joe, by chance, was giving his eyes a rest from the James Purdy novel assignment before him on the table when he noticed Guy taking an interest in him. They exchanged nods and then Joe returned to his reading. Joe assumed that was that. But the chair opposite him at the table was pulled out soon after, and Guy sat down, his handsomely built body not so much hidden as accentuated by the sweater he wore.

"Purdy," Guy said, gesturing to the book. "Interesting read." He gave a flirtatious smile that had undoubtedly snared many a co-ed.

"Yeah," Joe said rather timidly, trying to focus on the story. He didn't want to be rude, but he was always uncomfortable with new

people. Especially young straight men who could never know how neglected he felt in their world. He tried to concentrate above the roar of blood in his veins.

"Reading Forster, myself," Guy said, holding up the small paperback copy of Maurice *in his hand. Joe nodded in acknowledgment.*

There was an awkward silence between them, and then Guy asked, "Why aren't you out? I never see you having any fun around here." He spoke loudly. Too audibly for a college library. The librarian, a dissatisfied-looking man in his forties, gave a stern glance in their direction.

Joe was taken aback. "I-I don't know anyone," he defended, eyes still on the book. His face was beet red.

"That's not gonna change unless you go out and meet people." He stared for a moment at Joe, clearly waiting for a response. Joe could discern that Guy was not easily deterred by avoidance. In absence of a reply, he rose. But instead of leaving, he sat in the chair right beside Joe.

"Listen, why don't you come out with me?" he asked. "I'll take you to the frat. Introduce you to some people."

Joe now found the persistence a little annoying. "That's all right," he said, gathering his things. "I've got to go."

"You're a loner. I dig that. But I could show you a good time. Introduce you to some real hotties. I think we have some things in common. Similar tastes."

"I don't think we have the same definition of 'hottie'," Joe said quietly as he rose to leave.

Guy grabbed his forearm firmly. "I think we do," he said playfully, almost in melody. "I've been watching you. Waiting for you to come out... and play," he joked. "Come out and play."

There was a wicked, mischievous grin on his face. Joe understood that look.

THE *scene shifted numerous times. Like a tilt-a-whirl, events, faces, and dates passed by in blurred streaks and lines yet gave Joe full knowledge of the various happenings. Joe and Guy had become fast friends. Friends with the same definitions for the same words. It was a sexual free-for-all as Joe tried his best to forget Ben and the world of his past, which could offer nothing but hurt and loneliness. He didn't want to recall that world where dead boys and withered relationships resided. His life with Guy became an experiment in games and numbers. They passed eager college queers about like used T-shirts. Sometimes they would have two or three guys a night, sometimes apart, sometimes together in their shared dorm room. Guy even once set up a web cam for those with voyeuristic tendencies to watch as he did varying acts of titillation on willing participants. His sexual appetite amazed even Joe.*

After their nights of wrestling and sexual wrangling, they would crash on their futon together, high from drugs, drinking, and sex. In those gentle hours of pre-dawn they would talk, drift off in moments of self-realization, talk some more, giggle at the mundane, eat mini-fridge leftovers, and drink bottle upon bottle of water.

Once, in a conversation spawned by inebriate philosophy, Guy said, "I love water! Nothing better than water to make you feel cleansed." Staring at the plastic bottle adoringly. "Joe?"

"Yeah, Guy."

"What if... what if water is angels?"

Joe never knew what he meant by this. Soon Guy drifted to sleep. But those words haunted him long after.

Before long, though, it was over. All the partying and sex was done. Guy had graduated and gone on to a life at a larger school for graduate studies, leaving Joe behind to carry on a trend he found very hard to give up. It replaced his feelings of loss and anger, emptying him of longings for anything different.

In sex he had found a repressing agent.

WHEN Joe awoke from the sexually-induced remembrance, he was lying on his back below a large tree in the night, surrounded by the dandelions that tickled his naked flesh. Guy lay beside him, his massive chest rising and falling in the dark.

"Guy," Joe whispered as he pulled up a dandelion and touched it to his nose. "Good to see you again."

Guy grinned. "Good to be seen. Good to be known," he replied. "Was it good for you?"

Joe laughed. "Amazing," he said. "But you know if this were… I mean if we were alive, so to speak, that would be impossible. You would have killed me. You're a giant. Excuse me for saying so, but everything about you and the other fellas here is unreal. Your proportions, I mean."

"I know," Guy sighed happily. "Isn't this a place great! I can delve into whatever twisted sex fantasy I want. And, dammit, I've got a lot of them! It's just sex, after all."

"Is that why you chose to come here in that amazing bod? So you could do the fuck-impossible?"

Guy laughed loudly, scaring away a few of the glowflies that were hanging about. "No, my friend," he said. "There's a much more somber reason behind it. Something more serious. You see, I got sick back there in that life. Real sick. After I left and went to grad school, well, I got caught up in some bad things. I was a user. Even more so than when you knew me. And not the kid's stuff we did either. I did all kinds of drugs. I did all kinds of things to get money for the drugs. I didn't care what it did to the body I was so proud of in school with you. Flunked out of grad school soon enough, and then I got into the meth scene. And meth and sex didn't mix for me." He paused and turned over on his side, looking at Joe. "I got real sick, and then, one day, I died. Died right in the middle of fucking some greasy club kid who smelled of too much cologne. So after I remembered my self-destruction, I decided here I would have the most amazing body ever and really appreciate it. Be kind of invincible, you know. A body that could never fall ill. My fantasy body, like the kind the superheroes have in those comic books we all read as kids. I wanted to be one of those guys."

"Wow," Joe whispered. "I'm so sorry." He gently touched Guy's shoulder.

"It's over now, my friend. I'm here. I'm still learning lessons, but now I take them to heart. And I've never been so content."

"You look great," Joe whispered. "You seem happy."

"I do look great, huh?" Guy said with a play-sexy grin, flexing an arm for Joe that crowded the space around them.

"Well, at least you're humble," Joe kidded.

"Meh." Guy shrugged as he lay back on the ground and stared past the foliage at the sky. "I firmly believe humility is a form of dishonesty."

"We had fun back then, though, didn't we?" Joe reminisced. "Back when it was just about the sex?"

"Sure did," Guy agreed. He rolled closer to Joe with seductive intent, his penis falling onto Joe's leg with a slap. Joe playfully pushed him back onto the flowers and grass, and they rolled about giggling and laughing. The fireflies dispersed around them as if they were happiness given form and being—which, after all, was a possibility here.

Like this, Joe thought. *If it could always be like this.*

And they were soon both lost in the ecstasy of the act once more, intoxicated by the sweetness of discovery.

JOE stayed on at the Brotherhood, lost and happy, unaware of the days passing, not needing to bother with the worrisome ticking of clocks. He enjoyed the comforts that were provided him and the sheer abandon with which he was allowed to indulge his most fleshly fantasies—fantasies that could never have been fulfilled in his former lifetime.

He had more than one partner during his stay, but he preferred Guy, and Guy deemed Joe as a favorite in return. They had their history together, after all. Joe didn't know how the other brothers came to be at the fraternity, but he assumed they were past acquaintances of Guy's, lovers and one-night stands from previous incarnations. Added to Joe's and Guy's history, of course, was one simple and overwhelming truth that caused Joe not to want to leave the fraternity: Joe had never seen a body like Guy's. Who had? And he used whatever opportunity arose to play with it as he may. The broad chest and huge nipples, the strong back, the muscled legs, the bouncing mounds of ass, and the titanic penis with its balls that hung so heavily—were all rather buzz-inducing. And Guy, the Brotherhood's dreamy bull-colossus, loved the attention.

The other brothers harbored no resentment or jealousy toward Joe. On the contrary, it only increased their own desire for Joe. It was an accelerant for the fires, an oil for the chase.

Joe spent time, too, simply relaxing or walking about across the countryside, exploring with Declan the cherry blossom orchards and scattered ponds and reminiscing with both him and Guy. Memories that were very different but always held together by the slightest hint of similarities. Sneaking into dirty movies with Declan; filming them with Guy. They spent the dusk of many days strolling amongst the dandelions and evening mists until they were called in for a raucous dinner of pizza or fried chicken that would more often than not end in a food fight and invitations to carnal delights.

Joe felt accepted here. It wasn't the same kind of acceptance he had felt with Grandpa Joe. This was tribal, not kindred. With Declan and Guy there was the understanding of experiences shared, of the similar and same. They were like brothers who had fought in losing battles but held their own anyway against the weapons of a judgmental and hypocritical construct. They were war buddies.

One autumn-colored night, as Joe sat rocking in a wicker chair on the columned porch, Declan joined him. He came up from behind and sat crouched beside him, looking out onto the lawn and beyond to the trees, as if deep in some meditation or thought. The house was quiet for once. Games had given way to relaxation and sleep.

"I've given thought to what you said," Declan whispered in a voice as light as the fireflies whirling about them. "About what you said about Mom when you got here. I've decided I'm going to see her, Joe. I'm off to find her and make the Journey complete. I'm leaving tonight."

Joe was startled by the decision and the proclamation. "So soon?" he asked. But then he remembered it was he who had encouraged the trek to see Abigail in the first place. He settled back into the chair. "Good for you, Declan," he said quietly. "You're leaving now?" A stubborn lump began to form in his throat.

"Yeah. There's no point in waiting," Declan answered, breaking his stare from the lawn and the fireflies. "It's best to leave when the guys are asleep. They get real possessive, real fast."

"You're not going to say goodbye to Guy?"

"He knows I'm leaving. He recommended I do it at night. Maybe you should go now too. We could travel the road together for a bit. I could use a traveling buddy."

"I can't," Joe said forlornly. "Not yet, anyway. I need to tell Guy first."

Declan nodded in understanding. "Well, I'm off then," he whispered as he rose.

Joe stood slowly from the chair, and they embraced.

"Get out of here without them knowing," Declan instructed, still holding onto Joe by the shoulders. "You're asking for it if you don't."

There was a moment of silence as they took one another in for a last time.

"Until we meet again, brother."

Declan smiled and leaped off the porch. Joe waved, not saying a word, not yelling a goodbye for fear of disturbing the guys. Declan waved back as he ran for the trees, making his way to his mother's gardens. Joe watched until his form disappeared into the nonconforming twilight, that lump refusing to be dislodged from his throat.

THE brethren were upset at Declan's departure, but Guy assured them it was for the best. He explained that he had a journey yet to undertake and that everyone should be allowed to complete their soul journeys without any unnecessary obstacles, even if the obstacles were as enticing as the brothers in the fraternity. This placated them some. But it was also then that the Brotherhood began to eye Joe rather strangely. These were not looks of gall or anger but of warden-like watchfulness. Expressions anchored in retentiveness. Brian would constantly ask if Joe was happy, if he was having a good time. He repeatedly asked if there was anything they could do to make his stay better.

"They know you will be leaving soon," Guy explained one fresh morning. "You probably should have left with Declan. They'll find ways to keep you here."

"But then I wouldn't have been able to say goodbye to you," Joe said.

They both lay naked in the dandelions under the shade of the trees. Joe strummed Guy's ripped stomach with a flower. The brethren were being lazy, lounging about the lawn and porch on hammocks and quilts.

Suddenly, Guy rose to his elbows. "You should leave now. It's the best chance you'll have. Look at them." He gestured to the lawn. "They won't notice a thing. They're completely blissed out."

"What?"

"They won't expect it. You're with me, so no one has their eye on you. They won't expect me to let you go. They would think I, of all people, would fight to keep you here," Guy said.

"Joe, listen," he pleaded, grabbing Joe's hand. "You have to go. They're a rough group when they really want something. I tried to go traveling alone once, just over the hills, and they nearly ripped my balls off trying to catch me. The thing is, I love this place. I would never leave forever. It's *my* place. I love the brothers, but... this isn't your place, Joe."

"But I like it here." Joe paused. "I want to stay."

"No you don't, Joe," Guy said softly. His voice was sweeter than it had ever sounded. "Not like that. You have somebody waiting for you. You'll see. When you find that place, nothing else will matter. I promise. And you'll be glad you left here. But you've got to take that step. You need to go. You've learned what you can from me. In my selfishness, I guess I've kept you too long. I'm to blame."

"I have to go now? I can't," Joe protested. "I won't! Don't you want me around anymore?"

"You big baby," Guy whispered with a sad smile. "I'm sorry about this, Joe, but I can't argue with you on this. It's your time to go." He rose, a tower of flesh.

Immediately, the sound of a strong windstorm issued forth from Guy. His great chest heaved as he shouted to the house, "He's trying to leave! Joe's trying to leave!"

Every word shook the ground, causing birds to scatter and leaves to fall from the trees.

Joe looked up at him in horror and befuddlement.

"Sorry, Joe," Guy said again as he let out another roar to the Brotherhood.

Joe turned his attention to the house to see the mass of brethren rising from their naps on the grass or leaping from the porch.

"Run!" Guy said. "Run now!"

The brothers came ever closer, slowly at first, as Joe came to his feet. Joe recognized the obsession in their gazes, and, after a brief pause of confusion, he took off naked across the lawn and through the trees. Voices followed him, calling for him to return, to never leave.

"Brother Joe! Brother Joe!"

Joe looked over his shoulder once to see the magnificent, goliath figure of Guy waving a last farewell.

As he made his way through a dense area of forest, he heard the brethren still following, though he saw none of them. Their maniacal calls pushed him faster and farther. Running footfalls scuttled behind him through the brush and wood. All he could think of was being torn apart by a maddened group of possessive frat boys.

Ahead, a large mass of bushes and trees offered a needed hiding place, and Joe dove into them, the branches and limbs scraping his tender skin. In his haste, he had forgotten his jeans, which still lay in the dandelions with Guy. That was not his chief concern at the moment, however. He could find clothing elsewhere. He crouched down and hid in the brush, listening intently to the forest floor for the sound of approaching feet.

He waited until the calling and yelling of the brothers for his return had passed, and then he sat on the ground and waited some more. He waited to make sure all was quiet around him and that they were not ready to ambush him if he came out of hiding.

Joe waited in the thicket, alone and uncertain. The chase had made him tired, and the scent of the wildflowers in the forest lulled him into a drowsy, half-awake state.

As a breeze glided along the forest floor around him, he thought he heard whispers of memories....

THE new apartment droned an electronic chant with all its technology and high-tech toys. It was the best that could be found, on the tenth floor of a high-rise with a small deck that looked out over the areas of the city commonly referred to as the "better parts."

Joe had landed a fine job right out of college. Despite his playful socializing, he always managed to stay on top of things in school. He had somehow graduated near the top of his class, and with that came job offers, lots of them. He had accepted the one that would take him the farthest from his small-town beginnings and then proceeded to shop for apartments with his mother. She was so proud, beaming at what he had accomplished. The city was always a bit much for her, and she would rather have had him closer to home, but Veronica knew he had to find his own way.

Months had passed, and still he had not fully unpacked. Boxes were still sprawled around half-opened and looked into. Dishes were being unboxed little by little when he needed to eat, but mostly he ordered takeout. Only the bedroom, where he would spend most of his time at home anyway, was neat and orderly. The CDs were aligned alphabetically on the wall shelf, and fine art prints were framed dramatically in simple black frames. It was there that he would take his one-night stands and fuck buddies. They didn't care about the rest of the apartment anyway. What they wanted was between his legs.

Joe sat at the laptop that was perched on the desk Veronica had bought him. The room was dark but for the glow from the monitor. In the bed, the night's past fun slept tangled in linen sheets—a cocky man with huge sideburns that he thought made him look more attractive. He was married, what the world referred to as "on the down-low" in its ridiculous self-congratulatory terminology. Joe had seen the line from the removed wedding ring as soon as the man introduced himself at the bar.

Nights were a strange thing for Joe. He should be happy, he knew that, and he told everyone he was, but it was a lie. He had everything that everyone he knew wanted, and yet he was beginning to feel very bored... about everything. After his night's heavy fun—panting and rough words—he would feel content for just a few seconds before the tedium would settle in. The high of sex, like drugs, would slip away too fast. Then, as soon as the other fellow dozed off to sleep, Joe would climb out of bed, put on his blue terrycloth robe, and click onto the Internet, searching for something that might alleviate that unwanted feeling. It always happened that way. Every time he would hope for a different outcome. Maybe this guy was the one, he would think. But the "one" never showed up.

There was something, there had to be something in the billions of web pages that could help him. Some words or idea, something dazzling and amazing and life-changing floating about in cyberspace. An epiphany like he had been given that day at the fall festival a few years ago but brought this time not by a mysterious stranger but by bytes and megabytes and strange computer phrases.

An hour or so into surfing aimlessly through porn sites, travel sites, amazon.com, and bookstores, Joe stumbled upon a matchmaker site. "Sign up now!" it screamed at him in large, obnoxious letters. A scroll across the top of the page showed two dozen gorgeous men. "Meet the man of your dreams!" *They looked like models, all of them. Airbrushed, perfect, and impossible to attain.*

Joe looked at each picture, staring intently into each set of eyes as if he could discern the individual within. None of the faces did anything for him, and his mind began to zone out as his eyes kept watch. But then his eyes forced his mind back. There was something on the screen that had just left the picture scroll that caused Joe's heart to quicken before his mind could discern what it was. It was a photo, a face that he knew. Louis?

He waited again, impatiently, for the face to reappear. His toes curled in anticipation, his leg shook, and his stomach rumbled in a nervous rally. The night's guy fumbled about in the sheets behind him.

After a series of tense moments, the photo again appeared. It was Louis! His blue eyes pierced through the screen, shining hope and beauty and brightness everywhere. That, for certain, would wake the one-night stand. How could anyone sleep through such beauty?

Joe quickly signed up for the site. He filled in the information blindly, hardly comprehending anything his fingers were doing. He would write Louis. He could scarcely wait through the sign-up process. His mind was playing over a hopeful meeting far off, away from the computer, in some fantasy land of perfect first dates.

Finally, it was done, and Joe set about frantically searching for Louis. He entered criteria on the search, what he knew. But his fishing brought back nothing. After a half-hour of fruitless, irritating exploring, he gave up and went back to the sign-up page where he had first seen the photo. There it was still. His heart was about to burst as he clicked on the blessed picture.

We're sorry. This member is no longer active.

Joe's heart sank as real tears formed in the corners of his eyes and his lips molded around the word "No."

"Hey baby," a voice growled from behind. "Come back to bed and play."

"...TWENTY THOUSAND ROADS I WENT DOWN, DOWN, DOWN..."

HE HAD waited, hunkered down and naked, long enough. There was nothing to be heard but that which the woods naturally provided: a bird, a cricket, a whistling of breeze through the timber. These were not the sentient trees Joe had seen elsewhere, and that was a relief. If they had been, they might have given his location away. So Joe came from his hiding place at last while it was still light enough to do so. Even then, however, he walked through the trees, cautious and observant of his surroundings. He had no real idea where he would go if he did happen upon a brother, but that could be decided if and when it occurred. Now, he was just glad to be out of the thicket, however unclothed and bare. He set out at once to get as far away from the Brotherhood as he could.

The dense wood ended at last, and Joe found himself traveling upon a gravel road that ran alongside rolling hills of green under a magnificent cloudless sky. Sprouts of grass harmlessly invaded the middle of the roadway between deep, rutted tracks. Joe ventured down the road, arms folded, with no inclination of true direction. His mind swam with thoughts of confused ramblings and aimless sentences. In the end, there seemed to be no real purpose to his being here. Every time he found someplace that offered peace and joy, he was forced to leave it. He had had to leave everything that offered solace. There came into him a yearning emptiness he was sure he had felt before. Yet he couldn't remember from where he had known it.

"Great courage, Joe," he whispered to himself, the thought of the Stranger offering him some comfort.

The sound of gravel under wheel brought Joe's attention back from darker thoughts. Approaching him with easy speed along the hilly road came a brightly colored carriage (hot pink with bright yellow trimming) pulled by four horses, their manes and tails dyed shades of green and purple and blue. They trotted, proud and affluent. The driver, too, was dressed rather ostentatiously, with a pink ruffled shirt and shiny blue bloomers. Though he was a young-looking man, he had silver hair that was pulled back and tied in a ponytail. He hollered something at the horses as the coach neared. Joe's heart grew warm at the sight of the steeds as he remembered Buck and Phil. The four equines began clipping at a slower pace, and soon the yellow wheels came to a full stop at Joe's side.

The door of the coach opened with a furious commotion as a large, fleshy woman poured out. Joe jumped back immediately. It seemed to take quite a lot of energy for the woman to remove herself from the coach, and that was no wonder. She was dressed very exuberantly, miles past sophistication, with a satin gown the length and width of which Joe had never seen in either of his two remembered lives. Her dress was of a light violet shade highlighted with white lace. She looked like a plump grape. The neck of the ensemble plunged to reveal her fatty cleavage, and she wore a pearl choker around her throat that seemed in danger of popping off and scattering all over the gravel. Small round sunglasses did nothing to refine her face, and her hair stood piled up high in a tower of the same shade of violet as her gown. An overpowering aroma of lilacs trailed along with her. This woman was a sight.

Joe stood still, staring and mouth wide.

"Hellooo," the large purple woman said in a high voice of caricature. "My dear boy, you've got no clothes! Do you realize you are completely *au naturel*? Bette and I couldn't help notice it. You do realize, don't you? That you're in the nude?"

"Uh," Joe stammered. "I left my clothes behind...."

"No matter," she interrupted. "We'll get you fixed up right away. I just happen to be the foremost dresser in all the land." She said this with a twist of her wrist and a twirl to her voice.

She did her absolute best to stroll elegantly forward, fumbling a bit under the massive dress, and held out her fleshy wrist for Joe to kiss.

"Melva Jasmine," she said in a haughty tone.

Joe kissed her wrist obediently if hesitantly but looked up at her blankly.

"*Melva Jasmine!*" she repeated in response to his lost expression. "Surely you've heard of me." Her eyes grew wide behind her glasses in surprise and disbelief.

"I'm sorry," Joe responded. "I'm new here. I'm afraid I don't know much of anything."

"Oh, well, then that explains it," she exclaimed, her voice scaring the birds and annoying the horses. "You come with me young master... um... what did you say your name was again?"

"He didn't," the driver deadpanned from his seat. "You've done most the talking, you yappy old crone. The boy hasn't been able to say much at all."

"You be quiet!" Melva pointed at him, furrowing her thickly painted brow. "You're just there to drive me and look pretty. No talking! *Ever!*"

"My name's Joe." He felt like the self-conscious witness to a lover's quarrel.

"Of course it is!" Melva exclaimed as she clasped her hands together and smiled broadly. "Now, like I said, you come with me. We'll get you fitted into something snappy or dazzling or something just a teeny bit elegantly cumbersome. We can't have handsome young men walking about without clothes, can we? Where's the mystery in that?"

She grabbed Joe's hand and pulled him, willingly or no, into the carriage. It took her a while to climb all the way back in. Her bustle and muss seemed an entity of their own, with a tendency to be stubborn. But once that was accomplished, she handed a thick golden blanket to Joe to wrap himself in, and he fell to the seat opposite Her Purple Satin Majesty. Melva gave a throaty holler to the driver, and the coach began to move. Joe had no control over where he was headed now. But that was okay. It was nice not to have to decide on a direction for once.

Across from Joe, crowded into the seat with Melva and her gown, was an irritated-looking woman. She peered at the sea of purple with lordly disdain as she held a long cigarette between two disciplinary fingers. Her eyes were demanding, imposing, like they could see straight through a person and separate the truths from the lies. Yet she had the grace that Melva clearly lacked but desperately tried to convey. She wore an evening gown of dark blue, with a diamond butterfly placed just above her breasts.

By way of introduction, Melva said, "Joe, this is my friend Bette. Bette, this is Joe."

Joe, of course, knew immediately who she was. Ben would have fainted. Melva seemed a little hurt by his recognition of the woman.

"I'd kiss you," Bette said, her voice a caricature of itself, "but I just washed my hair." She studied Joe up and down with mild interest, then gazed out the window at the passing hills.

"We're dropping old Bette here"—the word "old" did not go unnoticed by the lady—"off at her summer home before we head to my lovely shop."

"Where do you live, Miss… Bette?" Joe asked nervously.

Bette did not turn to face him. Her eyes were fixed on the landscape outside the carriage. "A cabin," she said. "A cabin in the cotton. I had to fix it up at first. When I got it…."

"Oh, yes! We know!" Melva interrupted. "*What a dump!*" she mimicked.

Bette simply turned to Melva with an icy stare and said to Joe, "This one talks, Joseph. She talks *a lot*. Greer Garson at the 1943 Academy Awards has nothing on our dear, sweet Melva!"

Melva's jaws opened, and she made a noise like an agitated turkey, the flesh of her neck and face adding more to that resemblance.

Joe snuggled tightly in the fringed covering that felt more like a curtain than a blanket as Melva and Bette combated and chatted on and on about their own individual illustriousness. Melva was sure Joe would see her greatness in the fine art of fabrics and textiles once they arrived at the shop. Bette was certain that Melva was a second-rate drag queen in her last life. Flailing gestures of luxurious grandeur and biting whips of wit punctuated and spiked the carriage ride.

Joe hardly listened, though. The argument grew tiresome. He was soon under another thick cover, that of sleep. A dreamless, quiet sleep that not even Melva's voice and the ridicule of Bette could dissuade.

THEY were pulling onto cobblestone streets as Joe awoke. The bickering had ended. Bette was gone. Melva was still expressing her utmost admiration for herself, however, seemingly unaware Joe had dozed off at all. The carriage made its way past lyrically designed architecture and stylish citizenry. Joe knew the place; he recognized certain aspects of this city from blinks of memory. He was unable, though, to identify precisely where his faint remembrance came from. A book or a magazine? An old photograph? Something in his retention was reaching out to touch those graceful buildings and cobbled roads.

"Where are we, Miss Jasmine?" Joe asked, interrupting the old queen.

"Call me Melva!" she exclaimed, slapping him harshly on the knee with her big hand. "Why, my boy, this is Florence. Firenze! You know Florence, don't you?"

Joe sat up, letting the blanket fall just a bit from his tanned shoulders. "Italy?"

"Well, yes! Where else? This style, this elegance, it could be no other place."

Florence. Of course it was. He saw it now. All Joe's young life, he had wanted to see Florence. To see the art, feel the history, and taste the food. He remembered he studied it in college, yet he couldn't remember if he had actually ever made it there. But it was all in front of him now—the Medici Palace, the Duomo, the Uffizi. Every last sculpture, every romantic avenue.

It wasn't the modern Florence of which he had heard, though. This, instead, was a Florence without the pollutants of vehicles and the noise of technology. This was a youthful Florence holding a promise of art and enlightenment out to the world. Yet it still held every piece of art and sculpture and architecture that had ever existed in the city. Nothing had ever been destroyed here by war or feuds. Michelangelo's *David* still rested high atop the Duomo.

The citizens of this new "old" city were, of course, the height of fashion, and walked along the streets and ate at their cafés with style and dash. Their heads were held high and proud except for the younger men, who swaggered about in their tight black pants reeking of sexuality. Art was in their veins and flirtation in every glance.

The carriage stopped to the side of a large block of buildings, and Joe and Melva emerged. Joe stood wrapped tight in the gold blanket as the silver-haired coachman offered his hand to Melva. On the street, the Florentines strolled past with gallant strides.

"Buon giorno, Melva," men greeted the old crow with a tip of the hat.

"Good afternoon, Melva," the women said politely.

There were even some catcalls at the old dame from the younger men as she and Joe made their way down the boulevard.

"Don't they all look *fabulous*?" She gestured broadly at the people all about her. "I design their clothes, you know. Well, not *all* their clothes." She came close to Joe and said with a lower, condescending tone, "Some go elsewhere... *and you can tell.*" She chuckled at her own joke, giving a laugh that sounded like two badgers mating.

Joe was led past storefronts and crowds of swarthy, leering men and into a shop, the façade of which was much the same as those beside and across from it. The quaint charm of Florence lay in its antiquarian buildings of simple symmetry and balance. Still, he expected the look of the shop to match that of his hostess. He was expecting an overload of what she termed "fabulousness." Instead, on the outside the building was the same as most of the architecture in Florence, classic and artistic, yet uncomplicated.

The inside of Melva's shop, however, was another matter altogether. Vaulted ceilings with painted cherubs and various beautiful Florentines dressed in the manner of gods (the mightiest of which, of course, was the elaborate Miss Melva with her purple gown). And all of them were painted so preciously, with rosy cheeks and wide eyes. This was not Rococo; this was too much even to be termed that.

The shop floor consisted of rows upon rows of clothing. Garish, glittering stuff, each rack more kitsch than the next. It all lay somewhere between Renaissance and glam-rock. It was the sort of attire Joe could never imagine himself wearing.

Miss Melva removed her eyewear, revealing overly painted eyelids in three shades of violet. Her eyes were a very light blue.

"Have at it!" she said grandly, with excitement and pride. "Pick anything in the shop. All of it is designed by me, of course. I have a certain panache. Everyone says so. That's why I'm famous. Yes, so very well known in the best of circles. Go, go, go! Choose away! It would be an honor to have such a handsome young man wearing my frocks."

Joe clung to the golden blanket, unwilling to trade it for the elaborate clothes around him. He walked through the rows of clothing. Every so often he would finger a particular item so as to feign some interest. Melva would sigh in agreement. "Oh, that *would* look fabulous on you!" she would say.

Finally, after great faux deliberation, Joe decided on a shiny blue velvet jacket and pantaloons, much like those the silver-haired driver wore. It was to be worn with a ruffled white shirt, stockings and buckled shoes for the feet, and a matching captain's hat out of which bloomed a frothy blue feather. And this was the *least* embellished of the outfits. At least it didn't have golden stitchwork in flowery designs, as did most of the other garments.

"Oh, you *do* look the dashing gentleman!" Melva exclaimed as Joe critiqued himself in the mirror.

It did suit him, complimenting his frame and features rather appropriately. Still, he felt like a spectacle at a costume ball.

Melva took hold of his arm and stood next to him with pride. "We look every bit the handsome couple," she gleamed. "Don't you agree?"

"Yeah," Joe said, still staring into the bejeweled mirror. "We're something."

He turned to her. "Am I... I mean, are you next? Am I here on my journey to meet you?"

Melva smiled at him and gently took her large, fleshy hands and cradled his face. "No, my puppet," she said, softer than Joe thought she was capable of being. "You go on for that. I just saw you and thought you might like some clothes. We get travelers through here all the time. I keep a lookout for them. But you didn't know me. I have nothing more to give you than this delicious ensemble."

"Oh," Joe said, looking to the floor. "Thank you." Perhaps he shouldn't have gotten into the carriage. Perhaps he was now farther off from his journey's end than before. "Was I wrong to have come here? Where do I go next?" he asked.

"Just there." Melva pointed to the door. "Just out there, onto the streets of Florence." Her voice sang as she mentioned the city's name.

"But how will I know where to go?"

"You no longer need a guide, Joe. You have yourself. Just follow the cobblestones," Melva said. "You'll get there. You'll see."

Joe walked to the door and opened it, peering out onto the bustling city. He smiled and tipped his hat to the lady, then took his leave into a city he had known, but in a different form, in a different world.

"Wait!" he heard the shrillness of Melva's voice break forth. "I suppose it would only be proper and fitting for me to give you a true tour of the city." She hastened up beside him and once again looped her pudgy arm through his. "Shall we, love?" she said.

The warmth and style of Florence accepted the two of them into its evening air. They strolled past gelato shops and haberdasheries, past children playing by fountains and lovers kissing under sculptures as dusk fell. Joe was certain he would stand out walking along the streets in his flashy attire with an over-glossed queen at his side, but no one seemed to take notice other than to toss a flirting nod at him or give a naughty whistle from behind. The old dame received naught but respectful salutations. Joe saw cathedrals and churches, bakeries and pizza parlors, clothiers and cappuccino shops. It all smelled so wonderful and inviting. The magnificent whirl of a city most alive at night.

Melva explained to Joe the various quirks and complexities of the city as she knew them, the strange wonderfulness of the citizenry. He still listened courteously. Around them, music issued from everywhere: small bands on the street, guitarists on street corners, and acoustics from taverns. Gypsies danced in bright rags made of silk and finery. Children shared their gelati with their dogs. Joe found himself being lulled into relaxation by the essence of the city as he strolled along. Even Melva's voice became less of an annoyance. She merely became part of Florence, an acceptable variant in the voice of the city at night.

As they passed through the masses of Florentines in their piazzas, Melva and Joe came upon a crowd enjoying some nighttime entertainment. They were laughing at the frivolity of a play being performed on the stone steps that surrounded one of the magical lighted fountains. Joe and Melva moved into the inner rungs of the crowd. The light laughter of the crowd—lovers, men, and women—flitted into the air. Only Melva's rather boisterous guffaws somewhat disturbed the flow of the more gentle voices.

It was a romantic comedy of errors portrayed by two men *about* two men falling in love. Makeup was applied lightly to the handsome faces of the actors. Mistaken identities and the like were the name of the game, and the two men played all the roles. Joe smiled along with the Florentines. Whenever one of the lovers would make an especially humorous remark or clumsily fall or falter, Melva would elbow Joe in the ribs and snort in approving laughter. At times he was almost knocked to the ground by her ribbing, and yet it only made him enjoy the show more. It was a good time, after all. He enjoyed the night. He felt calm and pleased he had come.

The crowd soon dispersed after the appropriate applause for the deserving actors. The two bowed graciously and kissed one final time, much to the crowd's delight.

"Most exceptional!" Melva said loudly as she and Joe made their ways closer to the river Arno. "Very enjoyable, wouldn't you say?"

"Very enjoyable," Joe agreed. They walked slowly, still arm in arm. "That was wonderful. I think it would have made me uncomfortable in life, but here… it was just lovely, Miss Melva."

"Why so?" Melva inquired. "Why would that have made you uncomfortable, puppet?"

Joe thought before saying anything. He didn't want to sound self-pitying or full of remorse. "I think… I was never okay with myself. Not that I can recall anyway. I was never okay with being gay. I tried to convince myself I was, but when you're told all your life… you start wondering if everybody is right. Doesn't matter how many coming-out stories you read if you've always got someone there to push you back in."

"Rubbish!" Melva proclaimed.

"Why is it rubbish?"

"Well, without the aesthetic of gay men, there would be no culture. For the most part, the world would be boring stone facades and straight lines." Melva was adamant about her position. "There would be no sensual lines and orgasmic curves. There would be no swooning, my dear boy! Can you imagine a world devoid of swooning? Gay men have influenced every part of civilization: art, music, architecture, fashion, teaching, even war. Without gay men, culture as you and I knew it, as everyone who has ever lived knew it, would not have been. It's as simple as that."

Melva stopped and looked at him. The Arno flowed beside them, deep and heavy under the night. Melva's soft hands held Joe's chin. "When people said those things to you, puppet, they were denying their own inclusion into a world that lives through art and beauty and aestheticism. Wars and businesses come and go in every life, but the aesthetic and sensual qualities of the spirit lift us above those things. In your next incarnation, you might not be a gay man, maybe not a man at all, but you will be informed enough to know the truth. Beauty is eternal. It's really the only thing we can create that goes on forever."

Joe felt the shudder of truth crawl over his skin.

"Now, my love, I'm afraid it is my time to leave you," Melva said, her voice again climbing like a ladder into the night. "Can you make it alone now? And no puppy dog eyes!"

"Yes, ma'am. I can make it. Thank you."

"Well, you're very welcome," she said. "I should get back to my shop. Things to do!" she sang. "You just continue that way, along the Arno. You'll come to where you need to be soon enough. It won't be long."

She glanced at Joe like a grandmother who has spent too much time away from her grandchildren. "Oh!" she huffed, holding out her great arms. "Give us a squelch!"

Joe felt loved and secured in those arms. Arms that, when he had first seen them, looked cumbersome and too fleshy.

"I'll see you soon, love," she said as she wiped at her horribly dripping eye makeup. "Must get to the shop!" she exclaimed, rushing off so Joe would not see her cry. "Be careful! Just follow the Arno! I'll see you in the end, puppet! You'll make it!"

Joe grinned at the sight of that great mess of a woman as she hurried off into the night. He wondered if maybe this was his true grandmother and the one he had been stuck with in life was a mistake, a soul-match blunder. Melva, Joe thought, certainly felt like his grandmother now, the one he should have had.

Strolling by the Arno, he wandered upon a bright little café. It was empty but charming, with an outdoor area that looked across the river. He sat down at one of the lamp-lit tables, took off his hat, and crossed one leg over the other. He would watch the passage of the small crafts on the Arno and just rest a bit before going on. The lights and lamps from the other side of the river twinkled and glittered under the gentle darkness that cloaked the city. The lights were reflected, shimmering in the great pool that flowed out and away.

"Beautiful night, eh?" came a dreamy voice from behind.

A young man with graceful, almost feminine features had appeared. One leg was lifted onto a chair, and he was leaning forward on it, staring into the sky above the river.

"Yes," Joe replied. "Very relaxing."

"It's always like this here," the pretty young man said, bringing his eyes to Joe. "Always relaxing. Always serene."

He unlocked himself from his stance and, taking a bottle of wine and two glasses from the table where he stood, came toward Joe and pulled up a chair beside him. He set the wine and glasses in front of Joe and straddled the chair backward.

"Slow night?" Joe asked as the man poured the thick red wine into both glasses. Italian wine. *Real* Italian wine.

"Actually, I'm closed," he said. "But not to you." He raised his glass in a toast, and Joe replied in kind.

Florentines walked by them, admiring the river. It was less crowded by the Arno than it had been in the piazzas.

"I am Giuseppe," he gestured to himself with a slight bow of the head. His English was perfect. But then, Joe thought, it would be, wouldn't it? Language barriers were an annoyance from another world. The world that was crowded from shore to shore with ever-crumbling Towers of Babel.

"I guess you know who I am," Joe replied.

Giuseppe nodded.

"Were we friends?" Joe asked. "Maybe college buddies?"

"No. We weren't friends, Joe. We weren't anything. We didn't even talk. Not once."

"Well, then I don't understand," Joe confessed, sliding his index finger along the lip of his wine glass.

"You don't have to have known someone to impact their life." Giuseppe took a drink from his wine. He was a beautiful man. A sloped forehead, a thin nose and full lips, high cheekbones, and piercing gray eyes with arched brows. His brown hair was cut short and neat, and he wore a simple black dress shirt tucked into black slacks.

"I impacted your life? How? Or is this where it goes all fuzzy and I hallucinate again?"

"No. Nothing like that here, Joe." Giuseppe smiled. "I've got no tricks. You won't be seeing your story playing out in the waters of the Arno. I'm not one for that kind of magic. Never have been. I've always been one to focus on the future, not the past. We're just going to talk. Is that okay?"

"That sounds nice," Joe said. "I wouldn't mind talking at all. I would like nothing more than to just sit here and relax."

"Well, I'm guessing you deserve it. The Journey can be hard and draining. Plus," Giuseppe said more seriously, "you've got tougher things ahead. You're almost there, but these last few tidbits of memory are going to kick your ass, Joe. So just enjoy this moment."

Joe sat quietly, a bit jarred by the augury of the pretty café owner. He drank from the wine glass, looking out onto the waters. A group of teenagers came by, disturbing the night's placidity, and then disappeared down a side street.

"How did I affect you?" Joe finally asked. "Why is it that you are part of my journey?"

Giuseppe sighed. "You had graduated from college, remember? You'd gone on to a nice career as an editor for an up-and-coming book publisher. Books about mythology, folklore, and fantasy. You were very successful, in fact. You had a nice apartment in the city, co-workers who liked you, and a social life that often involved mixing business with pleasure. You had everything you could have wanted materially."

As Giuseppe spoke, Joe's memories of the time in between college and his meeting of Giuseppe were fleshed out and filled in, like a half-empty glass being filled to the top. Again he remembered all the joys, heartaches, and indifferences. Every memorable face and forgettable bus ride.

"I remember," Joe said, examining the wine in the glass. "I was doing very well, but something wasn't right." He frowned.

"No. You weren't happy."

"Not at all," Joe agreed. "I felt empty and alone. I mean, I had all these friends, this great job, sex every place I looked. Sex even when I didn't look...."

"But it left you feeling—"

"Incomplete. Disinterested." Joe sighed. "Was this life? Was this it? I was constantly asking myself that. There's a mopey song in there somewhere."

"But you had boyfriends. Lovers."

"Yeah, but they didn't give me anything but the momentary pleasure I was seeking. There was nothing more to them than that. I hardly knew them. Their faces now are as bland as the sidewalks I walked every day going to work."

"You came across an ad on a travel site on the Internet one late night. One of those nights after you had tried to drown the indifference with alcohol and sex. You decided one spring to visit Italy in order to get away from all the tedium and mediocrity."

"Florence," Joe whispered as a smile developed. "I wanted to see Florence. A gift to myself to maybe find whatever it was that was missing. I was so excited on the plane ride over. I hadn't been that giddy in years."

"But it was the same, wasn't it? The same loneliness from your life in the States was there lurking behind all the art and beauty."

"Yes," Joe agreed as the smile was whisked away. "No matter what, it was there. I went to the bars to try and meet men, but nothing seemed worth anything. They were just as insipid as the ones back home."

"Then, one late night, after you had chanced to find someone at a bar and came home empty-handed, you passed by a gelato parlor packed with tourists and Florentines. Every one of them was happy in their moment, eating their cones and freezes."

"Yes," Joe remembered. "They were all so cheerful. Such a simple thing made them so happy." He paused. "Wait! No. Not everyone was happy. Outside there was a young man, leaning up against a light pole, staring inward with longing. *That was you!*" Joe said, staring at Giuseppe.

"It was me." Giuseppe nodded.

"You looked so sad. There was such yearning in your eyes. I wanted to grab hold of you and cuddle you like a baby, like a little brother," Joe said. "Then our eyes met. You caught me watching you."

"But there was nothing but gelato on my mind."

"And nothing but sympathy on mine. You were a prostitute?" Joe asked. "A rentboy?"

"Oh, I was." Giuseppe sighed, peering into the sky. There was relief in that sigh.

"I passed you by, slowly."

"But then you came back," Giuseppe said.

"Well, I couldn't get you out of my head. That expression on your face kept haunting me. Your eyes. The sorrow and used emotion was too much, I think."

"So you reached into your pocket and pulled from it more *lire* than I had ever seen."

"I gave you enough to get plenty of gelatos." Joe smiled.

"Joe," Giuseppe laughed. "You gave me enough to open my own gelato shop."

Joe laughed as well.

"You changed things for me, Joe. Made me see possible goodness where I had never seen any before. And I thank you for that now. You had given me hope."

Joe looked earnestly at his host. "Thank *you*, Giuseppe," he whispered.

"Things turned around for you too after that."

"I don't remember that," Joe admitted, trying to wrest a memory.

"You won't either. Not here anyway," Giuseppe said. "That's for another place."

"God, I hate these cliffhangers." Joe took another drink.

Giuseppe chuckled under his breath.

"So what happened to you after that?" Joe asked.

"I got my gelato," Giuseppe said. "I was on my way home with it. It was delicious, and I was ecstatic. You made me happier than I ever had been. I mean, all that money was, of course, huge. But, in truth, it was that single gelato that made me happiest."

"And then what happened?"

"And then I was attacked. Robbed blind and my throat was slit," Giuseppe said lowly.

"Oh, Jesus!" Joe cried. He put his hands to his face. "I'm so sorry. Oh my God, I'm sorry!"

"Joe, it's okay," Giuseppe said, placing a hand on Joe's arm for comfort. "It would have happened that night whether you had given me those *lire* or not. Things are designed that way. They were hooligans, high on heroine and out to get more by whatever means. Do you understand me, Joe? It wasn't your fault."

Joe took hold of Giuseppe's hand and held it tight for a moment as he regained composure. "All the same," he said. "I'm sorry. It's a shame we didn't talk, or I didn't take you back with me to my room. Both of our lives might have changed right there. I think I would have liked to have known you."

"Well, we've got until you leave," Giuseppe said. "No need for regrets. There's plenty of time to get to know one another tonight."

Joe smiled, peering out at the river, the lights caressing its noble current. "Good. We shall," he said.

"Stay right there," Giuseppe said as he grabbed the empty bottle of wine. "I'll get us more drink."

He left and then returned shortly thereafter with a new bottle, as promised. People passed by the café in couples and sometimes alone, but all were enamored of the river and its coalescing with the nightfall. Joe and Giuseppe talked about the lives they had known or could remember. And as the dawn light began to drift into the sky, they understood that, yes, they would have liked one another, and they might have been great friends under other circumstances, for they had a mutual friend in Solitude. And so, mourning a friendship that was meant to be but had never taken true form, they pledged devotion to one another there, on the spot, with the air fragrant with morning bakeries and the taste of wine on their tongues.

Activity came back to the river in the form of fishermen and boats, and Giuseppe and Joe left the café and walked down the steps to the Arno. Joe knew the time was nearing for his departure. The ripples in the waterway told of something important forthcoming.

"You say I'm almost there?" Joe asked. "At the end?"

"Nearly," Giuseppe said. "It'll be hard, Joe, but you'll get through it. You're a strong soul in any life. Just like me."

Joe embraced him warmly. "It seems all my life I was surrounded by strong souls; I just didn't see them clearly."

"Ah," Giuseppe said as their bodies parted. "There you are."

He pointed to a small ship as it came out from under the Ponte Vecchio. A familiar sail came into view, flapping doggedly in the breeze.

"I'll be damned," Joe laughed as he caught sight of the tiny captain at the bow. "Petey!" he shouted, walking to the water's edge.

The little fellow still wore his shorts but had now donned a pirate's cap and an eyepatch as well. There was a belt attached to his waist and a wooden sword slung through it. He grinned widely.

The ship drifted slowly toward Giuseppe and Joe.

"Hiya, Joe!" 3P called from the bow. "Come on aboard! I know you can thwim!"

Joe laughed and slapped his hands together. Giuseppe grinned at his pleasure. "Go on, Joe," he said. "Go to your friend."

"We'll catch up more later?" Joe asked Giuseppe, almost imploringly.

"You bet," Giuseppe agreed. "We've got all the time in the world here, and a lifetime to tell each other about."

Joe grabbed him close, giving him one last hug, and then dove into the fresh, clean waters of the Arno.

3P lowered a rope, which Joe grabbed and used to pull himself aboard. Miss Melva's clothes were now soaked and probably ruined as Joe stood dripping before his young friend. He had left the hat behind inadvertently, but that was fine. He wasn't crazy about the outfit.

"Thath thum thnappy threadth, Joe," 3P admired. "But they're all wet." With a crinkled nose, he scratched his head under the skull-and-crossbones hat and studied the costume Joe wore.

"Yeah." Joe smiled broadly. "That's okay. They'll dry."

He glanced back to the shore and waved goodbye to Giuseppe. The café owner continued waving as they drifted from sight.

"You ready for another adventure, Joey?" 3P asked loudly, his fists placed firmly on his hips and his smile wide and cheerful, minus those few teeth.

"Sure am, Petey," Joe concurred.

"Good! I need a firth mate," he said resolutely. "Leth go then."

"Ay ay, Cap'n!"

And down the Arno they went, on to other legs of the same journey. Whatever lay ahead, they were ready. Dragons and demons, witches and mermaids, Scylla and Charybdis—none of them could stand in the way of the mighty 3P and his first mate, Joe.

"...PLEASE BE AWARE OF THEM THAT STARE..."

THE waters of the Arno eventually escaped Florence, flowing on past other banks of other towns and villages, other countries and landscapes. Every one of them was busy with a myriad of happy and blissful souls fishing, swimming, relaxing on the shores, spending given moments of joy and relief from former, harder lives. All were waiting leisurely for their next bump onward to another lifetime. Every so often Joe thought he caught view of someone with the same expression of wonder and concern on their faces as he. These were his fellow Journeymen.

3P stood at the bow of his tiny ship like a stern and proud captain surveying the passing lands as Joe did his playful bidding as first mate.

The banks soon broadened and then gave way altogether as the river emptied into a wide sea whose glassy water extended until it was seamless with the horizon. Large ships, larger than 3P's by a great margin, sailed from quaint ports into the placid blue. Aboard them, other proud captains of grand stature and refined bearing watched the inching away of the coast. Winds ruffled and beat the sails. Their flapping and the peaceful sounds of the water's mild turbulence made a sort of natural chorus with the seagulls and other birds overhead. It was a call to the sea.

The massive ships were easy for 3P's little boat to outrun and maneuver around. Enormous shadows were cast over the small vessel. Captains nodded and greeted 3P as he passed. In return, he did his best take on grown-up pretense and nodded solemnly. Joe found this extremely amusing.

Once out on the open sea, past the vessels of greater height, they trusted the current and relaxed. Joe and 3P lay on the deck and enjoyed a mid-day lunch, then a peaceful rest. 3P told Joe of his latest adventures with the seahorses as they sailed. There was not a compass in sight, neither a map of the world to be found. To have an idea of possible course or outcome would defeat 3P's inquisitive purpose. The boy would only have Joe steer in a certain direction when his whimsy so inclined him. Mostly, though, he did nothing at all, letting the sea take them onward of its own accord.

"This is nice," Joe said with his arms folded under his head. His coat lay spread out beneath him on the deck. The sky was blue and clear, and the sun was warm and comforting.

"Yeah," 3P agreed. He lay head-to-head with Joe. "I love jutht letting the thea take me thomeplathe. You jutht gotta trutht it."

They had been drifting a while and were now alone, a solitary speck on the massive face of the waters. It continued like this for a while, the two of them giggling over memories or yawning contentedly as the kind sea breezes swam over their bodies. So it surprised Joe when, out of the corner of his eye, he saw something approaching the boat. He turned his head sideways and saw more clearly the mast of another ship just a little larger than their own. Joe raised and supported himself on his elbows. "Looks like company," he said.

3P rose to see for himself, and then, with a gasp, he jumped to his feet, his hands firmly on his hips.

"What's wrong, Petey?" Joe asked, rising to his own feet at once.

3P didn't answer. He watched as the other boat dropped anchor, a solid *kathunk* into the water. On board there was a figure about the same height as 3P, wearing very much the same get-up but for a striped red-and-white shirt and a tiny jacket like the one Melva had given Joe, but with gleaming gold buttons. The little person bounded onto 3P's vessel, holding a hat as they did so, and landed with a thud on the wooden deck, immediately standing upright again. Only after she stood up straight again did Joe realize that it was a little girl with stiff, unmoving pigtails. Over her eye-patch she wore a pair of pink-framed spectacles. She stared first at 3P with challenge and then at Joe. Returning her glance back to the little boy, she exclaimed, "3P! We meet again!" Her voice came full force from her wide mouth. Joe chuckled to himself.

"Hello, Maddy!" 3P countered, not at all hospitably. "What bringth you to theeth parth?" It sounded more like an accusation than a question.

"Lookin' for bandits… bandits like you," she said with a leer and a dramatic step forward.

"Aren't you going to introduce us?" Joe asked through his chortles.

3P didn't budge from his position but kept an eye on Maddy. "Joe, thith ith my worth enemy! My greateth foe: *Maddy Mojingle*."

"The very one!" Maddy bellowed as she unsheathed her wooden sword.

"Now kids," Joe said, trying to calm matters.

"*En garde!*" Maddy thrust forward with the splintered blade.

"Have at you!" 3P hollered in return as their wood weapons struck with a smack.

They danced about the deck, striking dulled wood and making brave and heroic noises as they did so. Joe, seeing that nothing could be done, sat on the edge of the bow and watched the play, laughing and giggling at the sheer delight hidden beneath their fantastic minds. He remembered playing pirate with 3P himself; all the world and every character was created from their own ample imaginations.

Up and down the modest boat 3P and Maddy did their sword fighting, neither of them backing down to the other's claim of superiority.

"You are no match for my skill, 3P!"

"You are mithtaken. Take that!" *Thwack.*

Round and round they went. When they were done with their dance around 3P's ship, they vaulted over to Maddy's and continued their combat, ducking behind the mast and jabbing at one another without actually touching flesh. Every now and then one of them would make a fake cry of agony and then fall, but just as quickly rise with a loud "*A-ha!*" in a surprise show of fortitude and endurance.

Joe, still on 3P's boat, was so caught up in watching the play between the two that he noticed too late his own ship floating away from the anchored vessel. He searched, but there was no mooring to be found on Petey's ship.

"Hey!" he called to the little sword fighters. "Hey! I'm sorry to interrupt, but we've got a problem. Where's the anchor? I'm drifting off!"

3P and Maddy stopped abruptly and looked at Joe as he stared at them from the straying boat.

"There ithn't one," 3P called back. "I forgot to get one!" He shrugged an *oops*.

"You forgot to get one?" Joe whispered to himself. He was becoming slightly alarmed. "Well, what do I do?" he asked.

"Juth take care of her for me," 3P yelled. "Take her out! Travel the water."

"What? Aren't you coming back?"

"Joe, I have a fight to finith. Might take all day. You take care of my boat. I'll find her later, wherever you end up!"

Joe had to listen very hard to hear the last part. He was now quite a ways off. "But...," he protested in vain.

"Nice to meet you," Maddy called out and waved cheerfully.

Joe huffed in amused resignation, shaking his head. Soon he could hear neither of them. He only saw the two of them waving from the boat, peering across the waters at him.

So Joe drifted alone on the sea, farther and farther away from any known countryside, port, or past. Still, he wasn't fearful of his new situation. Gone was the anxiety associated with the new. He had finally learned to give up to the ways of this new place. He was certain, given time, he would end up where he was supposed to be, and that 3P would indeed show up again somewhere down the figurative—or literal—road. That's how it was here, after all. Things always worked out. The journey went on and on, with pauses and stalls but never any true stops. There was always a direction in some off-handed way, always someplace to go and some way to get there.

Joe rested his head upon his hands again, gazed out upon the waves and deep blue, and waited. There was no land that he could see. The horizon was water and sky. But there *would* be land. He just had to wait.

His mind was occupied, though, with other things. Curiosities abounded to keep him entertained. The little boat drifted past various orchestrations of creature and enchantment.

He passed a couple of handsome squads of mermen playing quite intently at water polo in some aqua-Olympics. Their arms and torsos were well-muscled and fierce, their backs scripts of muscular definition. Joe watched their lovely forms jump into the air in ruthless abandon after a sea-foam ball. A walrus was the referee. The ball once fell out of bounds, landing on the deck of the boat, and Joe threw it back their way. They thanked him with cheers and smiles and curious clicks. One even pulled up to the boat and gave Joe a kiss on the cheek. His wet lips made Joe just a little giddy.

The mermen disappeared from view, to Joe's slight chagrin (for he was very much enjoying the wet muscle), and cloud-divers soon appeared on the horizon. Men and women from clouds that drifted at varying heights above one particular patch of sea. These were the only clouds in all the sky, and they were assembled in only this small area over the water. The divers hit the water in graceful glides that created hardly a splash. Then they would leap effortlessly back to the cloud to do it again. Their ascension back to the diving clouds looked very much like running in the air.

And so things went. The journey Joe was on was never boring. It never had a chance to be. The boat floated on past all sorts of other friendly beings on their own journeys, past thousands and thousands of interesting and unique tales for each traveling soul. The sea, it appeared, was big enough for everyone. One big sea as big as the world. Everything from rowers to massive humpbacked whales to triton-wielding sea gods had more than enough room to move. Dolphins and selkies kept Joe and the vessel company as he drifted.

Day was lapsing.

As Joe closed his eyes on day's fading light, his head resting on the pillow composed of his jacket and his hands, he had the euphoric sensation of sinking, being overtaken or pulled beneath. It did not frighten or worry him. He rather enjoyed the soothing experience. It lulled him, scattering his thoughts like wooden boats on the sea, each carried on a different small current. And there was another feeling as well, one of a strange inner companionship. It wasn't that he felt the presence of another soul on the boat with him, but rather, he felt as if his mind were separating and he was quite literally in the middle of a decision. Two very good points were fighting for right and might in his mind.

He opened his eyes. The sky was still like an everyday borealis, flashing like sound waves of azure and violet. The water splashed gently against the sides of the vessel. Water whispers and liquid chirps flirted and giggled in the night. Joe stood and strolled the wood deck, looking over the side into the deep, bottomless sea. And though darker skies held sway above, he could still see his own reflection in the blackness of the deep. In fact, it seemed to throw light up, the sea set aglow by light from below.

Joe paused and studied his reflection again, leaning over the side. How happy he seemed now. He had never been this content, as far as he knew. Before, there was always something missing, something to be had. A vagrant part of the soul had wandered those dreams that are eclipsed at morning's awakening. The dreams that are never remembered as eyes awaken to the trials of the everyday.

But as he looked into the water-mirror before him, something changed. It was subtle, like a flower opening slowly to the sun. Joe saw a flicker of form, as if the figure in the water had moved of its own accord and was not merely mimicking Joe's actions. He passed it off as a trick of light and water. But then it happened again, and this time more obviously free of Joe's own form. As Joe rose from his leaning position on the side of the ship, the water-mirror boy leaned out over the water-mirror ship. The reflection's face still gleamed, shadows defining an eerie expression of transfixed calm. The smile grew ever more, even as Joe's own faded into slight horror.

The water-mirror boy mouthed something, but Joe could not comprehend it. There was a moment of complete idleness, as if each were sizing the other up. Joe leaned over the side of the boat once more. Then, to Joe's great astonishment, the water-mirror boy reached out from the sea, both pale hands breaking upward through the glassy sea, and swiftly took hold of his shoulders. Joe cried in terror as he was pulled down into the depths with nary a struggle.

Deeper and deeper he plunged, surrounded by bubbles and the thickness of water and the pitch dark of the sea. Somewhere in the midst of the confusion of the agitated sea Joe realized he was no longer being held by his mirror self. Still, he could not surface. He continued to sink as if sandbags were tied to his ankles. He had not had the time to close his mouth before he was pulled into the sea. But of course, the fear of drowning was moot here. He soon stopped struggling to ascend.

He was awestruck by the sights around him as he glided to the bottom of the sea. Dolphins swam lyrical ballets above him; a whale swam in the distance surrounded by billions of tiny fish; rainbow fish, mola mola, and mermen drifted past seemingly unaware of his presence. A great ocean liner lay perfect and in one piece, nuzzled in the sand and coral. On the side, in bold letters, it read HMS *Otherwise.*

He landed among deck chairs and railings. His movements were slow, controlled by the great force of the sea, but he was not hampered by its strength. The water-mirror boy was at the far end of the deck, near a set of doors that led into the ship. As he opened them and walked in, a glowing warmth flooded the deck. Joe immediately followed the water-mirror boy inward. He found himself standing in a hallway of staterooms. Every door was wide open, and light shone from them. Peering into each room, Joe was amazed by what he saw. Every room revealed a whole other world than what was on the ship, one with which Joe was more familiar. Snippets of recognizable places moved and slid over one another, as if all time was indeed happening at once. An Eternal Second, as Baker had said.

As Joe passed by each stateroom, he saw how the many frames of his life had been edited into a kind of collage that could walk and talk through one another without the slightest harm of bleeding out. No moment was ever desecrated by another's echo. After all, it was from one life, just differing stages of that life's growth. Childhood memories collided with but did not harm memories from later in life. They simply passed into one another and passed out like air. At seeing his mother, Veronica, in a memory from his childhood, he tried to call to her, to reach for her, but she did not hear or notice him. Still, his heart broke at the sight of her, looking so real before him.

Joe followed his mirror self down the long hall and witnessed his own meetings and introductions to new things and people. He should have felt a sense of nostalgia, he was sure. Yet there was something not quite right about these memories. Joe felt it immediately. Something in the way his other self moved, a sureness, a sense of the carefree, that he himself had never possessed. This was not a true memory. Even those he knew and saw in the overlapping places and events were not themselves. Not truly. Joe saw his mother frivolously laughing with her mother; he saw Declan content and gleeful; and there wasn't even a hint of Louis. Also, there were individuals he had never laid eyes on. But his mirror self interacted with these people as if they were old friends or very important in his life.

They took no notice of him as he walked past them, these happy, pale, glassy-eyed non-recollections. And he began to be okay with that. They were picture-perfect, cookie-cutter replicas of what his life had been. But in their eyes, he saw soulless, vacant glances. Eyes of glass and black. They fumbled through one another, not a bad memory in the lot.

And then, as Joe waded into a room that contained the memory of a glade he had never seen where stood a girl he had never known, he realized what was happening. The shock of it anchored him to the spot. His mirror self approached the pretty girl, and they embraced and kissed passionately, like teenagers behind a school locker. The sight of it stunned Joe to the point that, if the strength of the sea had not held him, he would have fallen down. *In this underwater existence, he was straight.* This was his life's curiosity incarnate. He had often wondered how his life would have been different—easier—if he were a heterosexual man. And here was the explanation, if skewed and too perfect. It was as if another dimension of being existed here beneath the waves, and it was horrifying because it was a lie.

And while it seemed that surely life might have been easier, at least more acceptable to others, had he been straight, Joe found himself squirming in extreme discomfort. This was in no way normal. Not to him. Everything he was seeing in front of him went against Joe's own nature. As he glanced into his own eyes, he saw his straight self was devoid of what made Joe the man he was. The battle, the triumph, the personality sculpting and the strength gained through it, were all gone. His character had been stripped away, and what was left was nothing but an assembly line straight boy. This girl wasn't whom he was supposed to be kissing. No, someone else was supposed to be in her place. Someone *not* female. Louis was supposed to be there, but he was nowhere at all.

Angrily, Joe grabbed his mirror self's shoulder and pulled him from the girl. He would not have it! Not in this or any other dimension or shadow existence. And at last, he was noticed. Both his mirror self and the perfect girl glared at Joe with ferocious stares. He stepped back into the hallway. To Joe's horror, those from the sliding moments of life also stepped from their perspective staterooms and stared at him, peering out of doorways. He looked around him. The other end of the corridor was just ahead. He would only need to pass a few angry-looking non-memories to reach it. So he began to inch toward it. Soon, there were thousands of people crowding the length of the corridor, pouring forth from the staterooms. Hundreds of Joes of all ages stared back at him, and they all began to creep slowly toward him with their soulless glances fixed and fiery.

Joe swam mightily toward the door, kicking furiously through the sea as the multitude of the soulless came forth. He fought against the strength of the water as it pushed its way into the hallway from the outer sea. As Joe viewed the sea of multiples and unfamiliar faces before him, the idea hit him that hell was not some scorching hot place full of literal torment. No, if there was a true hell, it lay at the bottom of the sea and was populated by every regret one ever had.

Finally free of the strangling corridor, Joe was once again on the deck. He swam past cabins and doors until he was at the bow of the ship, unable to go any farther. The crowd of thousands kept coming until they were nearly on top of him, trapping him in a semi-circle. He tried to rise to the surface to no avail. He was grounded by the sea, and he couldn't scream. The child Joes were the worst. Joe didn't see himself in them. Their glares, their wicked smiles, were worse than every tormentor he and 3P had ever encountered on the playground. These children would rip you apart as easily as they would wings off a butterfly. They were moving the fastest. They would get to him first, before any of the others.

As the relentless, menacing crowd approached, hatred the first clear emotion in their eyes, a thunderous rumble shook the sea. Above the towering ship, Joe saw a massive shape take form from the ominous water. A sperm whale decimated the crowd, crushing them or causing them to disperse like loose kelp. And as Joe stood motionless, confused as to what he should do, the mouth of the sperm whale opened and scooped him up. Terrified in the dark, watery belly of the mammal, Joe had not even time to think when another great rumble occurred within the creature's guts. Joe was regurgitated and spat out once again on the deck of 3P's tiny ship. He landed with a thud and rolled 'til he lay on his back, and after a moment of unsuccessful struggling to comprehend what had just passed, he allowed himself to fall, to faint, into a slumber.

"...MAGIC CRAZY AS THIS..."

STARS appeared in random clusters overhead as the little boat wandered with its lone sleeping passenger over the great sea. Soon, the darker colors of night faded into those of morning. Joe opened his eyes to the call of seagulls. Land was near. Still dazed from his underwater encounter with sea mammals and memory, he rose to meet the new day. A lovely island approached steadily from the edge of the sea. It was hilly, with lush vegetation and trees growing on its mountainsides.

The boat ran aground in the sand, and Joe disembarked without much thought. He was glad to see land. He left his now ruined jacket aboard the vessel and, once on the beach, took off his shoes and stockings. The sand was cool and refreshing as he walked slowly across a wide beach, which wrapped lovingly around the island. Birds called above him, sailing through the warm breeze. Joe headed for the green, full hills. He could have spent more time on the beach, enjoying the breeze, but he was intent on finishing the journey now. Every adventure had to end. How else would other adventures begin?

He spotted a trail taking off inland from the sandy beach. It curved its way through the flora, leading in between estimable hills. It was a well-kept path and was no trouble for Joe to cover. He followed it faithfully as it led him in a more or less straight line toward the slopes and peaks of the hills and ridges. He walked with very little obstacle through occasional bushels of heavy forest that whistled with soft, tropic breezes. He heard the calls of brightly colored birds and playful chimps as they noticed him from their perches on the fronds of indulgent palm trees. He stared up, trying to place the calls to the trees from which they came. It was a satisfying game. So enamored was Joe by the forest and its residents that he did not see the woman waiting for him until he was nearly on top of her.

"This belongs to you?" she asked crisply and curtly.

Joe jumped back in alarm, tripping over a thick, knotty root but steadying himself so he did not fall.

"This is your place?" she asked again, impatiently.

She was not a beautiful woman; she was not an unattractive woman either. In fact, Joe could not at first discern exactly who or what he was seeing. The voice was most definitely feminine, but the figure itself fuzzed and blurred as would a radio or television program with weak reception. With each flicker or fuzz, a different feature would appear, replacing the former nose, mouth, arm, or even the entire face. Sometimes even a more masculine characteristic would fade in, then quickly disappear again. The light of the world had been shut out by the large trees of the forest so that the eerie glow of the woman lit up the surroundings in quick gasps and glares. The path had widened out into a clearing, and she now stood in the middle of it.

"Do *not* make me ask again," the woman demanded. "Or do I need to sign it to you?"

"No. I don't think so," Joe muttered. "I don't think this is my place." He was at once nonplussed and annoyed by Her Blurriness.

"You're a mutterer!" she exclaimed with sarcasm. "How wonderful."

"There's no need to be so damn rude," he shot back.

The chimps and birds continued with their hoots and calls of curiosity, but they were quieter now, absorbed in the interaction going on below them.

"So," she said. "You still have your disrespect, I see. I guess that wasn't your mother's doing after all. It seems it's just a soul flaw."

"Still?" he said, ignoring her jab at him. "*Still* have my disrespect?"

She moved away from him, walking haughtily around the clearing as if she were a prospective buyer who was none too impressed. Her flickerings blinded the forest. She was like a giant firefly in a closed black box.

"Who are you, then?" Joe asked. "You clearly know me. But I can't say that I want to know you, or ever would have."

"Who I am now has nothing to do with you, *dear heart*," she replied sarcastically. At times her flickering was so rapid and bright, it seemed there was no figure there at all, just an over-abundance of bloated light. "Who I am now is a young woman in Turkey, sleeping in her bed. Right now, this young woman is dreaming of being on an island with"—she stopped and studied Joe—"on an island with you. Someone she has never known in that life. She won't remember it, of course. *I* won't remember it upon waking. Our bodies rarely remember that our souls take flight in the night while we sleep. These are souls which have been around for ages and have connections to other souls from other times."

She paused a moment in her carousel inspection of him, studying him once again. Then she raced at him in a furious rush. "Why did you call me here?" she inquired desperately, as if being with him, looking at Joe, was painful and torturous. "What do I need to tell you? Your journey has nothing to do with me any longer. You needed nothing from me in life, why would you need me here? Your grandfather...." But then she silenced herself and turned away, her light popping as in a storm.

Joe had been nearly blinded by her sudden surge at him. "I didn't call you," he said. "Jesus! You're my grandmother, aren't you?"

She huffed in exasperation. "Just now you realize? It took you this long?"

"I don't know who called you, but be assured it was not me," he said, crossing the clearing to the other side where the path continued on, intent on getting away from her. "I want nothing whatsoever to do with you. But you're wrong about me never needing you in life. There was a time I desperately needed your support, but you didn't give it to me."

"It wasn't...," she began to say as if in sincere explanation. "You can't just leave me here!" she exclaimed. "I need to know why I'm here, what this is all about. If not, I'll be forced to repeat this dream every night. We'll keep encountering one another until it's figured out."

"Absolutely not!" Joe shouted, silencing the forest creatures. "I will not keep running into you."

"Well, then, get your butt over here and let's figure this out!" She fizzed and fuzzed tempestuously.

"Don't tell me what to do! Not now. You have no right to be telling anyone what to do. Not after causing so much pain in so many lives."

"Pain? What about *my*…? I did what I thought was best—"

"For whom?" he said, approaching her. "For you, certainly. But nobody else. You were a mean, selfish old woman. Grandpa Joe, me, and Mom—we all deserved better than you."

"How dare you speak to me like this!" she flared.

"Why? You're not my grandmother here. For all I know, I might be the older of our two souls. Oh, wouldn't that twist your twat if that turned out to be true!"

"You don't understand," she hissed through the static. "You don't know me. You don't know my story. You don't know the pain your grandfather caused me."

"I don't see how anything you could tell me would help me on my own journey."

"Now who's being selfish! Oh, you always twisted the world so!"

Joe stood motionless for a moment, taking in the serenity of the forest around him, letting it bring him to calmness. But all he could feel was Grandma's blaring white anger.

"Why did you hate Grandpa?" he wondered sedately. "Why did you bother Mom and me with your bitterness? It was poison."

Instead of the expected angry explosion, Grandma was silent. Her flickering image even seemed to become less frenzied and clearer. Through the glow he saw a young, dark-haired woman. Her eyes showed, for a quick instant, a hint of remorse. She raised her arms as if expecting an embrace. "Dance with me," she said.

Joe wasn't sure how to react. He couldn't remember so much as a brush on the shoulder from her in life. However, in lieu of some awkward retreat and show of rancor, he went to her in an even more awkward embrace. Her arms crackled and fizzled as he touched them. His grandmother drew him close to her own body, and they began to sway. They danced peaceably in silence for a while, Joe having almost been enveloped by the light emanating from his grandmother, the suffocating brilliance of her. He closed his eyes tightly as she waltzed, transformed and mutated in their fragile entanglement.

"I never hated your grandfather, Joseph," she finally spoke in a voice that was so far from her own that Joe jerked. "I loved him more than anything. I was so much in love with him that the realization that he never felt the same about me made me the bitter woman you knew."

"Because he was gay," Joe defended.

"Yes." Grandma hushed him with a tightening of her grip on his arms. "He was so like my own father, I suppose I was destined to love him."

"How do you mean?"

"My father, your great-grandfather, left my mother when I was a girl. He left her for the arms of another man. My world then was filled with men who found more comfort with one another than in the company of women."

Joe at once opened his eyes to his glinting grandma.

"It runs in the family," she quipped. "On both sides, I guess. I hated your grandfather with the remainder of the hate I still held toward my own father. But I loved him more. It was my one life's mission to make for certain that, though my father left us in search of his own happiness, my husband would not. In this way, I would keep him. I think I knew your grandfather preferred men even before I decided to fall in love with him. Maybe that was *why*. But did he have to be so blatant about it? Did he have to go pick up men and not even have the decency to lie about it?"

They had stopped dancing but held one another still. Joe was able to see past the light as if through a veil now. "So, in trying to claim victory over your father, you almost destroyed the rest of us."

"We all do what we think we have to," she said. "I make no apologies, Joseph. I never will. Not even in the life I live now."

"But surely you can see—"

She put her hand to his mouth. He had to fight the impulse to throw it off. "It was self-preservation," she explained. "It had nothing to do with anyone but me."

"Bullshit!" he shouted, tearing himself from her grasp. "It had everything to do with everyone around you. You certainly know now that every decision you make affects all of us. This place has taught us that. What you did, it was just you trying to assert your dominance." He turned his back and walked to the edge of the clearing, ready to head down the path again. "Dammit!" he hissed. "I'm finding that anger is just as palpable here as it was when I was alive."

"I think that's why you called me, Joe. That's why I'm here," Grandma said, still standing in the center of the clearing. She made no effort to close the distance between them.

Joe knew what she was saying. He turned to face her again. "I don't know if I can forgive you, Grandma," he said. "But I think I can try to understand. Maybe."

"That's a beginning," she said.

"Why could we never talk like this in life?" Joe wondered aloud.

"Because, I think, Joe, we were both the stubborn sort. And we were both too hurt. And neither of us was willing to let go of our hurt and resentment."

"I think maybe you're right, Grandma."

And then, the serenity of the forest overtook them as carefully as would soft, gentle arms. Joe and Grandma were pushed together by their own need for understanding. As Joe looked into the eyes of the beautiful dark-haired woman, she transformed into the familiar form of the grandmother he knew and recognized. And she did something she had never before done: she smiled and kissed him on the forehead.

"I was not a terrible person," she said quietly. "Just easily distracted."

And no sooner had she said this than she vanished altogether like the fading light of a TV set. Joe was left holding nothing but a seedling of forgiveness. Perhaps it was something he could foster until she reappeared somewhere else in the afterlife, until her soul took the dream's exit from who she was now and met him anew to heal.

THE rest of the trek through the vegetation was not long. Joe had expected it to be after the strange meeting in the forest with his grandmother. To be honest, though, to describe anything as strange in the afterlife seemed redundant and obvious. He had honestly expected another lengthy, meandering walk through things he had never seen, perhaps more lessons to be learned. Instead, the path led to a wide-open area hidden between the hills. At the center of it, surrounded by tall grass and bushes, stood the crumbling remnants of what looked like an old abbey. It was mostly rubble, blocks strewn about through falls and tumbles. But there still stood a few walls from the structure, vestiges of Gothic arched windows.

With interest and admiration, Joe walked into the ruins. He ran his fingertips along the few remaining ivy-subsumed walls. Even here there was history. Even in this timeless world there was passing. There was no sense to the thought, of course. It was contrary to what he knew of the afterlife. But here *were* battered stones of a forgotten abbey. And here too was proof of time's passage by the growth of vegetation. Clearly, a history had sprouted through the cracks of the Eternal Second.

As Joe wandered inward, a notion of absolute wholeness, of home, came to him again. It was a feeling he had known in the company of only one soul he had met thus far, and it came over him like the sun over a shadow.

Down the crumbled stretch of hallway was an ancient wall that stood taller than the others, reaching higher into the air. In its large, glassless arched window sat a figure with one leg resting upon the thick sill and the other dangling to the floor. Even from this distance, Joe knew who it was. A flood of glee overtook him. He quickly approached the window, feeling his excitement and desire to be near Louis the Stranger grow.

The Stranger didn't seem to notice him. He still stared out the window onto the tree-crowded hills beyond. He was still nude, just as he had been when Joe had seen him in the barley, and his black hair tumbled down his bronzed shoulders in waves. His face still held the air of fatigue, and there was a wisp of a coming frost in the air. Joe admired him from the foot of the small stairs that led up to the wall, scared and adoring. Then he proceeded to venture closer; what could stop him? He felt the need to weep in relief. Again, what could stop him?

Louis turned slowly toward Joe. Tears dripped down his beautiful face. "You've made it here at last," he said. "You've come."

"I'm here," Joe responded, breathlessness owed to the moment. "But where is here?"

Joe could hardly contain himself. He held his arms to his sides, all the excitement and joy, the barely controlled emotion, gathering in two tight fists with white knuckles. "What's our memory? We have plenty, I know. I've seen you in bits and flashes all through my life, but there's more, isn't there? Our memory. My time with you. I feel it's important. Am I right, Louis?"

"It's very important, Joe," Louis answered.

"Then hold me, Louis," Joe blabbered, unable to control himself any longer. "Please!"

"I've waited for those words," Louis choked out. He stood up at once and wrapped his arms around Joe tightly. "It's Lou... you never called me Louis. My mother was the only person who called me Louis."

"Lou," Joe whispered through muffled tears as he kissed his lost companion's naked shoulder. He felt completely warmed and secure in the embrace, as if it were the only place he would ever want to be. Just like that. Standing there, in those arms, forever, through every lifetime.

Lou reluctantly drew back, still holding Joe, and placed his soft lips on Joe's own. Existence reacted to their reunion. Immediately, it was as if two halves became whole once again. The sky flashed colors overhead as they stood together: day to night, night to day. They stood motionless and kissing for so long a period that they might have been mistaken for part of the landscape, as vines climbed up their legs and grass grew around them; as dirt gathered and buried even more the scattered fragments of the abbey. They did not know or care how many lifetimes passed in the worlds closed to them. Only the keepers of time knew that lifetimes did indeed pass, possibly entire eras. And yet it was but a scant moment to Joe and Lou. All of it but a simple, longed-for embrace neither time nor death could contain.

When, at last, their lips parted, Joe clasped Lou's face with all gentility. "So, this is it? This is my place? This is your place? We're together?"

Lou frowned ever so slightly. "No," he said. "This is my limbo. This was where I decided to stay and wait for you."

"Wait for me?"

"You're my dream, my heaven, my bliss—whatever saccharine tag you want to put to it. We promised each other once, and I'm keeping true to that promise. Joe, without you I'm just floating about without anything real. So I chose to stay in this place until you came. I waited here until we could have our place together. You're my Journey's end."

"An abbey was where you chose to wait?" Joe smiled warmly through tears. "Were you religious? Was I, in the end?"

"Certainly not." Lou laughed. "No. This is just one of the places in my memory. One of the places I knew in that life. We visited it together, you and I. It was our third big trip together. But this place isn't always here. It just happened to be here today, the day you finally arrived. You see, here on the island, I can change my surroundings. I can see whatever I want from my past lives. But it's all just waiting, really. You see an abbey at the moment, but I can just as readily think of a circus I went to when I was four and... *voilà!*"

As he said this, the remains of the abbey around them began to deconstruct, seemingly taken down very rapidly, stone by stone, with an invisible army of hands. The vines that grew up their legs and the tall grass around them shrank back into the earth, and in their place, building up from the very ground, grew a tent, three large rings, exuberant trapeze artists, elephants, and tigers.

Joe looked around in awe. "Amazing!" he exclaimed.

"Yes," Lou replied. "It got me through, I guess. It's a fun trick. But it's not you."

"Lou, why do I feel like this? I want to know everything. I want to know it all now."

Lou smiled as if he were waiting for that very question, which, of course, he was. The circus devolved around them just as quickly as it had grown. The tent folded up, the animals disappeared into nothingness, and the trapeze artists flew high into naked space and never came back down. Then, up from the ground rose a huge cinema screen. A picture show was to be the key to the unlocking.

The film began as Joe and Lou settled on the grass. Joe could barely take his eyes from Lou, but Lou nodded him gently in the direction of the screen.

4, 3, 2, 1….

JOE sat on a park bench in the afternoon light. A picturesque day. The ducks swam in the lake, old men and children feeding them scraps of bread. (The smallest children sometimes threw whole slices at the birds.) Joggers, dog walkers, and women with strollers passed by him. The sky was mostly clear but for a few maverick wisps of cloud that resembled streaks. And yet Joe could not have felt more empty, unhappy, and alone. There was no enjoyment. Everything was monotonous. Florence had not changed that fact. The contentment of those around him only served to irritate him. He sat staring ahead at the ripples in the lake as they spread out to touch the banks.

Then, like a wake-up call flying loose from a Hollywood romantic comedy, a Frisbee hit him in the side of the head. Hit him, just as it would have hit Reese Witherspoon or Meg Ryan! Or Doris Day. Yes, he could have been Doris Day at that moment in some story where she first runs into Rock Hudson. The blow from the plastic toy startled him so much he dropped the ham and cheese sandwich he had been nibbling on, and it fell apart on the ground. Joe was barely able to reorganize his thoughts when, bounding up after the Frisbee with great slobbering breaths, an elated golden retriever nearly toppled him from the bench.

"Spooner!" a voice called as the dog licked playfully at Joe's face. "Spooner, get off him!"

The owner pulled the dog from its straddle atop Joe. The handsome face of the dog owner beamed down at him, and Joe couldn't help but smile through his depression.

Louis! At last!

"Sorry about Spooner," the man said... Lou said. He was dressed in blue running shorts and little else. But it was the eyes that first cornered Joe. They were beautiful, beautiful dark blue eyes that would hold Joe captive the rest of his life. He knew in that moment that things were changing. Fate, or some such arcane nonsense, was taking a turn—a favorable turn—in his direction.

He offered a strong hand, and Joe accepted.

They talked all afternoon, Lou and Joe, and into the evening, walking about the park while Spooner ran ahead chasing birds or fell behind playing with the other dogs. They settled into one another with the ease of life-long kindred spirits. Possibly they were; maybe those little run-ins and by-chance meetings were not coincidences at all. Maybe they were supposed to know one another and just kept missing their cues. Joe had secretly suspected as much. That first true meeting with Lou brought on by Spooner, though, almost made up for everything. Joe finally understood the allure of walking in the city park.

Soon they were on their first date—a comedic film of harmless quality. Then their second—a DVD on Joe's couch of a slightly more dangerous and sexy breed. (He had frantically cleaned up the apartment for the date, finally unpacking in record time.) And after various movies and museums, day trips and weekend excursions, things evolved into a solid relationship. Enough time had elapsed that Joe cheerfully agreed, without any hesitation, when Lou recommended they get a place together.

They scouted around and eventually laid claim to a very nice condominium in a very artsy district of the city. Life was at last passable for Joe. Breathable. And he loved their life together. And Lou loved him. And they loved living with their rambunctious, slobbering dog. The words, the smells, the closeness of home. With every sigh, Joe breathed, "At last, at last," almost singing the phrase like that old Etta James tune.

Joe introduced Lou to his mother, and the three of them dined and shopped together. Veronica loved Lou. But then, why shouldn't she? The two people Joe loved most in all the world, after all, would naturally become very fond of one another by association alone. She longed for the day when they would adopt. When she would have grandchildren to look after. She told them this repeatedly. Spooner was fine, she explained, but she wanted to wipe up baby drool, not canine slobber.

And, as the film ended, as Joe watched tearfully from the grass, the last shot was told with a kiss as the camera swooped around in epic majesty and the score swelled. They were in love, wrapped in each other's arms, in their apartment by the bay window with a happy hound.

Happy endings. Happing endings for everyone.

LOU threw his arm around Joe, and they kissed again like lovers at a matinee.

"Finally," Joe whispered as Lou kissed his eyelids softly.

It was then, as night settled on the pass between the mountains, that Joe understood why Grandpa Joe couldn't stay. Joe understood why he had to find his companion, his friend who had gone on ahead. Because there was no peace without him. There was no wholeness of being. An existence without Lou, Joe saw now, would be empty and barren. Now that he had remembered Lou, it seemed absurd he could ever forget him. How was that even possible in the first place?

Joe was content to remain there forever on their own island, though he knew that there was something else. There was still something missing. Strangely, though, he couldn't quite see any pieces gone astray. Everything looked fine. What could be better? So he stowed that notion behind more pleasant thoughts. For now, Lou was all he needed, and he wondered if he ever even wanted to go on, to find an end to the Journey or to ever leave for a new existence. That tiny missing piece could just as well stay missing if only Joe could stay with Lou.

The island was a magical playground. Fantasies were especially exciting here. Lou would often play jungle native, wearing a slinky loincloth, to Joe's stranded hunter. It was a fun game, as Joe would find himself in peril from a giant spider or wild beast and Lou would swing half-naked out of the forest with a hero's yell just in time to save him.

"How will I ever repay you?" Joe would swoon.

"Ugh!" Lou would respond.

There were many variations on their fantasies. Lou would win the World Series for his team as Joe watched in the stands of Fenway Park and cheered wildly; Joe would draw a sword from the stone and Lou would name him king, sweeping him away in an epic embrace; Lou would rescue Joe from burning buildings and fly off, kissing him as they went and wrapping him in his red cape upon landing. "I'll be your kryptonite, baby," Joe would tease.

It was always something.

Joe could relive any event from his life with Lou as well, as many times as they desired. Lou, too, finally together with Joe once more, played in their past memories while all the time creating new ones. They relived their first reunion in the park, dates and dinners, walks in the rain, and jogs on Sunday afternoons. They revisited all their most intimate moments.

To simply be in each other's arms was all they needed some days. They would wish the sky overcast and the weather just a few degrees cooler. Then they would curl up in a blanket on the beach with hot cocoa and listen to the waves. And it reminded them of a vacation they had taken once to the seashore in Maine where they made promises under the night sky.

On the first of these beachside excursions, snuggled up closely, feeling heartbeat match heartbeat, Joe gently ran his thumb along the dark skin around Lou's eyes.

"Why do you look tired?" he asked. "You've looked tired and pale since I got here."

Lou looked at him with concern. "I don't know," he lied.

There was one memory in particular that the two revisited again and again. More, in fact, than any other....

THEIR wedding happened in Veronica's back garden. She had received gardening lessons from her friend Abigail, who had passed away years earlier, and now flowers bloomed lovely and bright. She was elated when Joe told her Lou had proposed. She set about designing every last detail as if it were the wedding of an oldest daughter. Even the sprinkles of rain did nothing to dampen her mood. "Rain on your wedding day is good luck," she reminded the boys.

It was a small affair, fifty guests and a gazebo. Even Lou's sour-faced mother Emmy made an appearance, though it was apparent she did not approve. She didn't care that Lou was marrying another man. She thought of herself as a very open-minded woman. No, she simply believed her son could have done better than Joe. It was evident to Joe by the way Veronica sighed whenever Emmy was around that she didn't care at all for Emmy's demeanor. But Veronica was always pleasant to her.

Lou snuck into Joe's dressing room before the nuptials to give him a quick kiss. "Are you ready to be my woman?" he joked as he held Joe close to him.

"Barefoot and pregnant," Joe assured him with a smile.

"I love you, Joe. More than anything."

"More than chocolate swirl ice cream?"

"Well," Lou kidded.

Veronica came into the room with Emmy in tow. "Get your cute bottom out of here!" Veronica said to Lou. "You can't see each other before the wedding. Bad luck, bad luck."

"Mom, we've got the rain to balance it out," Joe said.

"Hush," Veronica said, swatting Lou on the behind as he made his way past her with a giggle. Emmy watched, unamused. Veronica looked at Joe and gleamed. "My baby," she said, kissing his forehead gently.

The ceremony itself went off without a single misfire or stumbled word. The rain was the only aspect that might have been construed as bothersome, but Joe and Lou loved it. It cooled them off in their tuxedos, a blessing from heaven sprinkling down upon them. There were no dramatic objections from lost lovers resurfaced, nor were there any loud children asking, "Mommy, why's it two men?" No, everything was quite lovely. Even Spooner got his part right and came down the aisle with the rings attached to a bowtie collar around his neck.

As the vows were exchanged and tears shed (most happily from Veronica), confetti fell down with the rain from cannons fired onto the happy gathering.

IT WAS always then that Joe and Lou would stop the memory, as if pushing a button. They would kiss under the frozen confetti and raindrops in front of the cheerfully static crowd. It was, after all, one of those moments in life one wishes would remain forever. Here on the island, that wish could be fulfilled. For Joe and Lou it was a wedding photo album brought to life, and they could be as cinematic as they pleased. Sometimes they would even play around their statuary friends and family, games of tag and hide and seek. Truthfully, the only thing missing was the sound of Spooner barking with them as he played along.

Nights and days came and went until their passing was hardly noticed. But still, Joe knew it would have to come to an end even before Lou, one fateful day, brought it reluctantly and more clearly to his attention. There was a much cooler whip to the wind that day. Lou had inadvertently caused it with his grief. He looked even more fatigued than usual.

Lou stood before Joe on the beach as the waves lapped over the sand. "You've got to leave, Joe," he choked out. "Just this one last time we'll be apart. Finish the Journey, and then we're together forever. You know, happily ever after and all that." His eyes held sorrow and aching. He had been trying to say goodbye all morning, but Joe did not want to hear it.

"No," Joe pleaded. "Lou, I can't! I can't be without you. They were all right. Grandpa Joe, Baker, Guy. They all said when I got here I would understand and I would never want to leave you." He sniffed, and his throat closed up. "You can't make me leave you. You're what I've been trying to find. Do you see that? I won't last without you."

"Joe, don't you understand? When you finish the Journey, we'll be inseparable. Nothing can tear us apart again, ever."

"But we could just stay here," Joe appealed. "We could remain and—"

"No, Joe. That's not how it works. You've stayed here too long as it is. You've got to finish things. See things through. Then you'll truly understand."

The form of Lou seemed to languish, to take on a transparent quality. Nothing had frightened Joe more since he had arrived in the afterlife.

"Great courage. Great courage, Joe...," Lou whispered as his phantom image faded from the beach.

Slowly, starting from the horizon's edge and then drawing near, the beach, too, faded away. The entire island began to bleed out of being. It darkened as if an eclipse had occurred or something had blanketed the sky. All turned to extreme shadow, then pitch-black. A coldness grew about Joe as he stood now in the void. A frost. The warmth and love Lou had offered him had been stolen away and was now replaced by fear and dread. Joe shook from the cold and the dark.

Lonesome, so lonesome.

There was nothing here. Everything had vanished. All life was dead.

WAITIN' ROUND TO DIE

JOE felt the uncomfortable twitching trembles of fear, though he wasn't sure he even possessed a physical form any longer. He couldn't see it when he looked down in search of his feet. All he could see was darkness. His senses had become mingled, and sight could just as well have been defined as touch. He had become part of the void that had encroached upon his consciousness. He couldn't physically feel himself any longer. All Joe was certain of was that there was nothing, and he was shivering in it in some form or another. Aside from his shivers echoing in the blackness, there was little else to hear.

Joe cursed the silent dark (at least he still had a voice to use for cursing) and called for Lou, pleading for his return, but he heard no response. He began to shout and swear in his anger and fear, afraid that, perhaps, he would remain there forever. He feared being locked in nothingness and supplied with the lingering taste of past bliss to feed his indignation.

Yet just as he was about to cave in to despair, another sound rose slowly all around him. It was a chorus, quiet at first and then growing. *Whale song.* That was what it reminded him of. The whale recordings he remembered from his past life. He had heard them on nature documentaries and listened to them on new age music discs to try to get to sleep on nights when his insomnia controlled him. Echoes from the deep. He had thought them beautiful once, but now they were only mournful ghosts.

Then, out of the suffocating dark, Joe saw a form appear. Like a Rothko painting, it separated the void into swaths of somber shades. A pinprick of light directly in front of him, in the middle of the Rothko horizon, began to grow, washing over stiff chairs and tables covered with magazines. Joe now stood alone in a dimly lit waiting room with ordinary white furniture. Music played low overhead. "Don't Stop Believing," Steve Perry sang. The afterlife's waiting room played the music of the 1980s.

Relieved he was out of the darkness, Joe peered out into the empty hallway. He called once or twice, but no one responded. At the end of the hallway, a light flickered through the glass of a door, and Joe felt the need to investigate. As he approached the room, the light grew stronger. He could make out flashes of form. He pushed open the door slowly, and the room was exposed to him. Illumination accrued until a young man was revealed.

"Lou!" Joe cried with happiness.

But he didn't hear Joe, for he was some other place, in some past remembrance. Lou existed there like a stage actor removed from his audience. He was dressed in pajama bottoms, his hair mussed from a night's sleep. His eyes were tired and his face drawn. But that was not new. He had looked very similar to this here in the afterlife. But he seemed ill now. Something was wrong.

"Lou?" Joe questioned, now with growing concern.

The light continued to grow until Joe could see Lou was leaning against a table shivering. Joe recognized it as the kitchen table at their condominium. Lou took some small pills that lay on the table and swallowed them, washing them down with a drink of water. He grimaced as the pills made their way down his throat.

Suddenly, Joe remembered without being shown what happened next.

"*Lou!*" he cried, his voice strangling the words.

Lou seemed to struggle to stand for a moment. Then his legs gave out completely and he fell to the floor, sprawled out in a motionless heap. Spooner ran to him, licking Lou's face and whining in worry, his tail sopping up the spilled water on the floor. Joe hadn't got up yet. When he did come into the kitchen that morning, tugged awake by Spooner, his world began its long, painful collapse.

As the light around the memory grew ever more present, Joe could now see he still did, in fact, possess a body. He was naked once again and now stood in a hospital. He knew the scene well. It seemed he was almost able to keep up with this particular memory. To know it before each moment was exposed to him. Every scene appeared before him like a virulent anamnesis.

He approached the bed where Lou lay. Beside the bed, his other self—the Joe of then—held onto Lou's hand, stroking it tenderly, continuously. Lou was awake and looked at Joe with love and fatigue. Lou had been ill for a week now. They had thought it was a simple cold or flu, that was all. But they knew better now. They had caught the cancer too late. In truth, Lou had been feeling ill for some time now, only he didn't want to worry Joe.

The treatments had worn him out. It had not gone well at all. The doctors had already informed Lou's family and Joe that there was nothing more they could do. Even a painless decline was too much to hope for. But Joe said nothing of this to Lou, and Emmy could barely speak at all. Veronica kept Lou's mother company as best she could. Emmy did not cry. Instead, she only asked why.

Joe simply sat by the bed and held Lou's hand, occasionally rubbing Lou's shaved head playfully. Joe would not shave, though, nor bathe. He barely remembered to eat. The only time he did was when he rushed home to feed Spooner. He ate out of habit, thoughtless mouthfuls of cereal and segments of oranges swallowed almost whole.

"Tell me again," Lou said, his voice scarcely audible. "Tell me about our house. The one we're going to buy when I get better." He coughed, wheezing for air until Joe helped him readjust the oxygen mask.

Joe smiled and leaned in closer to Lou. "Well, when you get all better," Joe said, swallowing a gasp of sorrow creeping up into his throat, "we're gonna buy a house in New England. Somewhere along the coast of Maine or Massachusetts, like where we went for vacation that time. Remember? It'll be an old lighthouse we'll fix up and turn into a bed and breakfast. We're going to be *that* gay stereotype, at least. Every morning we'll walk along the beach with Spooner, drinking coffee and wearing thick wool sweaters. When we tire of walking"—Joe struggled through bullying tear ducts—"we'll curl up with a big, heavy quilt and listen to our own breathing and the sound of the waves on the beach. On the weekends, we'll have these marvelous parties on the beach and invite all our friends. There will be singing and dancing and… food. Lots of great food. You know: lobster, corn on the cob smothered in butter, Cincinnati chili…."

"We should get another dog," Lou said. Every word took energy. "For Spooner. So he'll have a doggie playmate. They can do some ruff-ruff housing." He grinned groggily at his own joke.

"Sounds like a plan." Joe massaged Lou's head gently.

"Can we have horses? I've always wanted horses." His voice was stretched thin through the mask, making it very hard for Joe to hear.

"Of course we'll have horses. Two of them, and we'll ride out onto the beach with them sometimes. Won't that be nice?" He couldn't stop the tears. They were set to come no matter what. But Lou didn't see. His lids had grown heavy, and he trailed off for a while into his own dreams.

Joe stayed there holding Lou's hand for a long while until Lou opened his eyes once more with a look of realization.

"I'm fading, Joe," Lou whispered. Joe bit his lip and squeezed his friend's hand. "They want to put me on machines, Joe, to keep me alive." There was a struggle in his voice to keep speaking. "I heard Mom talking about it. I never made out a living will."

"Yeah," Joe sniffed. He didn't want to discuss this, but there was no use avoiding it. "Your mom is adamant about it. Didn't think she would ask your opinion on the subject."

"Don't let them do it, baby," Lou pleaded. "When I go, I want to go for good. I don't want to be kept here by machines. There are other places to see, and I don't want to be kept behind."

"But I tried talking to your mom," Joe explained. "She won't hear it. You know she doesn't like me anyway. Never has."

"Joe." Lou looked at him with eyes that held a certain fear. "Please. Don't let me be kept around here like that. Promise me. Don't let me be kept in a vege—" He took a breath. "Vegetative limbo."

Joe was breaking on the inside. He felt the jagged edges of his own pain tearing up his throat. "Oh, Lou. Don't leave," he cried.

"Joe. Promise me, Joe," Lou said through his own tears. He started to hack again.

"I—I promise," Joe answered, trying to settle him down. "Whatever you need. Whatever you want."

Lou relaxed and held as tight as he could to Joe's hand. "We'll be together again," he whispered knowingly. "You know why? Because some things just don't function that well without all their parts. That's my promise to you, Joe."

IT WAS later. Joe was in the same hospital room, still holding Lou's hand, but something was different. Something terrible. Despite Joe's best efforts, Lou's family had won out and Lou was hooked up to the cold life machines. Machines that beeped and droned without feeling or care, indifferently clutching to what needed to be let go.

Joe was scraggly, beaten, and unkempt as he held tight to Lou's hand. Snow was falling outside, hints of the beginnings of winter.

"I'm sorry, I'm sorry," Joe repeated over and over as he cried. This was the first time he had been let in to see Lou since he had been hooked up to the machines. "There was nothing I could do," Joe whimpered, asking for forgiveness, doing penance.

The thought of Lou's plea pealed through his mind. Here lay Joe's own life-loving mate, motionless, unable to object to his current state. Locked in his own body, a prisoner. *This is not right.* Joe knew he had to do something. He knew that even before Emmy had finally agreed to let him see Lou again. Lou would have wanted something done. And it was with those thoughts Joe had prepared himself that morning, that first day he was allowed in to see Lou.

Joe touched his love's face once more, softly sliding his fingers along the strong jaw line. He bent over Lou, kissing both closed eyes, *those beautiful eyes*, and his lips that were covered with tape and vulgar apparatuses. Lips he would never feel brush against his own ever again. That thought alone made him wince as if he had been knifed in the gut.

"I'm keeping my promise," Joe whispered.

He took the syringe from his coat pocket and emptied its contents into Lou. He did it quickly, allowing no time for thinking. If there were any thoughts at all, he might back out, and Lou would remain hooked up to machines, wasting away for the rest of his forced life.

Carefully and quietly, so as not to attract any attention from the nurses outside the room, Joe turned off the machines one by one and unplugged the monitor. With slow, loving movements, he removed the wires and devices from the body of his great friend so his soul could ascend unfettered to wherever it was he was bound. He leaned in to Lou's lifeless form and kissed him one final time on the crown of the head.

As he walked out of the room and down the hall past frenzied nurses who were just then rushing to Lou's bedside, he felt the surge well up in him. The great pinching rush of pain. He exited the hospital into the newly wintered air and made it as far as his own car when he gasped. Joe fell onto the side of the vehicle, reaching for any support he could find, however meager. The flakes fell down around him from the lonely gray sky. As he knelt by the car, his lungs couldn't seem to bring in enough oxygen. They were collapsing from his own grief. He gritted his teeth to bear what he could, aware that soon the hospital staff would realize what had happened and who was responsible.

He heaved until, at last, the strength came back to his legs and he was able to drive away.

HE WAS in the apartment now, and he watched himself—the Joe of then—sitting and waiting. The apartment was already too big and quiet. He was in a state of indecision at the kitchen table. The authorities would be coming for him, of course. They would call it murder and say what he had done was wrong. Joe knew otherwise. He could wait for their judgment or he could die. He could take his own life and be with Lou again. That was what he wanted most, after all. Life without him was a ridiculous idea. If only love were enough to defeat everything that sought to rend it.

Spooner laid his head on Joe's lap and looked up at him with sad, understanding eyes. Veronica would take care of Spooner. Joe knew that. And thus, his decision was made. It was his only option in the end. He gave the dog a ruffle of the ears and a big hug. He would have said, "I love you," but he couldn't get the words out.

In the bathroom, Joe searched for the razors he had purchased for Lou at a Dollar Tree before Lou had collapsed. The package was still unopened. Spooner barked in the front room, most likely having spotted a squirrel or rabbit out the window.

"Spooner will be fine," he assured himself, and he sat down on the toilet seat, studying the blades in his trembling hands. They would cut deep, and he would simply float away out of this life.

But before he could run a blade into his flesh, he was distracted. From the corner of his eye, he saw movement at the bathroom door. Something too big and too quiet to be Spooner.

"Emmy!" Joe said, rising from the toilet as he caught sight of Lou's mother staring at him from the doorway.

He dropped the blade to the floor and came closer to her in awkward staggers, trying to find the words to explain.

The things love makes one do! The things one does for love.

The look on her face told him she knew what he had done. He looked down at her hands as he heard a click. The gun she held fired and tore a hole through his chest. His world dimmed, then faded altogether.

Echoes. Various echoes....

JOE was once again in the dark, desperate void. The whale song spread out around him as he sobbed, at last remembering it all. Remembering his entire other existence. And he began to howl and push forth from his inner self every ounce of loss and grief, of guilt and longing, of despair. It filled the universe to the brim. When the whale song quieted once again, all that could be heard were his own echoing howls that told of a life not quite full.

Then they, too, ceased, and Joe felt himself collapse to whatever ground lay beneath him in the blackness. And he wept, depleted of the energy to do anything else. He was too tired to continue with one more step or speak another word. He was surrounded by the dark and his own sobbing reverberations, and he decided he would not move. He could no longer go on, especially now, without Lou. How could he ever forgive himself?

He closed his eyes and lay like he had in the mists after he had lost Baker. The darkness entombed him, and he was thankful for it. This was no more than he deserved.

"WHAT'S it doing?"

Joe heard voices in mid-conversation, his eyes still shut, but the despair taking on a lesser weight.

"I think it's sleeping."

"Why does it sleep here?" the first voice responded. "Let's wake it."

A hand touched Joe's shoulder and shook him gently. Joe reluctantly opened his eyes, and there was light again. The blackness had retreated. A beautiful morning light now shone. Joe felt soft sand beneath his cheek and saw, as the world formed around him, that he lay on a beach, but not the same beach where he had last stood with Lou on the island. Waves crashed into the shore a few yards off. The colors in the horizon of the sky were those of a blessed new day. Glorious things to come. The sky was all vibrant pink and warm orange streaks. He could hear the call of seagulls overhead. The air was crisp and nourishing, like water. Even upon opening his eyes he felt replenished.

Joe rose to his feet with help from a pair of strong, capable hands. He was surprised by his sudden acquisition of attire. He was dressed very nicely now, apart from his bare feet, wearing khaki pants rolled up at the bottom and a thick gray turtleneck sweater. He brushed the sand from the clothes as the faintest sense of felicity began to sink into him. The darkness that had found its way into his soul was emptying from him like draining water.

"Are you okay?" he was asked. Two men stood in front of him, both beautiful. One was of alabaster skin, the other was darker-skinned. They wore nothing but small, tight, white shorts and to Joe's delight, they had wings, white and fluffy and pure as snow.

"I'm fine, thanks," Joe responded to their curious, innocent glances. He sniffed back the last of his sadness.

"We're on our way to a party," the first winged man said. "A White Party. Would you like to come?"

Just then, Joe caught sight of a third figure, a very familiar figure, standing apart, waiting. Joe grinned. "No, thank you," he said. "I have some things to do around here."

"Okay then," the second winged man said. "But if you change your mind, just follow the beach."

As the two took their leave, Joe stopped them momentarily. "Wait!" he called. They regarded him with beatific smiles and clear eyes. "You're angels, aren't you?"

"Of course we are," the first angel said. "Gay angels are all the rage in heaven."

Joe laughed as the two angels walked off.

"You all right there, bud?" the third figure said in his lazy drawl, still unmoving from his spot.

Joe approached the folkie, running through the sand toward him. "Baker!" he cried as he flung his arms around the hippie, almost knocking him over.

Baker laughed. "Guess I was wrong," he said. "There are angels after all."

Joe laughed again. Things were coming about. Breath was coming back to him. Disassembled moments were taking form again.

"...BRIGHTEN MY NORTHERN SKY..."

"GOOD to see you too," Baker said, patting Joe's back in their embrace. "Lost you back there, didn't I? That storm was a big'n. Gabriel Ratchet causin' a ruckus. I was worried, but you made it here fine without my help."

Joe released him. "It would have been so much better with your help, though. I was so lost, Baker. There were so many times I wanted to give up."

"Naw," Baker smiled. "You done just fine. Now you're here."

"No more journey? No more surprise memories?"

"Not until your next life," Baker said. "Not unless you wanna go adventurin' in this one. There are surprises in every life if you're open to 'em. Good ones and bad."

"Then this is for me? This is my place?" Joe asked, looking out onto the dawn over the sea. It was quiet. Like some new world at the infancy of its creation, not much seemed awake just yet. Only the birds and the water. A few crabs crawled along the beach. The sky still had an air of mystery to it, as if it were waking from the darkest of storms.

"Of course it is," he answered his own query. It felt right.

"Part of it," Baker replied. "There's more. Much more."

They stood admiring the tides for a while, unfettered by time. As Joe watched, new details caught his eyes and ears. They were small things—a smooth polished rock, a strand of seaweed awash on the beach, the sound of the tide.

"C'mon," Baker finally urged as he led the way up the beach, his guitar still resting faithfully on his back. "Lemme show you the rest of your place."

The sand was cool, thick, and soft. Joe glided through it. The sky was getting ever lighter as they walked on, a queer lessening of severity.

"It was so lonely there," Joe said. "There in that dark place. I thought I could just not exist. I wanted to fade away with the grief."

"We all go through it," Baker assured him. "Some do better than others at the end. Yer last memories were particularly hard. That's why it was difficult for you. The more difficult the memory to face, the more you learn. Might mean the less you need to go back, and the closer you are to the Ultimate."

"Will I see Lou again?" Joe's heart ached just thinking of him.

"Didn't he tell you you would?"

"Yes," Joe replied.

"Well, then, smarty, what d'ya think?" Baker glanced at him and grinned. "You'll see all the people you loved if you stay long enough. From every life. Even those you knew just a little. But those beings who were really important, the ones who are part of you, those you'll see sooner and more often because they ain't whole without you either. It's the connections we make that make us who we are."

"Does that mean you?" Joe asked, knowing the answer. "When were you going to tell me, Baker? When were you going to let me know, Dad?"

Baker stopped and smiled. He chewed on a toothpick between his teeth. "When did you know? When'd you figure it out?" he asked.

"When you told me how you died. Mom told me you were a singer. She never said quite how you died, only that you were away and she had just gotten pregnant with me. I just put it together on the mountain that night."

The winds from the sea ruffled Joe's hair.

"And I remember, too, seeing a picture of you when I was little.

Just one, because Mom hurt too much from losing you to have your face spread throughout the house. I barely can recall it, that photo."

Baker flung an arm around Joe. "I was waitin' for the right moment to tell you," he said as they continued walking. "I shoulda guessed you'd get it figured out. You're smart like your momma."

"Thanks," Joe said. "I'm glad we finally got to meet, Dad." The awkwardness of the word, and the notion, could not be excused. It would take some getting used to, even here.

"Me too, kid. You turned out real good. You turned out a fine fella. Wish I'd a been at your weddin'."

Joe breathed deeply, inhaling the words his father had just spoken. That simple sentence made up for all the absent years and missed birthdays.

Though the beach continued to stretch on around a bend where the tracks of the angels led, up ahead was a wooden stair that zigzagged up a grassy hill. The morning breeze played with the blades. Atop the hill stood a lighthouse, tall and white, with a black keeper's lookout. At the base was a cozy two-story cottage. It overlooked the cliff of the hill, peering into the serene waters. Joe breathed a sigh of satisfaction as he and Baker waded through the cool sand.

As they climbed the creaky wooden stairs, Joe caught sight of a figure with strong waiting shoulders and a tapered waist at the top of the hill.

Lou!

Lou stood smiling brightly, his hair being tossed by the wind as. He was no longer without clothes. Now he wore a white turtleneck sweater and, like Joe, khakis. Joe's heart leapt at the sight.

"Run to him!" Baker urged his son, giving him a slight push on the back.

Joe took the advice. Up the stairs he raced until he nearly tackled his love with his embrace. As they kissed and hugged, they made promises they knew now they could keep. These promises could only become more valuable the longer they remained in this ageless, graceful place.

"I'm so sorry for what I did, Lou," Joe whimpered. "Can you forgive me?"

"Nothing for me to forgive, babe," Lou responded. He no longer looked tired or sick. That had all been washed away. "You set me free. You rescued me from the mists."

"You're not going to leave me again, right?" Joe asked, looking into Lou's misty eyes. They held to one another tight, still fearful that one or the other could be whisked away.

"Never again," Lou promised.

Baker mounted the top of the hill just in time to see an exuberant golden retriever joining Joe and Lou's reunion.

"Spooner?" Joe exclaimed in surprise. The dog jumped onto them with ebullience.

"Yeah," Lou said, still unable to control his smile. "He got here when you did. Apparently he got out and was hit by a car just around the same time you left the world. I just saw him moments ago, right before I spotted you on the beach. But I know you've seen him here before. He had other things to do before he could join us."

"And he got here before me?" Joe said as he and Lou rubbed and massaged the elated animal.

"Time ain't the same here," Baker said. "It takes some longer than others to arrive. Sometimes it all depends on what happened to them, how they died and what was left unresolved. Plus, you two did spend a while on that island doin' who knows what. And, Joe, Spooner *is* a dog. Not many worries in that shaggy ol' head."

"Well, we're here now. Our family's all here," Lou said, kissing Joe on the forehead.

"Yes, we are," Joe agreed, hugging Spooner and leaning into Lou. He looked over his shoulder at Baker and winked.

JOE'S days were filled with family from then on out. They were family in the broadest and most complete sense of the word. There was no sadness. They had no worries. Only the constant fellowship and love of the ones he cared for most existed in this place.

He took walks along the endless stretch of beach with Lou and Spooner (who had found another dog friend to play with); had romantic midnight picnics on the sand, followed by carefree naked swims in the water; and took to horseback riding along the beach on the backs of Joe's new friends, Phil and Buck. (Phil was always the least cooperative, so Joe would ride him.)

Sometimes they would invite all their friends to beach parties that would last all day and into the night. They could last all week if they so desired.

Baker would play guitar by the fire along with his heroes Nick Drake and Townes van Zandt. Others would join in a sing-along.

3P would arrive with Maddy Mojingle, his "greatest foe," and they would play pirate on the sand with Spooner and his doggie friend. When Claire the Bear happened by and caught sight of the two youngsters, she, along with her various animal friends, would join in the fun.

Guy would wear clothes (but just for these occasions) especially designed to fit his extra-large frame, and he and Giuseppe would stay by the fire, listening to the musicians and creating a spark of their own.

Even Melva would come, commenting on the various outfits that adorned the guests and *very* eager to design some specific threads for Guy. "That's a lot of man to clothe," she said, clearly up to the challenge.

Lou's friends came as well, those important to his life and journey. He, too, was surrounded by all those who had seen him through lifetimes of existing, or at least the lives he could remember thus far.

But for their part, Joe and Lou would simply sit back and enjoy the company, relishing the comfort and love around them. They knew everything had been worth it, the good *and* the bad. They thrived on the knowledge that all their journeys had a reason. And they realized forgiveness was the greatest gift they could give themselves or anyone around them.

On one such night of seaside camaraderie, Declan—he of the eternal beauty and the auburn hair—came walking down the wood stairs to the beach. He strode slowly, taking in the frivolity that played out before him. Along with him came a youthful and radiant woman with her hair pulled up under a large, floppy hat. She wore comfortable jeans and a plaid button-up shirt. Declan escorted her, their arms entwined. Joe ran to the stairs and hugged Declan, holding him tight. Nick Drake crooned by the fireside.

"You remember my mother?" Declan gestured to the woman. He was smiling, content at last.

Joe's eyes flew open wide. It *was* Abigail! She had become more youthful, aged backward. But there was no doubt it was Abby. Joe smiled warmly.

"Nice to see you again, Abby," Joe said, taking her hand. Lou sauntered up beside him.

"You as well, Joseph," she said graciously. "And thank you."

"For what?" Joe asked.

"For convincing this one"—she nudged Declan playfully—"to come see me. It's made all the difference to my gardens."

"You're very welcome," Joe said. "This is Lou." He curled his arm into Lou's.

Declan shook his hand genially. "Hi, Lou," he greeted.

"Wonderful to meet you," Abby said. "Veronica will be happy to see you two together again." She winked, turning her attention back to Joe.

"My mother?" Joe asked, startled by the statement.

Spooner began to bark excitedly, his tail wagging, as he raced up the steps past the foursome. He jumped onto a woman who ruffled his fur with delicate hands and laughed with fragile syllables. She looked at Joe with an expression of triumphant reunion in her eyes. Warm ripples cascaded through Joe at the sight of her.

"We came across her on our way," Declan said as he and his mother stepped aside. "She just arrived herself. Spooner here was part of her journey. He raced ahead, though. I guess he was impatient to see you."

"Mom!" Joe cried. He ran up the remaining steps and embraced her. Lou watched from below with a smile.

"Oh, my boy!" Veronica said. "You look so good! Oh, honey, you look so lovely." She took his face in her palms and kissed it a million times.

Baker, his attention drawn by the clamor caused by Spooner, rose from his seat around the fire. He slipped past Lou, Declan, and Abby at the foot of the steps and, half bewildered, climbed the stairs.

"Veronica," he whispered out through choking sobs as he stood finally at the top. He held the guitar by its neck. His hands were shaking.

Joe let go of his mother, wiping his eyes, and she set her gaze upon Baker. The guitar slipped to the ground as Baker rushed to her, swooping her up in his arms, twirling her about as they smothered one another in kisses and tears and laughter.

Joe glanced back at Lou, and he knew this was it. The warm ripples coursing through him told him so. There was nothing any better. Nothing could even pretend to be.

FOR Joe and Lou and those souls they knew, adventures in the new wide-open world came as epic or as lazy as they wished. There were great romantic sunsets or quiet walks in the rain. Days would pass in groups and bushels like entire eras where Joe and Lou would see nothing of their friends. On other days, however, quite on a whim or as if by happenstance, a friend would be seen crossing the beach below and would be greeted with much joy and jubilation.

They ventured away from the lighthouse as well. There came many occasions when Joe and Lou would take to traveling with Spooner across the universe, across the never-ending map of consciousness. Joe took Lou to Florence and drank wine with Giuseppe by the Arno, then danced in the piazzas until the sun shone in the morning sky. They hiked every mountain they could find or came across, hitting the heights of Everest without loss of breath. Joe took Lou to Grandpa Joe's villa, now disappearing into the mountain. It had no reason to exist now that Grandpa Joe no longer needed it. They trekked across rolling hills of Kentucky bluegrass and sailed passively on the blue waters of the Caribbean. They attended a ball at the Emerald City and camped for a night with Artemis the Huntress.

When they ached for home, they would head back. Spooner always led the way back to the beach. On their return, the lighthouse would shine like a symbol of truth, hope, and love. The sea lay before it like a peaceful mistress.

Baker and Veronica spent much of their time hidden away behind the foliage of Baker's tree house. They would lie all day and night, naked and wrapped in sheets, letting the sunlight sprinkle in from the canopy and feeding each other fruit. Baker would play for her as she sang for him. Their lovely ballads could be heard throughout the land, calming the beasts that would gather outside the tree to listen to the beautiful lullabies. When a few nights had passed, Joe came to join them with Lou and Spooner, and they drank, played, and danced.

"This *is* heaven, Joe," Veronica said once. "Don't you let your father tell you any different. This is *my* heaven."

Joe and Baker also set out, the two of them quite content to be alone together as father and son, and found passage by way of a phoenix to the City of Thought. Baker, still wary of the city's inhabitants, fashioned a helmet made of a borrowed turtle shell. He soon lost it, however, as they flew over the formation of a new range of mountains. It really didn't matter, though. The people of the city didn't seem to care much for his thoughts. In fact, they flinched when his words floated near him, as if his thoughts needed to be washed. Joe only laughed at this. But it was a gorgeous city, esoteric and full of secrets.

After the passing of thousands of days and nights, Declan and Abby visited Joe at the lighthouse one evening. Autumn was in the air. Declan, it seemed, was to be the first to return to Earth. He had been there so little time previously that he wanted another go at it. He felt the pull. Abby held on to his wrist lightly as he told Joe of his decision. A going away party was immediately decided upon, and everyone Declan knew was invited.

The soiree was held at the cottage in Abigail's gardens. Leaves were falling, and the trees were clothed in their new coats. It was a wonderful affair, crowded with those Declan had known and loved. There were cheers and wishes of good travel all around. Declan embraced them all individually as they said good evening once the party ended. He held to Joe especially tight.

"I'll see you there, brother," Joe whispered.

"I hope we have better luck," Declan smiled.

Joe was not there to see Declan fade from this existence, but Abby said it was just an ordinary moment in another day.

"There we were in the garden, the back one by the pond where the child cherub stands, working on planting the fall tulips, and he just stood and looked to the water. I knew it was time. There wasn't a word," she said, her voice gentle with ripples of warm remembrance. "He looked to me and said goodbye... silently, with his eyes. He walked to the pond slowly, past the tree and the cherub, and went into the water. He just kept walking until he was totally submerged and then no longer in the world at all."

Soon after, Abby too disappeared. Though she had told no one she planned a return to Earth (there was no party), they all knew that was where she had gone. She had a reunion with her son to get right, even if this time she was his sister or brother or best friend or friendly neighborhood mailman. The gardens and the cottage disappeared eventually, becoming part of the forest again. They had returned once more to the whole to be recycled by some other consciousness.

Joe knew the itch to return was making its way into others around him as well. He saw the look in 3P's big eyes at Declan's going away party. There was a longing there, but it was a new itch that was just beginning. Joe still had more time to play captains and superheroes with his young friend. He had at least until 3P's brother and sister arrived and the little one was able to see them. They would keep him around for a bit longer as he guided them through the afterlife.

Yet even with all the leaving, there was still so much to welcome. So many fresh events happened every time one turned around. New souls were arriving from past lives. There was always someone else who needed welcoming. Joe loved how every day was a sort of rebirth.

THE night fell over the ocean. Bright colors were, for once, replaced by the single shade of dark blue sky dotted with a billion stars. A winter season was wished for and had come in response. The air was perfumed with salt and beach-scent. Snowflakes descended lightly. On the beach below, the gathering was uninterrupted, the reunion of souls that took place continuously.

Baker played the guitar, looking lovingly at Veronica as she sang along and everyone else danced and played about.

But Joe and Lou stood on the bluff, beneath the lighthouse, holding on to one another. They looked out over the skyline, the waters and the sky melding into one. Everything was one. They hugged one another, admiring that which had finally been given to them. Each appreciated the merits of their own spiritual journeys. Their lips met softly under the night sky. Flakes caught in their eyelashes. Joe had never felt such contentment, such ease, purpose, and sense of place. It tickled him so, and Lou as well. And they began to laugh, letting each syllable of laughter fly with diaphanous wings into the evening, giving joy its due.

This was life; this was death. And miracles happened here. They were everyday and obvious. And things Joe and Lou were told could never be real did occur. In this place, in this glorious existence, there *were*, in fact, talking bears and men with wings and boys who could tame waterfalls and chances to right wrongs and pick up from where goodbyes left off. In this place, there were reunions every day—*every single day.* In this life they could love whom they wanted and live how they pleased. There were no rules. No restrictions. Just the will to be and the knowledge that there was no other way....

ERIC ARVIN resides in the same sleepy Indiana river town where he grew up. He graduated from Hanover College with a bachelor's degree in history and has lived, for brief periods, in Italy and Australia. He's survived brain surgery and his own loud-mouthed personal demons.

Visit his blog at http://daventryblue.blogspot.com/.

Also by ERIC ARVIN

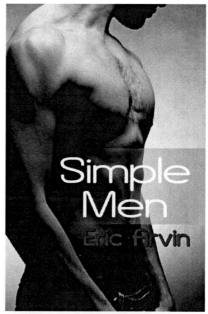

http://www.dreamspinnerpress.com

ARVIN

Arvin, Eric.
Woke up in a strange place
Central Fiction CIRC - 1st
fl
01/12

CPSIA information can be obtained at www.ICGtesting.com
Printed in the USA
BVOW030457281111

277000BV00006B/183/P